Praise for *Wish You Weren't Here* (The Rooks, Book 1):

T0347187

Home Sweet Hell

THE ROOKS
BOOK THREE

GABBY
HUTCHINSON CROUCH

Farrago

This edition published in 2023 by Farrago, an
imprint of Duckworth Books Ltd
1 Golden Court, Richmond, TW9 1EU, United Kingdom

www.farragobooks.com

Print ISBN: 978-1-7884-2407-3
Ebook ISBN: 978-1-7884-2408-0

For Nathan, who I'm pretty sure still hasn't noticed that the first book is also dedicated to him.

CONTENTS

CHAPTER ONE
Last Christmas

Think about life. The continuation of being, a gene passed down and down from an amoeba to a fish to a reptile to a mammal to an ape that stretched upright and grew a brain so big that it became dangerous. The continuation of a set of chemicals, a spark of life, trundling on for millions and millions of years on this one ball of rock and water, floating in space, unaware of its own miraculousness. Millions of years of fighting to survive, to get enough food, to not be the food, to pass on the gene and be outlived by at least some of one's offspring. Millions of years of this upright deadly ape fighting – fighting other life, fighting itself, fighting for resources, fighting for territory. Every day striving to keep the rain off its head, warmth in its blood and food in its belly. That big brain growing even more. And still the deadly ape fights for resources. And still it fights for territory. And instead of sharp rocks it now has weapons that could kill the whole world in one day. Still striving to keep off the rain, and calling this rent, or mortgages. And houses and flats are built and nobody can afford them and yet they must be bought and more must be built. Still striving to keep its blood warm, and pouring carbon into the air to do so. Still striving to keep food in its belly, and chopping down the forests to do so. Still working, working, working to keep life going. Accidentally making life more and more impossible in the process.

Sounds awful, doesn't it?

I was a part of that endless cycle of strife once, accidentally playing my part in making the fight to continue life a little harder with every year of my own survival. I even procreated, and was survived by my offspring. And then, I left the endlessly repeating battle called life. I died, suddenly and violently and in the dark, my living baby screaming and terrified in my arms. Unbeknownst to me, beings from beyond this sphere of rock and water, beings far more powerful than the deadly upright ape, had formed their plans and decided that I was no longer of use to them – I was expendable. And so, I was expended. Is that a term? How about this, instead – they'd watched all of this chaos unfold in front of them like directors watching a scene from the darkened stall seats of a theatre and they'd decided that I'd played my part, by giving birth to my daughter. And so these beings sent a hook to come and yoink me off the stage. No, that's still not quite right. Look, it's difficult to think of apt metaphors for the unfairness of the cosmos when one is dead.

However you want to put it – life, and life's architects, were done with me. And yet, I wasn't done with life. Like that gene passed down and down, I persisted against the odds. In growing those dangerous big brains, we deadly apes developed something else that would drive us on to fight, to strive, beyond the simple passing along of the gene. Call it love. Call it hate. It may be a combination of the two. It may even be faith. Faith in a deity perhaps, or simply in there being something beyond shelter, heat and food. Something grander. Something about my big ape brain remained after my body died, and I continued upon this ball of rock and water as a ghost. I was driven by love for my daughter, or hateful rage for those who allowed me to be killed and wrenched my daughter from me. Or maybe even driven by faith – faith that my daughter and her adoptive family can save this ridiculous, miraculous ball of rock with its persistent gene, from the plans of those watching from beyond, who have grown weary of watching it and wish to end it entirely.

Yes, the constant continuation of mortal life is tedious – one might even say that it's gone into a terminal spiral now, and its demise is only a matter of time. But, for us deadly apes, it's all that we have. It's small and precious and without it we have nowhere for our love and hate and faith to go. Trust me. I should know. I'm dead and death is, if anything, even more tedious than life.

The living might disagree. Certainly, the living people I currently haunt might disagree about the comparative tediousness of my own personal afterlife. I primarily haunt my daughter Charity. She can't see me, but her adoptive older brother Darryl can see me as clearly these days as he can see the living. Luckily – or sometimes unluckily – for Darryl, he is a clairvoyant. Charity and Darryl live together in a small two-bedroom flatshare, along with Darryl's husband Janusz. Janusz can't see me either, but Darryl often points out to the others where I am, and Janusz flashes a handsomely sympathetic smile in my general direction when he does. Sometimes Charity tries to talk to me, but ghosts are silent even to psychics like Darryl, so my responses are interpreted painfully slowly, usually through a sort of convoluted game of charades, which annoys me as well as Darryl, Charity and sometimes even, in spite of his winning, patient smile, Janusz. Frustrating as it is, I can think of few ghosts with as pleasant a set up as I have. It must be awful for most ghosts. Imagine being stuck haunting the living strangers who have moved into your beloved home – strangers who resent those cold patches in the corners where you cower, who flee when you try to ask them what they're doing there, and what happened to your loved ones. No wonder the lingering dead are usually so upset.

The living people that I haunt know all about the frustrations of the dead. They are ghost hunters. Darryl has the power to see the dead. Charity has the power to send us from this living world into one of the many other dimensions beyond – whether that's the restful nothingness of an endless desert dimension called 'the Waste', or the cold, dark, wet dimension of the Demons, or the bright, clean lined, uncomfortable-looking dimension referred to as 'Head Office', or one of many other realms beyond this living world that we little people don't even know about yet. Charity used to be Death, the Grim Reaper, a mortal chosen by the beings from beyond to gently usher the dead out of the living world and through to the Waste. When she found out about this – that, as she had always suspected, she truly was the Chosen One, carefully curated and groomed to ease the ending of the mortal world – she immediately quit in a fit of pique.

That's my girl.

She still has the power to move ghosts on from the mortal realm, even after resigning as the Grim Reaper, but she chooses to only do this if a ghost truly wants to leave. The ghost hunting business wasn't set up by Charity or Darryl, but by their parents – adoptive, in Charity's case. And their parents, a month after their children moved out of the old family home, are still convinced that nothing has really changed and that their silly, helpless, full-adult children will come crawling back begging for their old bedrooms any minute now. There are slightly more parents in this situation than you're probably expecting. Their names are Brenda, Richard and Murzzzz. I think I might have loved Brenda, once, but now those feelings hurt. I used to get on OK with Richard, too, and tolerated Murzzzz. Richard and Murzzzz are sort of the same person, since they comprise of a man in his sixties and an impossibly ancient Demon, inhabiting the same body. There's also a priest living with them called Grace Barry who isn't really a priest at all. She's almost certainly not even really called Grace Barry. It's

4

complicated. But then aren't all families complicated? I suppose that's just life for you.

Do I... miss it? Life? I think maybe I might miss it. Perhaps any life, no matter how complicated, no matter how painful, is preferable to this... drifting. Aimless, doing nothing, days melding into nights melding into days until time becomes a meaningless sludge. Look at them, my living babies. They have no idea what that must be like.

Charity honestly had no idea what day of the week it was. She wasn't even a hundred per cent certain on the year. It was, you see, the sludgy week after Christmas, when all the time bunches into itself and forms a sort of single, fuzzy, soft, temporal nest that only ever seems to untangle itself after the first couple of days of the new year. The week where you used to be able to work out just about where you were in it by checking the *Radio Times*, but streaming services had put paid even to that. There was a weirdness to the week besides that, and she couldn't put her finger on it being due to any one thing.

She, her brother and brother-in-law had only just moved out of the family home, mere weeks before Christmas, and there were still half-unpacked boxes lying everywhere. The important stuff had been unpacked, like the kettle and her Funkopops, but sometimes she'd still trip over a box of the men's wedding souvenirs, or catch Janusz rooting through a stack of her Manga books for some mislaid paperwork. It was no surprise that most of the false alarm ghost hunting calls her family got were for people who were still in the process of moving into a new place. Of course objects were always going missing in a new place – it was down to general human disarray, not ghosts. Charity knew that the ghost in their flat would never stick their insurance paperwork between issues of *My Hero Academia*. That was very obviously Darryl's fault, and Charity had said as much. Not that they'd listened.

And there was another weird thing. She'd gone from being one of three grown 'children' in a family home to being the single housemate to a pair of husbands. The dynamic had changed, and she wasn't exactly sure she liked the new energy to it. She'd always had the smallest bedroom, being the youngest, and never having found anybody she particularly wanted to share her bedroom with for more than a few nights, but now her single room felt more like the only bit that was her space in a couple's new marital home. It was taking some getting used to, and the flat still didn't feel any more 'hers' than the old house had done.

Moving out of your parents' house was a whole thing, she got that, and comparatively speaking, thirty-one was a bigger age than usual to be going through that rigmarole. It kind of made it more of a wrench. She'd always been there with her family, knowing they weren't her birth family – but her family nonetheless. The baby. The princess. The one with the really awesome powers. They'd needed her psychic ability to 'pop' the dead away to other realms so much in the family business. It had made her feel special. Chosen. And now, she knew that her specialness was real. Now, she knew that her very real special-ness had led to a cosmic plot, to whittle down the old ghost hunting team that had once comprised of her adoptive parents and her birth parents. Now she knew that Murzzzz, the Demon living within her adoptive father Richard, had allowed Charity's birth parents to die in order to spare Richard and Brenda Rook. Now she knew that powerful beings from beyond had intended Charity to be instrumental to the end of the world. Charity was, to put it mildly, not a fan of these revelations. It had driven her to leave the old home and, while she always found it hard to stay angry at Brenda and Richard for long, a discomfort remained.

It wasn't a sharp, insistent rage any more, but a dull ache of background upset and distrust. And it wasn't going away.

In spite of all of this, Charity, Darryl and Janusz had spent all of Christmas Eve and Christmas Day back at the family home, and hadn't talked about those unpleasant revelations, or indeed any of the terrible things that had come up during their just-about-successful efforts that had saved the world twice in November – because it had been Christmas, and one doesn't dwell on those things at Christmas. They had talked as usual about how lucky they were to get two Christmas dinners in a row due to Janusz's insistence they have a Polish Christmas – *Wigilia* – the night of the 24th. And they'd talked about the food, and the weather, and stuff in the news, and complained about the quality of the TV shows on offer even though between their various devices and subscriptions they could access pretty much any TV show or movie in existence. None of them had mentioned that this was likely to be the last Christmas that they, or anybody in the world would know – even when 'Last Christmas' had come on Janusz's Spotify *Wigilia* Megamix playlist. They'd all just sort of looked at each other, known what the others were thinking, and then carried on eating their piero-gi and continued their conversation about plans to repaint the hallway. Grace Barry had said a little prayer before both dinners, to a deity and a cosmic system of moral order that Grace Barry now had proof did not exist. And, although Brenda had rolled her eyes, nobody had stopped Grace from saying grace. They were all clinging onto their own happy lies. Who were they to deny Grace doing the same?

After twenty-four hours at her old house, all of them stead-fastly refusing to say aloud any of the awful things that silently gnawed at them, Charity had gone back to the small, cramped flat filled with boxes and her brother's marriage with a sigh of relief, and a renewed sense that she'd made the right choice.

It had taken her until the next morning for Darryl's general presence to start really annoying her again.

And now, it was the twenty... somethingth. Or the thirty somethingth? Could be New Year, even – Charity wasn't quite sure.

'Charity?'

'Mm?'

'Charity.'

'Mm,' she grunted again, in a louder and more irritable tone, which she hoped more emphatically conveyed the message: 'Yes, I heard you the first time but I'm busy, so if you wanted any response more detailed than a grunt, you are bang out of luck.'

'Could you please pause your video game?' Janusz asked.

'It's the middle of a fight,' complained Charity, but paused it anyway because it was Janusz who had asked.

'Thank you.' Janusz was frowning at his laptop. Janusz was always frowning at his laptop, these days. The man looked uncannily handsome even with his brow all furrowed over a bit of admin. Charity was honestly amazed at how much her brother had lucked out when a routine call-out had turned out to be from an astonishingly attractive Polish bisexual with a ghost pirate in his kitchen and a thing for gangly, awkward British men. And here was Charity, cuter than a button, and still with absolutely no need for a double bedroom of her own. Bit unfair, frankly. Usually, she'd tell herself that it was fine, she was still young and she still had time to find a Janusz of her own. But, y'know, the world was sort of on the brink of ending.

'So, we should really work on clearing this job constipation,' said Janusz.

He meant the work backlog. Neither Darryl nor Charity corrected him.

'There's a cluster near Exeter,' Janusz continued. 'Maybe we can go down there, see how many we can fix—'

Charity groaned. 'Not the South West. It takes ages to get to and we have to drive past Stonehenge.'

Darryl shuddered. Charity knew that bringing up the Henge would get him onside. It was, according to her clairvoyant mother and brother, 'absolutely heaving with the dead'.

'We don't *have* to drive past Stonehenge,' sighed Janusz, with the soft weariness of an utterly non-psychic man who actually really liked Stonehenge but knew that he would never see it again because his husband was absolutely terrified of the place. 'But we probably should drive, so, um… Charity, me and Darryl were wondering if maybe you could message your mum? We've had trouble matching schedules with the other half of the family lately, and we think maybe—'

'Maybe it's because Mum's still sulking that we moved out?' Charity unpaused her game and immediately got her poor avatar kicked in the face.

'We just thought maybe she'd respond better to you,' said Darryl. He sighed faintly. 'I mean, she never made a secret of how you're her favourite.'

'Janusz is her favourite,' Charity replied, wrangling with her controller.

Neither man tried to argue with that.

'But, you know,' continued Darryl, 'ever since you and Mum had your little…'

Charity's avatar was grabbed by the leg and flung across the screen. She screwed up her face in annoyance.

'Are you going to refer to what went down at Helsbury as "a little falling-out"? All those years of lies?'

'They kept important things from me too, Charity!' Darryl put in.

'Yeah, but your stuff wasn't as important.'

'Charity, they didn't tell me I'm part-Demon!'

'Yeah, well, that's just a You Problem, isn't it? My problem affects my poor birth mother's ghost too. I've got other people's feelings to take into consideration.'

'And *I've* got a husband.'

Ugh. Rubbing his marriage in her face again. Charity's avatar was knocked off his feet and lost the last smidge of his life bar. She rolled her eyes. Darryl snorted a small, affectionate laugh. She frowned at her brother as she restarted from her last save point. Darryl shrugged with a little smile, and indicated to a corner of the flat's small living room.

'Constance rolled her eyes at exactly the same time as you. I just thought it was cute.'

'I think what Darryl was saying,' added Janusz, with the patience of a year one teacher trying to steer a chatty class back to the lesson plan, 'is that we've all found out a lot of unpleasant things the last couple of months, and the atmosphere might be a bit more tense with your parents than usual—'

'Because they chose a Demon over us,' Charity reminded him.

'But,' continued Janusz in that same teacherly tone, 'they're still half of this family, and half of this business. And also they're the half of the business that has a car, which we sort of need unless all the ghosts are going to decide to suddenly focus their activity within the ring road of town. We should really get back to the ghost hunting work again, partly because a lot of prospective clients have given up waiting and gone to rivals – and yes that includes Aurora Tavistock, which I know none of you will be happy about...'

Both Darryl and Charity tutted at that name.

'Aurora Tavistock,' growled Darryl, his voice full of distaste.

'That bloody fraud,' agreed Charity.

'Exactly,' said Janusz. 'And also, we should step up the ghost hunting because, you know, of the ongoing attempt to end the world. And because the last two times they tried to end the world, we were the only ones who could stop it.'

Charity sighed, wearily. Her avatar got kicked in the face again. 'Fine. I'll call her. After I've cleared this level.'

Grace didn't 'live' with Brenda and Richard Rook. She wasn't a member of the family, nor was she a housemate or a lodger. The little priest didn't have her own room in the three-bedroom family home – she slept on the sofa, even with two of the bedrooms standing empty for weeks. Brenda Rook still referred to those rooms as 'the kids' bedrooms', and kept the beds made with old bedding sets: Catwoman in the case of Charity's old bed and David Beckham in the case of Darryl and Janusz's, even though Janusz supported Poland and Darryl had never expressed any interest in football in front of Grace. That duvet cover seemed to date back to Darryl's teens, so Grace could tell what that was probably all about.

Grace didn't complain about the sofa. It was big enough for her with her little legs, and comfy even if it was made of leather, of which she wasn't sure she approved. The sofa was fine, because she was a temporary guest. Her home, the rectory house on Coldbay Island, had been destroyed back in November when she'd met the Rook family. Well, to say it was 'destroyed' was a bit of an understatement. Her old home had been ripped from its foundations and physically thrown at the family as they'd made their escape, and then the entirety of Coldbay Island had vanished, expunged from the physical plane and from history. Brenda Rook was being a good friend and putting Grace up for now until she was back on her feet again, able to get back to a normal life. And that was fine. It was fine. It was fine.

Except that it regularly kept hitting Grace that it wasn't, in fact, fine at all. The rectory house on Coldbay hadn't really been her home – she'd been placed there by strange, immortal beings who called themselves Celestial Executives... and who other people called 'Angels'. She'd been placed there as part of a trap, to usher the Rooks towards aiding the end of the world. Her whole life was a lie; an invention; a story she'd told herself to shelter her own mind from the truth.

She wasn't really a priest. She wasn't really called Grace Barry. She wasn't really a small, middle-aged woman. She wasn't really a human being at all. 'Grace Barry' was what the Executives called a 'Suit'– a human-shaped disguise for Celestial Executives to walk the Earth incognito. At some point, a part of Grace had rebelled against the Executives' plan, and decided that she wanted to be on the side of the Rooks. Whether it was because she liked the world, or liked the Rooks, or just liked being Grace Barry too much, Grace had no idea. The Angel within her had wiped itself from Grace's memory. All she knew was Grace, and Grace was a lie. A lovely, tiny lie in a big, colourful, ethically-knitted cardigan, but a lie nonetheless. She wasn't a temporary guest at the Rooks, until she got back on her feet. She wasn't really 'alive' in the traditional sense. She wasn't even sure whether Angels had feet to get back on. There was no permanent normal life for her to get back to. She was a temporary guest because the world was very likely to end really quite soon, and Grace didn't know if they could save it this time.

It kept hitting Grace Barry that Grace Barry wasn't real and, in those moments, she would feel panicky, because how could that be true? She felt so real. So full of love for the world. And so, in the weeks following her discovery that she wasn't real, Grace had been putting as much effort as possible into being as Grace Barry as she possibly could. She followed every instinct that told her 'Grace Barry should be doing this'. That involved volunteering at a local homeless shelter and a charity cafe, and doing delivery runs for the food bank on Saturdays with a middle-aged man who kept showing her pictures of his cats. There was to be a bring and buy sale in support of 'Save the polar bears' in January which she was very excited about, even though Brenda enjoyed pointing out that a polar bear would cheerfully attempt to eat Grace as soon as look at her. She found a peace in it – in doing things that she believed Grace Barry would do and in manifesting her as a real person somehow. It pushed the panicky feelings back down and relaxed her again.

And nothing relaxed her quite as much as feeling the black eye. Shortly before Christmas, she'd intervened in a dispute in the street, between a very shouty man and a hurriedly retreating, tearful woman. For this, Grace had had some very sexually violent things screamed at her, and she had been punched. The man had not been arrested, the woman had run away crying and Grace's eye was still discoloured and sore even now, but she wouldn't change a single thing. She'd acted on impulse, not even thinking it through and she had felt so utterly like Grace at that moment. The black eye made her feel even more real. It made her a flesh and blood little human, fragile and flawed, not an Angel playing make-believe in a costume. And every time she blinked, it would hurt a bit, and remind her. Blinking had become one of her favourite things to do.

Cradling her tea in her favourite cup – a faded, chintzy affair with a cartoon kitten and a declaration that nobody should speak to her until she'd had her coffee – Grace blinked, experienced the faint pain in her eye and exhaled. Despite the cup's message, Grace was ambivalent about kittens and coffee, and enjoyed a chat at any time of day. It was her favourite cup because it was the one the Rooks had declared to be 'her cup', and having her own cup made her feel good, and real, and wanted, and human, and *Grace*. Brenda's mobile was ringing.

'Brenda,' she called, from right next to the ringing phone, in a voice no louder than that of the ring tone. 'Phone.'

'Is it Charity?' called Brenda from upstairs.

Grace looked. 'Yep.'

'I *knew* it,' called the faintly muffled voice. 'She always rings while I'm in the loo. It's like she's psychic.'

'She *is* psychic.'

'Yeah, but… you know what I mean. Tell her I'll only be a mo, would you?'

Grace answered the ringing phone, and didn't put any thought into how she just knew Brenda's lockscreen PIN. Just *knowing* stuff like that wasn't a very Grace Barry thing to do, so she ignored and instantly forgot it.

'Hiya, Charity,' said the eternal Angel, the all-powerful Celestial Executive dressed in the body of a small, bruised priest. 'Your mum's just popped for a wee.'

CHAPTER TWO

Not Exeter

'Exeter, though?' Brenda sighed down the phone. 'What does Janusz want to go there for?'

'For hunting ghosts,' called a male voice over the line, tinged with a faint Polish accent and a general air of handsomeness. 'Sorry to interrupt – you're on loudspeaker.'

'We'd have to drive past Stonehenge, though,' said Brenda.

'We're not fans of Stonehenge, Janusz,' added Richard. 'Sorry – should say – you're on loudspeaker too.'

'There's nothing special about Exeter, kids,' continued Brenda. 'It's no more haunted than the places within our own ring road. Why bother travelling? Last time we had a road trip we got trapped in a haunted service station.'

'*Told* you she'd be like this,' murmured Charity's voice, on the other end of the phone.

'Maybe that's because I've been doing this since before any of you were born, and I'm very good at keeping tabs on where supernatural hotspots are,' Brenda retorted.

'Only because Janusz set up those alerts for keywords on local news websites for you,' blurted Darryl's voice.

'Please don't bring me into this again...' came Janusz's voice, quietly.

'I'll have you know, we Rooks were excellent ghost hunters long before the internet came along,' Brenda told her assembled audience, and anybody else who might be within a ten-metre radius.

'Yes, we know, Mother,' came Charity's voice, 'back in the day you relied on local papers and microfiche—'

'And on Murzzzz,' added Richard. 'Murzzzz was very good at keeping tabs on supernatural happenings all over the world. Better than microfiche. Better than Google.'

The voices of the younger adults on the other end of the phone fell into a stony silence.

'Sorry for insulting your precious Google, kids,' mumbled Richard, into his coffee cup.

'Why don't we do a few jobs closer to home for a bit eh, kids?' Brenda asked. 'Grace is still finding her feet here after all, and after all, it's Christmas.'

'It's not Christmas any more...' Charity attempted.

'Yes,' Brenda continued, 'a quick local job and then you can all come back home.'

'And we don't live at home any more,' continued Charity, with a heavy we've-told-you-this-already sigh.

'Just for chippy tea!' Brenda interjected. 'Then you can get back to your little flat where you're very happy, I'm sure.'

'But the clients in Exeter,' sighed Janusz, in the tone of a man whose argument had already been defeated, crushed into a fine dust and stomped into the ground so that no other arguments could grow there.

'There'll be clients right here in Rutherford!' Because they were using her phone for the call, and Brenda wasn't entirely sure how to go about using two apps at the same time, she took her husband's phone off him to check the local paranormal

Facebook groups. 'Yep. Weird sightings at Sunnyside Primary School.'

'Oh, there's always weird sightings at schools, Mum, and it's never a ghost,' Darryl replied. 'It will just be tween girls winding each other up.'

'There was a ghost at that boarding school!'

'That boarding school was 200 years old and had a history full of misery due to being a boarding school! The whole Sunnyside estate was built on an empty field in the nineties, probably the worst thing that's happened there was a kid falling off a climbing frame, or a conker related injury...'

'Still going on about conker injuries,' sighed Brenda.

'They're dangerous, Mum,' argued Darryl, 'Charity nearly had my eye out that time.'

Brenda continued to scroll through Richard's phone. '*And* someone's reported happenings at the bowling alley. That's only a ten-minute walk from the school, we can do both in an afternoon.'

'What sort of "happenings"?' asked Grace.

'A "pervading sense of evil",' Brenda replied, reading from the post.

'That's just bowling alleys,' said Darryl, 'they always feel like that. It's the acoustics and the black lights. Remember when you were sure 10 Pin Wonderland was haunted, babe?'

'You said it was just balls,' came Janusz's voice.

'Just underfloor balls,' said Darryl. 'It's a waste of our time, Mum. The jobs are racking up and the world's not getting any less doomed.'

'Well, if you want a real supernatural hotspot, we should go to Winnipeg,' Brenda stated.

'What, in America?' asked Charity.

'Canada, princess.'

'Same thing,' mumbled Charity.

'What's up with Winnipeg?' asked Darryl.

Brenda shrugged, still scrolling. 'Ghost hunter community over there's become overwhelmed recently and nobody's sure why.'

'So you'd be happy to go all the way to Canada, but not Exeter?' asked Darryl.

'Don't have to drive past Stonehenge to get to Canada,' replied Brenda, matter-of-factly. 'I don't know why you're arguing for a West Country mission, Darryl, you're more frightened of the Henge than I... oh shit on a biscuit!'

'What?' chorused various members of the family at Brenda's horrified curse.

Brenda was glaring at the phone. 'Aurora Bloody Tavistock!'

'She's in Canada?' asked Richard.

'No, she's here!'

Richard didn't quite have the temerity to take his own phone back off his wife, but he did shuffle up behind her to look over her shoulder at the screen. 'Here? In Rutherford?'

Brenda jabbed at the screen. 'Her stupid scammy psychic sideshow is at the Lamada Inn Conference Hall on New Year's Eve.'

'That's not for like a week though, right?' said Charity, over the phone.

'Princess, that's tonight,' Richard told her.

'Is it? Bloody Hell, where did that week go?'

'I mean, that's all we need,' continued Brenda. 'Aurora's travelling snake oil show defrauding everyone, giving proper psychics a bad name.'

'Does...' Grace already started regretting the question when she was only one word into asking it. 'Does it really matter? If she's just one of these cold reading fakes who scams the living, surely that has nothing to do with real ghost hunting work...?'

It was a good job, thought Grace, that she wasn't a real mortal being after all. If she were, then the glare Brenda gave her right then would surely have withered a poor mortal form away to some sort of human-shaped raisin.

'Grace,' said Richard with his usual Richardly patience, 'you know that ghosts are attracted to seances. The hokier the better. They remember the cues from when they were alive. When they see Aurora Tavistock with all her silly crystals, loudly claiming she can commune with the dead, they flock to her. Ghosts are even more desperate to communicate with the living than the living are with them.'

'That's the irony,' added Darryl, over loudspeaker. 'Aurora Tavistock's shows are always absolutely heaving with the dead. She just doesn't realise it – the fraud. And after an hour of desperately trying to get through to the living world only to be ignored...'

'You're left with a hall full of ghosts who are even more frustrated and upset than they were before,' murmured Grace, picturing the scene.

'Exactly,' sighed Brenda. 'And who do you think keeps getting called by desperate staff weeks later to clear up after her?'

'So it might be nice to be out of town for when Aurora comes to annoy all the ghosts,' reasoned Charity, over the phone. 'Maybe ring in the new year at a nice historic Roman city, with a beautiful Gothic cathedral, and—'

'We are not going to Exeter!'

Exeter had no particular cause to mourn Brenda Rook's reticence to visit. Tourism-wise, it was doing just fine, and besides, leisure industry revenue was, amongst all other issues, not going to be a problem for long – what with the world being on the brink of ending. Among the many people who *had* recently been to Exeter were Aurora Tavistock, and her tour manager-slash-PA, Yemisi. Not that they'd taken much time to see the sights. Their tour was one of conference rooms in mid-level chain hotels. Yemisi was getting to see a lot of out-of-town leisure estates and a lot of wet car parks, occasionally dotted with thin, sad trees and bedraggled strips of brown amongst the varying greys of concrete and tarmac. The whole country was becoming one big sludge. Motorway. Leisure estate. Car park. Hotel. Conference room. Always the same buffet breakfasts of serve-yourself scrambled eggs that managed to be lukewarm no matter how quickly you ate them and the same slim square of white bread, making its plodding way through a little conveyor belt over a grill that didn't quite manage to toast it but just make it vaguely crunchy. Dark green carpets. Dark green curtains. White walls. Faded framed prints of the countryside. Always the same conference hall chairs – why were they *always* the same chairs? Burgundy velour, worn at the seats, with little bits on the legs to interlock them, which would always dig into Yemisi's shin when she had to move them. Showbiz, baby.

And it was showbiz. Really. Yemisi knew that what Aurora did was all show… but *what* a show. Aurora was the best in the business – if the business was putting on a spectacular hour for a couple of hundred people to marvel at, then go home lighter of cares and worries and grief. And cash – a tenner for the ticket and another thirty or so a head for souvenirs and merch. Yeah, this tour was going really well. It helped that Aurora had been on telly and the front pages of a couple of tabloids – mostly due to her claims that she was in regular contact with the ghost of Princess Diana – but Yemisi was pleased with her part in its success. Goodness knows, most of the actual legwork was down to her. Maybe after this tour, Yemisi would move on and up, do a tour for a mid-level pop band, or a YouTuber, or one of those comedians who was always on *QI* or something. Aurora would easily find a new twenty-five-year-old who didn't mind rainy car parks and cold eggs and being treated like a general dogsbody. Showbiz, baby. Yes, Yemisi would move on and up really soon. She had been telling herself this for a whole year, now. There was just... *something* about Aurora. When she spoke there was nothing but her voice. It filled you... filled you so much that everything was taken up with the act of listening to her. Confidence and showmanship, Yemisi supposed. During her act, it was just easier on your brain to believe her, even if you knew it was all show. It was like a pantomime or like one of those big, silly, brightly coloured superhero movies. You knew Robert Downey Jr. couldn't actually fly. And yet... When Aurora did her big, silly, brightly coloured show, it felt to Yemisi as if there really could be loads of clamouring ghosts in whatever green-carpeted, burgundy-chaired conference room they were in that day. Showbiz!

Yemisi really wasn't sure why Aurora had insisted on booking the Rutherford Lamada Inn for New Year's Eve. Showbiz or not, Yemisi would really rather have taken New Year off, and surely people would have other plans that night? They wouldn't want to spend it at a seance. And then, when she'd been proved wrong – tickets for the New Year's Eve show had actually sold slightly faster than the rest of the tour – Yemisi had pivoted and wondered why they hadn't make a bigger thing of it. Maybe taken the show to Manchester or Glasgow instead – even London. But, no. Aurora was set on Rutherford.

Yemisi had not yet been to Rutherford, but she already knew that there was nothing special about it. Just another Home Counties new town, hurriedly thrown up after the war, with grand dreams about green spaces and gleaming concrete long since faded away. She hadn't looked at the high street, or the shopping centre where Aurora was due to do a book signing, but Yemisi could already name all the shops and coffee chains that she would find there, and predict all the faded signs now covered in PVC banners for temporary pop-up shops offering vape juice and phones unlocked with no questions asked. She already knew there would be buildings with signs for once proud high street names, that wouldn't even have phone cases or knock-off handbags for sale in them, but would be standing empty and forlorn – fallen soldiers in the war they were losing against the internet. Even the decay of these places all looked the same. She hadn't even looked Sunnyside leisure estate up and she could already tell you what restaurants there would be surrounding the Lamada Inn. She already knew what she'd have for lunch, and for dinner. And for breakfast she knew she would have room temperature eggs and barely singed white bread with a rock-hard inch of butter.

She wished she could see in the New Year in her beloved London. Go to a decent restaurant and get some proper food, put together by a human not an algorithm. See her mates. Hang out with her brothers. Dance. Smooch some cutie-pie. Smell the brilliant stink of a proper city again, not some sad grey satellite off an A road. Go to a coffee shop with silly too-low sofas and even sillier too-high bar stools – and absolutely no interlocking burgundy chairs.

But Aurora was set on Rutherford. And when Aurora was set on something, you went along with it. Showbiz, baby.

Since their tour was via Britain's glorious grey road network, neither Yemisi nor Aurora would see Rutherford train station. They weren't missing much. It was much the same as any mid-sized train station in the country. Not one of those tiny country stops that consisted of nothing but two platforms, a level crossing, a footbridge, an automated ticket machine, a single perspex shelter and a general air of foreboding, but a four platform affair with an awning, a couple of coffee booths, a vandalised toilet and a very small branch of Boots the Chemist, in case you needed a post-train paracetamol, teeny tiny bottle of shower gel or a sandwich with crisps.

Nobody at the fairly nondescript train station paid any attention when a youngish man of slightly above average height and attractiveness disembarked the train, and the cashier at the very small branch of Boots scanned through his paracetamol, shower gel and vegan falafel wrap with crisps just as she would do for any other customer. She just about took note of his accent when he smiled and thanked her but, even then, she assumed he was a very polite American when he was, in fact, from Winnipeg in Canada. Why indeed should anybody at this very standard train station pay much attention to a polite vegan who sounded American but wasn't? Yes, if they knew him they'd know he was special, but isn't that true of everybody? That's how Krish saw it, anyway.

Krish Patel sat on one of the benches outside the station, which had been cleverly and deliberately designed to be as uncomfortable as possible to keep people from lingering – or worse still, resting – on it. He ate his falafel wrap, hoped the paracetamol would get rid of his headache, berated himself yet again for forgetting shower gel, and wondered what he was supposed to do next.

And nobody who passed by him knew that Krish Patel was Death.

CHAPTER THREE
The Big Clock

Darryl finished hoovering the bits of the small flat's floor that were currently accessible, and found that it had only taken ten minutes and now he had nothing else to do. He had even carefully hoovered around the small patch of cold behind the sofa where Constance stood, watching Charity's video game with the mutely agog wonder of someone who still considered Sonic the Hedgehog to be cutting edge. He had already told Charity that her birth mother's ghost was watching the game in fascination, which had spurred Charity on to keep playing it, using the flat's sole TV. Darryl decided not to sit in the middle of the sofa, between his sister and his husband, since that would mean having a dead woman looming over him. Instead, he perched on an armrest and glanced down at Janusz's ongoing admin.

'Sorry the phone call didn't really work out as well as we thought,' he said.

'It worked out exactly as well as I thought,' mumbled Janusz. 'Just, not as well as I'd hoped. Sunnyside is fairly new, yes? Not just the school – the whole estate?'

'Whole town's new,' replied Darryl with a shrug. 'Rutherford was all forest and fields until the sixties.'

'Like Helsbury services,' noted Janusz. 'And that whole place was haunted as anything.'

Darryl nodded. The whole family knew from experience that just because a building was fairly modern, it didn't mean it couldn't be haunted. Helsbury, their last really big haunting problem, had been a motorway service station built in the sixties, ostensibly in the middle of nowhere, but which turned out to actually be the site of a plague pit and a haunted ancient tree that was very, very angry about getting bulldozed and having a Caffè Nero and a petrol station stuck in the middle of its territory. There was never any such thing as a new space. Civilisation was built on the bones of more civilisation, and sometimes those bones were furious about being built upon. This still didn't mean that a primary school and a nearby bowling alley were definitely haunted though – it really was likely to be just kids and balls.

'I actually remember a lot of Sunnyside estate getting built though,' added Darryl. 'Sometimes I'd go and watch the building site, and I never saw any ghosts all angry because when they were alive it was a medieval village or anything like that...' Janusz cocked a handsome eyebrow and Darryl trailed off, slightly embarrassed at the admission he used to go and watch building sites for fun. 'I was a kid. I liked diggers. And there wasn't much else to do before the internet.'

'Poor *zabko*,' replied Janusz with a faintly mocking, symmetrical smile. 'I could never understand such hardships while I was growing up.'

'Ha ha,' added Charity in a very little-sisterish singsong tone. 'Darryl forgot his husband had a harsher childhood than he did.'

'Don't make fun of my husband's Soviet childhood, thank you.'

'Post-Soviet mostly. And her birth parents were murdered by Demons and then technically Brenda sort-of-kidnapped her,' replied Janusz, 'so she gets a free pass.'

'I could see dead people! As a baby!' Darryl folded his arms. 'You're all picking on me.'

'You don't actually think Sunnyside's haunted, do you?' Charity kept her eyes glued to the screen as her avatar lobbed handcrafted grenades at a monster and then hid behind the same tree over and over again. 'That was just Mum clutching at straws to keep us in Rutherford until we decide it's more convenient to go back the old house.'

'She's actually right about the uptick of posts to local paranormal groups,' said Janusz, going back to his laptop. 'Mind you, from our emails, there's been an uptick everywhere. Might just be an end of the world thing. Did either of you check up on Winnipeg?'

Darryl shook his head. He wasn't aware he was expected to have checked up on what his mum had said about Winnipeg.

Janusz sucked through his teeth. 'I did. They're overrun. One of their main guys there is suddenly missing and everything. Maybe this is the next part of the plan to end the world – fill it with too many ghosts and Demons so we can't fight back no matter how hard we try.'

Darryl stared at Charity's game, aware that, right at that point – and ever since Helsbury, in fact – they weren't actually trying at all.

Ghost hunting wasn't just Darryl's job. It was his life. It had always been his life. He had always seen the dead, just like Brenda. His first memories were all of his mother hurriedly ushering him away from 'the scary sad people'. He'd been on his parents' missions since he was little – his parents' reasoning being that it was hard to get a babysitter when your only friends are also ghost hunters, and besides it was probably safer for him to be by their side because that way they knew they could count on Murzzzz protecting him.

That was before he'd known that Murzzzz was kind of one of his fathers. Before he'd known that, since both Richard and Murzzzz had been present at his conception, Darryl himself was part-Demon. That was before what his mother kept referring to as the 'Longest Night', the night when Murzzzz had abandoned Constance and Harry Xu to their deaths so that Brenda and Richard could live – so that Murzzzz could carry on existing on Earth in Richard's body, helping to raise the Xus' psychically-gifted, orphaned daughter, and watching his part-human son grow into a man... a man-Demon.

The Demon side of Darryl had only manifested a handful of times – when he was scared, when he was cornered, when his family were under attack and when Darryl felt he had no choice. He hated it. Hated how it made him feel – hated the strength, hated the rage. And he hated that people kept calling his Demon form 'cute'. It wasn't cute. It was horrific! Yes, it was fuzzier than most Demonic forms. Yes it had big, bright eyes and dainty fangs and a little lion cub roar. Yes, it looked less like a traditional Demon, and more like an Ewok mixed with a seal mixed with a pussy cat. That was clearly just what happened when you mixed Demon and mammal DNA. But it was still demonic. It still had deadly claws and a brute strength hugely beyond his own understanding. And, it... *he*... had accidentally hurt Janusz, the last time he'd taken that form. Darryl's eyes darted briefly, guiltily, over to Janusz's wrist. The bandages were off, now, but scars from the gouges his Demon claws had cut into his husband's arm remained. He had acted on instinct – grabbed his husband to stop him falling – but the monstrous, sharp jagged claws had shredded Janusz's skin and left him scarred. It was a mercy that there had been no nerve damage or worse, but the three discoloured, puckered claw marks still stained his beloved's wrist. Darryl had promised solemnly he would never, ever hurt Janusz, not after he had been hurt so many times in his youth. But the Demon had hurt Janusz. Well. The Demon was never going to get the chance to break Darryl's vows ever again. Darryl had gone thirty-five years without allowing the Demon form to emerge before, and he would go however many years it took without ever letting the Demon out again. He would swallow it down, dissolve it, reject it. It was no more a part of him than last night's veggie burgers, still winding their way through his gut. They didn't need the Demon. They had Murzzzz for protection... actually, no. Sod Murzzzz. They didn't need him either. They didn't need *any* Demons, Demons were selfish, heavy-handed brutes that had such long lives that they couldn't help but think of mortal lives as anything but silly, ephemeral playthings, no matter how much they protested that they cared. Demons lied. You couldn't trust them. He didn't trust any of them – not even the one inside himself. And now, he was in a situation where he'd told his own parents that it was Murzzzz or him. And they'd chosen Murzzzz.

Demons. Were. Toxic. Arseholes. And he wasn't going to let one control his marriage the way Murzzzz had done with his parents'. In fact, he wasn't even going to give the Demon inside of him the satisfaction of so much as thinking about it any more. That'd teach it.

They were doing the right thing, right? Carrying on with the ghost hunting even after everything they'd found out? They were helping the dead – not to mention the living. They were going to save the world. Right? So, why were all of them so reticent to take up a new ghost hunting job? It wasn't just the Stonehenge issue, surely. Why was *he* so reticent?

He looked at his husband's wrist, and continued to think about the Demon inside of him.

Charity carried on with her game, even though she was terrible at it. She could tell from the way Darryl had avoided sitting in the middle of the sofa that Constance was still there, right by her shoulder, watching her play. Playing a game for the amusement of a ghost instead of actually getting out and doing any ghost hunting was almost certainly the opposite of what she was supposed to be doing – what she had been raised by mortals and chosen by beings from beyond this world to do. She still retained her psychic ability to usher ghosts away to the dimension of the dead, even after officially quitting the role foisted upon her – the role handed out to selected mortals. A steward to ease the apocalypse. The role of Death. The Grim Reaper.

Charity had spent her whole life convinced she was cosmically special. Finding out that this was literally the truth actually really sucked. Learning that there had really been an argument between immortal beings about how best to groom her for the role – an argument that had culminated in the deaths of Constance and Harry Xu – it made her feel rotten. Angry and helpless. It made her feel like she still had no more agency than a crying baby. So she had quit as Death. But now what? If she stopped doing the ghost work completely, wouldn't that be a more definite way to turn her back on the role the immortal beings had imposed on her? Was that even something she wanted to do?

She was a Rook, and Rooks hunted ghosts – that was just their thing. But now, she knew that that hadn't been Constance's wish for her. Constance and Harry's will had said Charity was supposed to have been raised as a normal girl by her non-psychic aunt in New Zealand. What a different life that would have been – just doing normal girl stuff, not understanding her powers and feeling pressured to keep them under wraps instead of being pressured to use them for work. She could have been like a sort of ghosty Harry Potter, but with an exotic Wellington accent. It still wouldn't have been perfect, and it still wouldn't have been Charity's choice. But then, neither was this life. She hadn't been consulted on a single element of any of this.

She'd always loved comic book superhero stories. And now, she'd discovered, even that hadn't been her choice. The Celestial beings had deliberately fed a string of stories they knew she'd relate to into the mortal world – stories about superpowered kids, plucky orphans, Chosen Ones with an angsty backstory and an inescapable destiny. But actually having an angsty backstory – especially one where you know people died – so you would be pushed to follow your destiny was horrible. And the trouble about being the Chosen One was that nothing about that choice was yours.

Was she still following this bullshit 'destiny' without even knowing it? Was sending the dead into waste really helping? Or was it making things worse? She knew Brenda would just write this off as anger that Brenda hidden the truth from her. And she *was* still annoyed about that, but there was more to it. For the first time in her life, Charity was genuinely unsure about what she should do. So, for now, she decided she was going to sit in her onesie and play video games.

In the game her avatar was killed. She stifled a sigh, and started from her save point again.

'It's that end-of-the-year malaise,' announced Brenda, 'isn't it?'

'Hmm?' asked Grace.

'You were judging me for not wanting to go to Exeter,' said Brenda, picking up a glass from the draining board, 'but honestly, I could tell that the kids' hearts weren't in it either. Post-Christmas droop and all that. If we went, they'd only complain the whole time.'

'I wasn't judging you,' protested Grace.

'Oh, please. You're an Angel. Judging is in your nature.'

Grace winced. 'I'm pretty sure they...' she screwed up her eyes and forced herself to correct her wording. '*We* don't like that term. We prefer "Celestial Executives". Well, *I* prefer "Grace" And I'm not judgey, when have I ever judged you?'

Grace watched Brenda pour out her second large glass of Baileys of the day. It was only a little after 1 p.m. OK, so maybe Grace was judging just a little bit, but she had the decency not to say so out loud.

Brenda noticed her expression, and gave a little shrug. 'It's still Christmas. Everything's all sludged together. Give it until after New Year. New start. Aurora Bloody Tavistock will have sodded off from my home turf and I'm sure the kids'll have seen sense by then.' Brenda still watched Grace's expression. 'Look. At the moment, every time we go off to do a big job, horrible things from the past get dredged up, regrettable things are said, feelings get hurt and it all ends in a mess. Oh, and one of your lot inevitably tries to end the world. I know that'll happen again, if we go to Exeter, or... or wherever. Might even work, the next time. And if it works... well. I'd just like everything to be in order at the end. Have the kids back where they belong.' She paused, and took a long drink of warm liqueur. 'Make peace with Constance,' she added eventually, with a Baileys Moustache. 'And for that, I'll need Constance to start haunting this house again, and for that, I need Charity to stop all this "renting a flat with her brother" nonsense and come home. And, then, then it'll be fine. We can all stop accidentally hurting each other, and get back to rolling the boulder of trying to save the world up the hill of attempted apocalypses.' She took another sip. 'We could even go to Winnipeg.'

'Are things really that bad in Winnipeg, or do you just fancy going to Canada?'

Brenda shrugged again, but at least did so with a small smile, this time. 'Little of both. I hear people are very nice, over there. Canada is the Paul McCartney to America's John Lennon.' She finished off her glass. 'You do know who The Beatles were? Do you get references to things from before you were planted on Earth in that human skin?'

'We call the human forms "suits", remember?' Grace said. Well, *she* called her human form 'Grace Barry'. 'And yes, I know about The Beatles. And Nat King Cole and Tchaikovsky and Rembrandt and… and *The* Rembrandts and the theme from *Friends*. And *Friends*. And the spin-off about Joey that didn't really work, and that time Matt LeBlanc hosted *Top Gear*, and—'

'OK,' replied Brenda, 'I get it, you have a full fake memory bank of human art and pop culture. You can stop listing stuff about *Friends*.'

'Sorry,' said Grace with a cringe, 'you know when you sort of get into a loop and you're trying to think of a different subject but you can't?' Another thought hit her and she couldn't help blurting it out. 'They were paid a million dollars an episode, you know.'

Brenda stared at her, a strange look on her face – half fondness, half troubled.

'What?'

Brenda shook her head, faintly. 'Just wondering. You would never have actually watched *Friends*. Your memory of it isn't real. It's there because the character of Grace Barry would have watched *Friends*. Got to wonder what about you is really *you*. And, you know… what's there because it was written for Grace.'

'Does it really matter?' asked Grace.

'Probably not,' replied Brenda. 'Maybe I'm just curious because I like you. And I wish I knew who I liked – a character or someone behind the character. Is my friend Monica Geller, or Courtney Cox *playing* Monica?'

Grace smiled, proudly. Brenda liked her. She had a friend! 'You...' she stammered, happily. 'You think I'm a Monica?'

Janusz spoke four languages competently and had passing understanding of a further three. After his mother tongue, English was the language he was most fluent in and still he had trouble deciphering a lot of Facebook posts. Honestly, it was one of the harder aspects of his job, and that was coming from someone who was no stranger to getting flung around churches by angry Demons. From what he could tell from the Facebook posts he was scrolling through, there had definitely been an uptick in paranormal activity in Rutherford. Perhaps this was to be expected as the world reached its end. It was easy to feel overwhelmed by that fact, like there was no point in trying to fight back against it any more. But it was also easy to think, 'No. *Pieprzyć to*. I'm finally happy with my life, and no attempt to end the world is going to rob me of that while I still have the energy to resist the apocalypse. Even in my capacity as the admin guy.' And so, Janusz did what he was best at – he did admin. Could admin put a stop to the end of the world? Probably not, but he was going to try.

The local forums strongly suggested a lot of ghostly activity was around the Sunnyside estate, but that there was also a secondary hotspot at the Oakpines Shopping Centre. Oakpines was a comfortable walk from the flat, and even closer to the old house. They wouldn't even need the car and they could go this afternoon. This would, as she pointed out, mean Charity would have to get out of her onesie. Nevertheless, after complaining and repeatedly dying in her video game for another five minutes, she got up and went to her room to get dressed, declaring loudly she was only doing this as a favour for Janusz. Brenda gave a similarly limp objection over the phone, before agreeing to meet them – as a favour for Janusz – by the big clock at three.

Considering the violent and messy way the past few ghost clearances had gone, Janusz got changed into a jumper that he didn't mind getting ripped or stained. As he pulled on the ugly penguins jumper from the back of a drawer, he breathed a little sigh of relief that he'd managed to talk them all into doing a job together. Janusz was very aware of how much the family liked him. If he could utilise that into getting them all off their bums and saving the world a little bit, then surely that was for the best. They could start up the fight again, small scale and local at first. He believed in the Rooks, still. He believed they could save the world, if they put their minds to it – if they actually worked together. He just had to show them. Get them to sort out a relatively minor problem in their own town by appealing to their laziness and their pride. They could stop an encroachment on their home turf. And not just an encroachment from paranormal beings – becoming the big heroes in their town's only remaining shopping centre would be a pretty big middle finger to Aurora Tavistock on the day she arrived in town for her show. He knew that the family would enjoy that. And nobody had to drive past Stonehenge. Whatever was haunting the shopping centre could end up being a really good thing for his family and the world, if not for this terrible jumper.

His husband popped his head around the door.

'Charity's just having a quick five rounds of toast before we head out. Do you want a… hey!' Darryl's face lit up. 'You're wearing that jumper I bought you last Christmas!'

'Yep,' replied Janusz with a weak smile.

'And there was me thinking you'd lost it in the move,' added Darryl, happily.

'I found it,' replied Janusz, and mentally kicked himself for not pretending he'd lost it in the move, along with those 'sexy' pants. Oh well. Maybe a Demon would spit acid on it or something, and do him and the world of festive men's fashion a massive favour.

The Oakpines Shopping Centre had neither oaks nor pines growing anywhere near it, and it never had. An attempt at some saplings along the front had been made in the seventies when it was built, and swiftly abandoned a few years later in order to widen the road. Nevertheless, a wispy nineties redesign of the logo still stood fast on the large plexiglass canopy above its sliding doors – the silhouettes of a pine in front of an oak, in a single swishing line of weather-faded green. Ghosts of trees that never were. Nobody ever really questioned it, except for Janusz, with his twin interests in linguistics and pointing out things that made no sense to him.

Oakpines was a smallish indoor shopping centre, with a mezzanine, a couple of refreshments stands, and twenty-one shop units, eight of which now stood empty. Even the two-level department store you had to walk through to get out of the multi-storey car park was deserted now. The walk from car park to mezzanine was a sad trudge along an MDF corridor promising a new development that was meant to have opened two years ago. Oakpines had never, even in the nineties heyday of shopping sprees and Americanisms, been grand enough for anybody to refer to it as a 'mall'. However, in its prime it had once at least been a decent place for teenagers to while away a couple of hours and a tenner or two on clothes, or CDs, or amusingly oversized American-style cookies. Its main feature was, at least, still there. The 'big clock' – a large, overly intrinsic affair of twisted chrome, hanging over a small, murky fountain. Every town has a place where teenagers would agree to meet up, in the days before mobiles made coordinating social gatherings child's play. With some towns, it would be a particular statue, bandstand or monument. Rutherford had the big clock. It still just about worked, even though it was permanently set to British Summer Time these days and the little metal model birds that nestled amongst the chrome no longer chirrupped a song on the hour – they just sort of silently bobbed about. The fountain beneath it also still just about functioned as a fountain, although the water was little more than a trickle now and stank like an old log flume.

Darryl, Janusz and Charity perched on the marble effect lip around the fountain, between cigarette scorch marks and signs saying not to use the fountain as a bench, waiting for the other household to join them. Charity tucked into a sharing bag of chocolate-coated pretzels, which she did not share. It was, thought Darryl, just like the old days – except in the old days it was Charity who would be with a boyfriend and Darryl who would be the third wheel, still proclaiming to a wider society, which remained largely hostile to his true romantic interests, that he simply hadn't found the right girl yet. The shopping centre was much emptier than it had been in its heyday – both of shops and of people. In the old days, they would never have managed to get a prime perch like this, right on the fountain. They'd have had to linger near the escalator. Now, only a few elderly folk and mums with pushchairs wandered about, even though it was mid-afternoon at the start of the post-Christmas sales. No gangs of teens skulked like murders of crows – strutting squads clad in glossy black, cawing wordless belligerence and making a mess of the bins. It was sad, really.

Sadder still were the ghosts. Darryl could see them lingering about: hazy, human-sized patches of shadowy misery, all of them alone. A couple of dozen. None of them bothering anybody. Just… waiting. He was sure that they hadn't been there when he'd been in the centre before – at least, not in these numbers. He'd always felt relatively secure going to Oakpines, in part because it was fairly ghost-free. It wasn't that the ghosts would try to attack him – they rarely did that unless they were very agitated. Considering the best way to agitate them was to try to make them leave the mortal world, he only really had himself and the ghost hunting work to blame for the vast majority of ghost attacks. He just didn't really like being around lots of ghosts. You try spending your whole life being able to see the lingering dead stuck in their unending sadness and see how *you* feel about having a day out to buy a T-shirt, a DVD and a fancy ice cream plagued by hordes of clamouring spirits. No, he'd definitely only ever seen a couple of ghosts in Oakpines before – there was Limpy below the mezzanine balustrade and Heart-Clutching-Guy near the fire escape of what had once been Debenhams. Ghosts usually stayed where they'd died, and not many people had died in the shopping centre.

Which begged the question – why were there so many of them now? There would have to have been some sort of mass catastrophe in the past few months to explain this many ghosts here now, and while Darryl wasn't exactly hot on Rutherford's local news, he would have definitely heard about that.

It took ten minutes of waiting around, listening to Janusz complain about how 'Oakpines' made no sense as a name, before the other lot showed up. Brenda greeted them by telling them to remind her in a bit to tell them about 'the absolute state of Sunnyside retail park'. The others all said hello to one another with the same cold, vague courtesy as they had at Christmas. With every subsequent meeting, they felt even more like two households who tolerated one another, and certainly not one big happy family. Had they ever been one big happy family? Darryl wasn't sure, but there was a new awkwardness to them now, a brittleness. The family had become like a delicate, cracked vase. The cracks were so obvious, but nobody dared do anything about them. Everyone was being so careful not to push a finger against one of the fracture lines, and risk accidentally making the whole thing shatter.

'Well,' exclaimed Brenda, looking around herself, 'what happened here?'

'Local forums have reported a *lot* of disturbances here the past weeks,' Janusz told her.

'Yes, I get that,' replied Brenda, 'it'll be all the ghosts hanging out here – but *how*? They never used to be here and now there has to be over a dozen... oh no!' She cut herself short with a cry of genuine shock and despair.

Darryl looked around, trying to see what paranormal disturbance had upset her. 'What is it?'

Brenda pointed to an empty shop unit. 'That designer shoe outlet that was always having the "seventy per cent off closing down sale" closed down.'

'Who saw that coming?' asked Charity.

'Well, quite,' replied Brenda. 'It kept that closing down sale going for over a decade. I think it was some sort of tax fiddle, but it was a tax fiddle that got me these for fifty quid.' She gestured down at her stilettos.

'I'm a bit more worried about where all these ghosts came from, Mum,' attempted Darryl.

'A psychic can care about a ghost infestation and the state of the local economy at the same time, Darryl,' Brenda snapped. 'It's called multitasking.'

'I brought most of the things we need for a seance,' added Janusz, helpfully. 'Well – almost all. The crystal ball was left at your place, I think...?'

Richard nodded serenely, pulling it out of his backpack. 'It was in the garage.'

It would be a lie to say that their crystal ball had seen better days. In truth, it had been a state when they'd got it half-price from a Halloween section at the start of November a few years back. It was plastic, hollow, with a thin crack in it, a splodge of wood stain from where it had been resting in the garage and a mysterious sticky patch that collected dust to form a blob of mucky felt. None of the rest of their seance equipment was of any better quality. There was a metre of dusty black velvet, a few pewter pentagrams and a job lot of Cranberry Crush scented candles, bought purely because they were bright red. It was the sort of hokum that would jog what was left of ghosts' memories into being aware that this was indeed a seance.

Darryl was aware that his mother hated seances. It wasn't just because they were 'the sort of airy-fairy wiffle-woo that fraud Aurora Tavistock would pull', but she also felt it was—

'A waste of time.'

'Oh come *on*,' groaned Charity. 'We've been over this, Mum!'

'Yes, we have! In Helsbury, where the silly seance didn't work at all.'

'But the seance in Coldbay Island *did* work,' argued Janusz patiently, setting the pentagrams on the floor.

'One time,' Brenda reminded them, 'and that's when we knew all the ghosts' names and how they'd died. All that's happened in any of your attempts to hold a seance since then is we've wasted precious time and energy. And Darryl threw a fit and nearly died, so you should know better, actually.'

'I didn't "nearly die",' Darryl protested. He looked to Richard and Grace. Usually they sided with him on the seances.

'It was a bit scary, son,' mumbled Richard.

'Of course it was, it's always scary! Scary's our job! Scary's been our job even before terrifying burning eyeball rings started ripping holes in the sky and trying to end the world! It's fine! Grace? You're an all-powerful being from beyond our ken – tell Mum, would you?'

Grace just pulled an apologetic face and shrugged meekly at Darryl.

'But you know what *did* work in Helsbury, when our backs were to the wall?' Brenda added.

'Was it you being right?' sighed Charity.

'It was you, princess. Doing your Chosen One stuff.'

'Not the Chosen One any more, Mum. I chose not to be.'

'Still, though, you know what I mean. Doing things the old way. Me and your brother find the dead for you and you pop them off into the great beyond. Murzzzz and Grace act as bodyguards and Janusz does the spreadsheets. Bish bash bosh. A tight unit, working together.'

'We're not doing that any more,' chorused Darryl and Charity, wearily.

'It's mean to the ghosts,' added Darryl. 'Look at them.' He gestured around himself at the lonely patches of sad figures. 'They're not bothering anyone but there's too many of them, and the only way to find out why that is, is to ask them. And the only way to ask them is—'

'Is to let the dead use you as a vessel, Darryl, and then have a namby-pamby chat about their feelings until they get overexcited and choke you to death.'

'They've never choked me to death, Mum.'

'You don't know that.'

'Yes, I do! I'm not dead!'

Brenda did have a little bit of a point about the seances. They didn't always work, and the ghosts using Darryl's part-Demon body as a vessel through which to speak wasn't a pleasant experience. Often, there were so many of them trying to speak through him at the same time that they would make him pass out. And, yeah, sometimes they got a bit chokey. But he'd always been fine afterwards. Just about. And it was the more ethical way of dealing with them. He preferred it, Charity preferred it and, most importantly, Janusz preferred it – and Janusz always made the better choices. He made Darryl a better person. Darryl recycled diligently these days and he was even vegetarian now. Except on Christmas. And on Polish Pre-Christmas Christmas. And some Saturdays. Still, he was better than he used to be.

'We'll try the seance first,' he announced, in what he hoped was a firm tone. 'For starters, it means *he* can stay back.'

Darryl pointed at Richard, but he didn't mean Richard. He meant the Demon dwelling within Richard. Richard gave him a hurt look. Darryl was sure he'd known what he'd meant but Richard had a nasty habit of looking hurt on Murzzzz's behalf.

Brenda took in what Darryl had to say, and then ignored him and turned to Charity.

'Darryl's right,' said Charity.

Brenda huffed.

'I'm not popping any ghosts away until we've at least *tried*, Mum.' Charity nodded at Janusz, Richard and Grace's handiwork. A passable seance scene had been created on the floor next to the fountain with chalk sigils, sickly sweet smelling red candles, the velvet and the plastic crystal ball. Janusz had added crescent-moon-shaped glitter confetti as a finishing touch, this time. It looked horribly cheesy. Cheesy enough to work, thought Darryl.

Charity held her hands out for the others to take, so that they could form a circle. Again, the only purpose this served was that ghosts expected the living to hold hands in a circle for a seance.

Grace took one of Charity's hands. Brenda refused the other hand, folding her arms instead to show she didn't intend to do any such thing.

'Mum,' sighed Charity, wearily. 'We'd get this done quicker if you just—'

'If I just brainlessly went along with every harebrained scheme you kids come up with, even though I have been running a ghost hunting business since literally before you were born...' Brenda trailed off, locking eyes with Constance. Darryl glanced at the ghost of Brenda's dead former best friend. She had the sort of judgmental expression that women had a tendency to reserve for beloved friends and family who they'd had an epic falling-out with. 'Oh, don't *you* start,' growled Brenda, and grumpily accepted Charity's outstretched hand.

The family sat together on the floor as Darryl had a tendency to collapse into a heap during seances and he didn't want to fall too far if he did. He prepared himself to be flooded with the minds of the dead, but knew that it wasn't on him to invite them in.

Ever since their first successful seance, on Coldbay Island, Darryl had become convinced that the one who actually compelled the ghosts to speak wasn't himself, or Charity, or Brenda. He believed it was Grace. He had started to suspect that Grace was far more psychically powerful than she realised quite soon after meeting her. He had recognised that she was capable of summoning spirits and dispelling Demons with a strength that even put Charity's considerable abilities to shame. Of course, they had then discovered that Grace wasn't human at all, but an Angel who had been sent undercover and decided to rebel against the plan to end the world. So really, the whole psychic power thing made absolute sense now. It was likely that Grace was capable of far, far more than just summoning the dead to seances and punching Demons so hard they flew straight through the fabric of the universe and back into the underworld. She just didn't know it yet. Darryl didn't know whether Grace was aware that she was the one summoning the ghosts – because it *totally* was her summoning the ghosts. When Grace used her powers, something about her hurt his face. He wondered if it was the Angel within her, pushing itself slightly outside of the tight constraints of the small human body it had chosen to wear.

Grace closed her eyes, and seemed to concentrate, and Darryl's face started to hurt. Darryl felt the lingering dead rush to him suddenly. He let them into him – all clamouring to speak – and the shoving, tumultuous minds pushed his own mind back, back, back, so far back that he no longer connected with his body.

He didn't exactly pass out. He was aware that it looked to the others as if he passed out, but it was more like being pushed to the back of a crowd. Sometimes he was so far back that he had no idea what was in front of the crowd. And sometimes, like this time, he was just about able to make it out.

He was aware that the ghosts speaking through him weren't making any sense. They were too confused, too far gone and too many – pushing and shoving to be the one to say a few words before someone else butted in. None of them could say how they'd ended up in Oakpines. The closest thing to any sort of useful information was that a lot of them seemed to be waiting for something – but then pretty much all of the ghosts the family had ever been able to communicate with believed they were waiting for something. The beings that ran the universe from dimensions beyond told lies to the dead people stuck in the mortal realm. They raised their hopes that there'd be answers and a resolution one day, and then left them there, corralled into hotspots where misery could beget misery. It seemed that the other dimensions harvested the energy of their ghostly suffering. This energy helped to power what the family called 'Hell holes' – vast portals between dimensions to facilitate Demons travelling to the mortal plane on some sort of sadistic minibreak – and, if that wasn't bad enough, those portals were also now being used to attempt to end the world.

When they had tried this before, the ghosts had asked after the one they had been told to wait for, and the same name came up over and over again – the Manager. Having actually met the Manager more than once, Darryl was aware that the dead's hope that an irritable, officious floating nightmare of interlocking flaming rings and eyeballs would be willing to do anything to help them was an extremely false hope indeed. The Manager did technically have the power to be helpful, just not the inclination. The idea that the Manager would help was a lie, but Darryl could understand how the lie might have come about. This time, he couldn't make out anybody asking for the Manager at all, which was unusual. The person that they *were* asking for, on the other hand… he could see this not going down well with the rest of the family.

They were asking for Aurora Tavistock.

CHAPTER FOUR
Please Do Not Touch The Displays

'What?' asked Brenda, in a tone that should by rights be capable of turning people into stone.

Darryl sagged against his husband like a five-day-old party balloon. His mouth hung slackly open, and the various voices of the dead tumbled out of it.

'Is Aurora Tavistock here?' the ghostly voice of a youngish woman repeated her question.

'No,' Brenda told the ghost, frostily. 'And where did you hear that name?'

'She can help us,' said the voice. 'She's the best.'

'She...' replied Brenda, in a voice that could tarnish all the silverware within a ten-metre radius.

'Is...' continued Brenda, in a voice that could curdle milk inside a cow's udders.

'Not,' concluded Brenda, in a voice that could make a rainbow start crying.

'Is Aurora Tavistock here?' pleaded the ghost voice, unperturbed by Brenda. 'Someone said she'd be here.'

Brenda turned to the rest of the group.

'I will put up with my children being turned against me,' she announced. 'I will put up with being lumbered with an amnesiac Angel in disguise. I will even put up with repeated attempts to end the world. But I will *not* tolerate this sort of professional slander. *Whomst* is telling the *ghosts* that Aurora Bloody Tavistock is the medium to go to while I am sitting *right here*?'

'Can you remember who told you to wait for Aurora?' asked Grace, levelly. 'Can you remember who you are? And why you're here? Did you die in this shopping centre?'

But the voice of the young woman was gone. Now it was a man with a Scottish accent.

'Death,' he said, softly.

'Yes,' said Janusz in a kind tone. 'Yes, you're dead. Do you remember dying?'

'No,' replied the Scottish voice. The voice was rather sweet, and sleepy, the sort of voice you might hope to hear saying 'Good morning' to you from beneath last night's rumpled duvet. 'No – Death. Death is here.'

'There *are* a lot of dead people here,' Grace agreed.

'Death,' repeated morning-after Scotsman, sounding confused. Before he could say more, he was replaced by an older sounding man.

'Aurora Tavistock?' asked the new voice.

'No!' Brenda broke hands with the others in frustration. 'That's it, that's enough. This is impossible.'

'Is Aurora here?' asked a posh sounding woman, from Darryl's lolling mouth.

'See?' Brenda asked the others, exasperated.

'The Grim Reaper.' It was the Morning-After Scotsman again. Then quietly, '*That* Death.'

Oh. Brenda glanced at Charity. Her daughter looked concerned.

'I'm sorry,' she told the voice. 'I quit all that, a few weeks back. I can still help you though, if you'll let me—'

'Not you.' The voice didn't sound angry, just confused. 'The other one.'

'What?' Charity asked.

'Aurora Tavistock?' The sleep-rumpled Scotsman was gone again. This new voice sounded like a teenager.

Charity blinked and said to herself, 'The other one…?'

'Where's Aurora?' Another new voice. Another man. An angry man. 'Where is she? I've been waiting!'

Not all of the ghosts were within Darryl. Many were still standing gathered around the seance circle. Brenda could see ghosts well enough to make out most of their faces. They all looked impatient. People who had been waiting and waiting after being told to stay here until help and guidance came along, and now that the seance was here, it wasn't what they'd been promised. They'd been promised Aurora Tavistock, for some awful, nonsensical reason. They were frustrated. They were angry. It was a different anger to the one Constance followed Brenda around with. That was a patient, personal anger that could easily keep bubbling on for decades. This was the frustration of a crowd that had suddenly, after an unknowable length of time, found a focus to vent itself on. A seance was not the way. Hadn't Brenda *told* her silly children? This was not the way!

'That's it. Seance over.' Brenda got to her feet.

'But Mum,' attempted Charity.

'But nothing. They're turning sour, princess.'

'*You're* turning sour because they all want Aurora Tavistock.'

'Princess.' Brenda looked around at the surrounding ghosts. Darryl was still a drooling mess so, right now, Brenda was the only one who could see the bubbling anger of this crowd and had the wherewithal to say anything about it. 'We need to do this old school.'

Charity groaned. 'I knew you were going to say that. We're not going back to the old ways, Mum!'

There was an angry vibration coming from the ghosts. Brenda couldn't feel it yet, but she could see it – a buzzing of the air.

'Break up the circle, wake your brother and get popping,' she ordered.

Charity looked up at her with all the ferocity of an adorable cartoon penguin. 'Shan't.'

'Fine. Fine! Fine by me!' Brenda grabbed Grace by the neck of her cardigan and tried to hoist the little Angel-disguised-as-a-priest up to her feet. 'Grace, you can punch Demons back to Hell. You're just going to have to do the same thing to these ghosts.'

Grace looked horrified. 'I don't want to send any poor lost spirits to the Demon realm, they're not doing any harm!'

Darryl started choking. The ghosts were overcrowding him again, sending his overwhelmed body into shock. Typical.

'Well, somebody needs to do something.' Brenda glanced down at Janusz trying to pat his choking, shuddering husband awake, then over at the nearby wall above the fountain. The big clock hanging on the wall had started to shake in its brackets, little broken metal songbirds and all. She let go of Grace's cardi, and turned instead to her husband. 'Murzzzz,' she said. 'Can Murzzzz do it, in a pinch?'

'Not Murzzzz,' snapped Charity.

Even Janusz shook his head at Brenda at the mention of Murzzzz's name. So. *That* was still an issue, then. Apparently a bigger issue than Darryl literally choking in his husband's arms and the buzzing frustration of a number of ghosts making the big clock rattle violently, like it was the bars in a rioting prison rather than an overly ornate public timepiece set an hour too fast.

Brenda got down on her knees to try shaking Darryl out of his seance-trance a little more vigorously than his gentle husband was doing. Fortunately, it was at that second that Darryl took a deep breath in and focused his eyes on Brenda. Unfortunately, it was also at that second that the big clock was wrenched off its moorings and hurled at the group.

It landed mostly on Darryl, as the majority of supernaturally flung objects always did. There was just something about him that was a magnet for bad luck and poltergeist projectiles.

'Ow,' he complained, which meant he was fine for now.

A small metal bird bounced off Brenda's head. It wasn't that heavy.

'Stop whining,' she told her son, hauling him up to his feet, 'and help us out. Your silly seance just made them all more angry and confused.' She turned to Charity, who was trying to untangle the clock's intricate filigree minute hand from her hair. 'Princess?'

Charity stood up, leaving the minute hand hopelessly entangled, like a sad, lopsided chrome hairpin. 'No, Mum. I meant what I said.'

The angry vibrations from the shopping centre ghosts weren't dissipating at all. Throwing the clock had neither worn them out nor provided a catharsis for their frustration. If anything, it had just got them even more agitated. And just like a gang of emotionally drunk men after a silly little football match, the first patio chair to be hurled was unlikely to be the last. This was not a good time for Charity to decide to put her colourfully trainered foot down.

'Charity, princess, I let you have a go at doing it your way, I have been nothing if not— pFFFFFTTT.'

Brenda's perfectly good argument was suddenly and unpleasantly cut short when the fountain turned its stinking trickle of stale water into a pressurised jet of stinking stale water and was no longer flowing sadly down into a pool full of used fizzy pop cans and wet cigarette ends, but spurting straight at Brenda and Darryl's faces.

'Dear?' Richard fretted. 'Are you O— ARGH!' The jet of awful water turned its ire on Richard. Somewhere deep within him, Murzzzz growled with the shock, but managed to stay hidden inside his human host.

'Princess!' Brenda entreated her daughter, as she wiped water and running make-up off her face. 'We're under attack.'

'It's just a bit of gross fountain water,' argued Charity. 'Nothing we can't handl— oh COME ON.'

The jet of water hit Janusz square in the chest.

'I didn't even say anything!' Janusz protested, trying to hold his bag out of the water's way. At least he had had the where-withal to wear that horrible jumper.

Brenda held out a hand towards him. 'And now they're attacking Janusz! It's beyond the pale!'

'I'm not doing it, Mum!'

There was a bang from the display window of a nearby clothes shop. One of the mannequins was standing right at the window, its blank face pressed against the glass. As Brenda watched, the mannequin slid back a couple of feet and then forwards again, at a ferocious speed, smacking the glass with a deep thud.

'I have a duty of care,' continued Charity.

'But you don't any more,' Brenda argued. There was a differ-ent bang. Two child-sized mannequins had joined the adult one in being repeatedly flung against the window, like a horrible cross between a zombie movie and a crash test. Brenda kept a wary eye on them as she tried to talk sense into her girl. 'You're not the Chosen One any more. You quit. You don't have to lead the dead by the hand through the desert or any of that Anubis nonsense. I get that you're still angry at your father and me, but—'

'It is not about that, Mum! I still want to help the dead.' Charity had to raise her voice to a shout to be heard over the mannequins banging against the windows. There were mannequins in two more clothes shops doing it now. A pop-up boba tea place had an overly cutesy fibreglass model of a cartoonish cow that was also now repeatedly smashing its big round head against the door to the shop. 'I just don't want to do it for "the Man"... or the Angels, or whatever the Manager is— HEY!' The stream of terrible water turned on Charity. 'I am *trying* to help!'

'You see?' asked Brenda.

'Um,' squeaked Grace, who by now was the only dry one left, 'you guys do realise there are other people here?' She indicated to a woman standing with a pram outside Superdrug, watching the scene, frozen in terror. The baby in the pram was screaming – a frightened scream. 'Shoppers, shop workers...'

Brenda then noticed the ashen face of a blue-haired girl in the window of the boba tea place, her lip trembling as she watched the large, hollow cow mascot trying to smash its way to freedom.

'What do we do?' Grace asked, desperately. 'I've never been in a haunted building with the living caught up in it all before.'

There was a louder bang from one of the clothes shops, and a scream from within. One of the windows had smashed under the relentlessly butting head of a mannequin. A heavy-looking metal bin close to the terrified mother and baby started rattling the bolts holding it to the wall.

Charity's determined expression wavered in the face of the onlookers' fear. 'I'm not just being difficult because of the... you know, the falling-out. I won't simply banish the dead without their consent any more, Mum. It's horrible.'

'*All* of this is horrible,' argued Brenda. Bits of shopping centre were getting thrown at her, but this wasn't as distressing to her as seeing her usually confident daughter now so hesitant about using her ghost popping abilities.

'We have to help them,' Grace said. Brenda turned to face her and something about Grace's demeanour hurt Brenda's face. Something about Grace seemed to extend outside of her little body – an eye-melting light that couldn't be contained like a… like a halo.

The fountain tried to turn its force on Grace, but the water simply bent around her. From the look on Grace's face, she hadn't even noticed the water. She was too upset by the unfolding scene and by the twin fears and frustrations of the living and the dead. It was as if the water bent around Grace *because* she hadn't noticed it, like physics only worked for her if she paid enough attention to it and remembered that water should make her wet.

'Grace,' said Richard, in one of his deliberately level tones, 'we're on it, please try to stay calm. You're getting a little… rrrrrrrrrr…' Murzzzz shifted ever so briefly into focus. The Demon looked worried and sheepish – as if he hadn't meant to do that – and then he shifted again less than a second later, and became Richard again.

The boba cow finally smashed its way fully out of the shop, ripping off its horns and pulling the door off its top hinge as it did. The blue-haired girl screamed. There was more screaming and banging from the Timpson's next to it – an older man in an apron was pounding on the shop door trying to no avail to escape the key-cutter machine that was rattling towards him. The woman with the pram was still rooted in fear – the bin next to her was very nearly free of its bolts.

Darryl turned to his sister. 'You've got do something.'

'Oh, don't you start. We *were* doing something!'

'And it made things worse.' The fountain water hit him again. 'Argh! Do something else!'

'We're not going back to the old way, Darryl, not after all the hurt it caused...'

'There must be another way,' he shouted.

Grace was getting far, far too bright. Brenda had never had a headache that flooded every part of her head with a completely even level of pain before, so this was quite an experience.

'Grace,' said Charity, 'you need to stop that, if we can feel it, so can the others.'

Indeed, the woman with the pram had lifted a hand dreamily to her head, and the baby's cry had become one of discomfort as well as fear.

'Grace!' warned Brenda, as screws from the overhead lights started jingling to the floor.

'Someone has to do something,' breathed Grace, in a quiet tone that still somehow sounded loud and clear above the din of the haunting. 'Death is gone. But... but there's something else, someone else... They're going to him, he's here!'

'Grace!' shouted Richard. One of the overhead lights crashed to the floor, inches from where he stood. 'Pack it **in, Angel!**' Murzzzz emerged from Richard. Murzzzz was part of Richard's fight-or-flight mechanism, and things *were* getting pretty fight-or-flight-y.

'No!' Darryl fought against the torrent of water to point an angry finger at Murzzzz. 'Not you!'

'**Somebody needs to stop this,**' growled the Demon.

And then, it stopped.

It completely stopped. The mannequins stopped headbutting the windows. The lights stopped unscrewing themselves. The bin stopped trying to throw itself at the woman with the pram. The fountain stopped spraying them and the fibreglass cow lay lifeless, hornless and forlorn a couple of feet from the boba place's busted door.

Brenda looked around to see what had mollified the ghosts so suddenly, and saw… nothing.

There were no ghosts.

There had been dozens!

She turned to Darryl, confused, looking for a second opinion. He wiped the filthy water from his eyes and squinted around, before turning to her with a bewildered head shake.

'They've just… gone, Mum. All of them.'

'Wasn't me,' announced Charity, defensively.

'We know,' replied Darryl.

Of course it hadn't been Charity. Charity was incredibly psychically gifted, she could send spirits packing one after another in matters of seconds, but she had to concentrate on each one in turn. She couldn't just do away with dozens in the blink of an eye. It hadn't been Murzzzz either. Brenda knew how Murzzzz worked, he was more hands-on than that – or claws-on, since Murzzzz didn't have 'hands' per se.

That left Grace. Grace, whose immortal power had started to spill out of her right before the ghosts vanished. Brenda's head didn't hurt any more, and when she looked at Grace, all she saw was the same small woman as usual. The uncanny, painful 'halo' escaping from her form had vanished along with the dead. Grace frowned back at Brenda, a picture of befuddled innocence.

'What?'

'Was it you?'

'I don't understand.'

Grace seemed to mean it. But just because she didn't understand the situation it didn't mean she hadn't done something otherworldly and just not realised. Grace's mind had a nasty habit of compartmentalising the Angel in herself away.

'I think you might have just popped all the ghosts away,' Brenda told her.

'No, I... I wouldn't.'

'You *were* worried about the living,' Richard reminded her, fully Richard once more. 'And you were making me feel all hurty about my face.'

'It wasn't me,' panicked Grace.

'You said someone else was here,' added Janusz. 'Just before the ghosts went. Who did you mean?'

'I...' Grace retained her expression of miserable confusion – the daft amnesiac immortal. 'I don't know.'

'Oh. Sorry.' The voice was youngish, and male, and polite, and vaguely American. 'That would be me.'

Brenda and the rest of the family turned in the direction of the voice. A man was standing a few feet from them, near the escalator. He was either forty-ish with a good skincare regime, or thirty-ish and not in need of a good skincare regime. He had soft, dark eyes, gentle as a restful night, and a guileless smile.

'That's not to brag or anything,' he added, approaching them with as much menace as a blossom wafting towards one on a gentle breeze. 'Just, I heard you guys arguing and I didn't want you doing that over something that I was responsible for. So. Thought I'd just fess up instead.'

The family just stared. Brenda was sure she recognised this young man. Her memory flipped through its database of male American ghost hunters in his age range.

'Excuse me for asking,' added the young man, courteously, 'but are you Brenda Rook?'

Brenda nodded, still trying to place the man.

He beamed. 'Awesome! Huge, huge fan.' He turned to Charity. 'That means, you must be Charity,' he added in even more reverent tones.

'Meep,' squeaked Charity.

'And I'm Darryl,' added Darryl in the quietly irritable voice he always used when he was feeling left out.

'Of course you are,' grinned the man.

'And I am his husband Janusz,' added Janusz in the flatly professional tone *he* always used when Darryl spoke to a man over a certain threshold of handsomeness.

'Cool,' beamed the man. 'Love your sweater, by the way. Super festive.'

Janusz fiddled self-consciously with the soaking, stinking, ugly Christmas jumper. 'A present. From my *husband*.'

'Awesomesauce,' replied the man with the same open smile.

Something clicked into place in Brenda's brain. Not American. Canadian. The missing ghost hunter from Winnipeg. Krish Patel. He was here. *What was he doing here...*? Wait, didn't Patel's name ring a bell? Hadn't someone mentioned it a while back? Maybe during the battle for Helsbury? And if he was telling the truth about popping all those ghosts in one go, how had he done it? She'd heard Patel was good, but not *that* good – not able to do a complex, dangerous clearing by himself in a heartbeat when it would have taken their whole team hours.

'You must have a bunch of questions, and that's cool, I'm happy to answer them,' Patel told them. 'Maybe once I've had something to eat. The work always leaves me with the biggest carb craving. But the short of it is this – hey guys, name's Krish. Angels literally blew up my work phone and told me to come here because, it turns out, I'm Death.'

CHAPTER FIVE

You Don't Know Him,
He's From Canada

Yes.

That was it – the immortal powers running the universe from afar had said when Charity quit her role as Death that she would be replaced.

What they hadn't mentioned was that her replacement would be absolutely hot to trot and have a cute foreign accent. Krish Patel was one of the top Canadian ghost hunters, wasn't he? Oh. Charity *loved* Canadians. They were full of foreign glamour but so courteous with it. Was it OK to exoticise North American men like that? Charity decided within half a second that her experiences of having exactly the same thing done to her East Asian origin self at comic conventions by Anime-addled Englishmen meant that it was totally fine for her to do it to a bloke with a nice accent, as long as she did so with dignity and respect.

'A snack,' she said, far too loudly. She cleared her throat and started again. 'I know how hungry moving on ghosts can make you. Let me get you lunch, or early tea or whatever, and we can talk about this whole "Death" dealy.'

'You're buying lunch for Death?' asked Richard.

'Until quite recently, Dad, you were making dinner for Death every night,' Charity reminded him. 'It was just that none of us knew it, yet. Also, Death has a name. Right, Krish?'

'Right,' replied Krish. 'Also, I don't want to come across as difficult or anything but I'm vegan – I know the cliché is that we yammer on about it all the time, but I'm just putting it out there before you go to the trouble of buying me a ham sandwich or something...'

'It's fine!' Charity jabbed a thumb at her brother and brother-in-law. 'These two keep trying to do the vegetarian thing, so we're used to it.'

'What do you mean, "*trying* to do the vegetarian thing"?' asked Darryl.

'*Oczywiście*, he would be vegan,' muttered Janusz. '*Czy normalny wegetarianizm nie jest wystarczająco dobry?*'

'Oh hey, you're Polish?' beamed Krish. 'My college roommate was from Płock. Learned to speak it so I could talk to his mom when she visited. And also so I could speak to his dad when *he* "visited". His dad had been dead awhile, I think I helped him find peace.'

Janusz's expression twisted into an unusual expression of guilt at getting caught out in the act of saying mean things in his first language.

'It's OK, I'm used to people getting funny about the veganism, it's not that I think I'm better than you or that "normal vegetarianism" isn't good enough" like you say. It's just a personal choice, and anyway it's pretty easy to go vegan in a big city like Winnipeg. You probably just have fewer options in a small town like this.'

'We have options,' retorted Darryl, defensively.

'The community cafe where I volunteer has a vegan menu,' added Grace, helpfully.

'That sounds perfect for me,' smiled Krish. 'Where is it?'

Grace's face fell. 'About two miles away. Also it's shut this week.'

And this was why usually when Charity offered to buy a hot guy lunch, she didn't do it with her entire family and an overly 'helpful' Angel in tow.

'The boba place,' Charity said, indicating the shop where the blue-haired barista was now gazing in stunned relief at the broken door, 'also does yakisoba, and there's a tofu option. Hence the name. Boba and Soba. Come on.'

She linked arms with Hot Death and started guiding him towards the smashed-up shop. As she did so, the woman with the pram finally shook herself out of her torpor and began shakily pushing the pram in the direction of the group and the car park.

'Did you feel that earthquake?' asked the woman as she walked towards them. She gazed, wide-eyed, at the mess. 'It's nuts. Here? All that fracking, I reckon. The Greens had a pamphlet about fracking and it said about earthquakes.'

Charity nodded at the woman earnestly. 'Yeah, fracking'll do that,' she agreed.

'Shouldn't be allowed,' muttered the woman, carrying on back to her car. 'There was a petition, but they never bloody listen, do they?'

Charity paused to pick the boba place's fibreglass cow mascot up off the floor. It was a real shame. She'd liked that cow. Maybe she could be fixed.

'Kawaii Cow,' sighed the blue-haired barista, as Charity carried the injured mascot back to her home in the shop.

'A victim of the earthquake,' Charity told her, silently thanking the pram lady for coming up with a believable explanation for what had happened.

'Earthquake,' repeated Blue-Hair, still shell-shocked. 'Yes. It'll be all that fracking. There was a petition.'

After a needlessly long conversation about whether the blue-haired barista was absolutely sure the noodles weren't egg based and the sauce didn't contain any fish extract, Charity bought Krish some hot food and a delightfully chewy drink. And while she hadn't actually popped any ghosts recently and technically had no need to carb-load, she bought herself some boba and soba too, because it was tasty and besides, if they were both eating it made it look more like a date. This was for Krish's benefit, Charity told herself. With their food, they sat together in the most attractive part of Oakpines – next to the Christmas tree display. It was the same large plastic tree and same slightly faded decorations the centre had been using for the past decade, and it had been toppled by the 'earthquake'. Dusty baubles and fake presents were scattered about the floor in a considerable radius and the plastic star lay sadly next to the doorway of a closed-down record shop, with one of its points smashed off. To say that this was still the most attractive part of Oakpines was a sad indictment of the general state of the shopping centre even before the 'earthquake'.

This didn't bother Charity so much. She was a bit more bothered that her entire family, plus Grace, hadn't cottoned on yet that this lunch with Krish was supposed to be an unofficial date, and had also gathered around to talk to him. Well, most of them had. Darryl had complained that Charity hadn't bought him or Janusz a drink while she was in the shop, and had stalked off to get some himself.

'So,' said Brenda, 'you can see ghosts *and* you can move them on.'

Krish nodded, politely. 'Ever since I was little.'

'Multiple abilities – that's rare,' noted Charity.

'My Darryl has three abilities,' said Janusz, in the same defensive tone he'd been using ever since Krish showed up.

'Yes, but he's part-Demon,' replied Richard.

Krish raised his eyebrows in surprise at this.

'You're not part-Demon, are you?' Richard continued. 'Or maybe was one of your parents a Finder and the other a Deliverer?'

'Never knew them,' Krish replied, breezily. 'They died in a freak road accident when I was little.'

Charity gasped, mid tapioca ball. A tragic backstory!

'Technically I was dead too, for about twenty minutes,' added Krish in his cheery, conversational tone. 'Got a scar here that's...' he trailed off, pointing to the side of his head. 'Well, you can't really see it, because of my hair.'

And he really did have lovely hair. Thick and black and glossy. *And* it covered a tragic backstory scar? Charity was definitely going to have to date this man.

'Anyhoo, that's possibly why I have my powers.'

'A brush with death,' breathed Charity, reverently, '*and* violently orphaned. I just did the "violently orphaned" bit.'

Krish nodded. 'That's your birth mom, right?' He indicated to an empty space at Charity's side. 'It's so cute she's still with you. I never saw mine again, no matter how hard I tried. They must have moved on straight away. And I didn't used to be *that* powerful. I was Winnipeg Good, not World Leading. So, I was pretty stoked to get asked to be, you know, Death, the Grim Reaper, the final guide – whatever you want to call this gig. I like to think I can bring a bit of positivity to the role, you know? Less the Grim Reaper, more the...'

'Nice Reaper?' Charity interjected.

Krish beamed. 'I like that. Also, after I agreed to the job, they really superboosted my ability to move spirits on. Coupla dozen angry ones came up to me next to that bookstore over there before I could get to you, and swoosh – off to the realm of eternal peace for them.'

'Yes,' grumbled Janusz, 'very impressive.'

'Thanks,' smiled Krish.

'However,' continued Janusz, 'as we were *just* discussing when you decided to show up and take things into your own hands, you should know that just popping people away like that without their consent is actually very problematic.'

'Oh, is it?' Krish asked. 'It's how I've always done it, I assumed that was how you guys worked, too. And I felt like I should act fast since, you know, there were babies about to get crushed? Don't worry, I'm super gentle. A few of the ghosts even understood what I was and why I was here.'

'The Scottish guy,' muttered Charity.

'He was Scottish? Cool! I'd love to see bonny Scotland.'

'While you're sightseeing,' Janusz added, 'your own home town is overrun with spirits and the ghost hunter community there think you've gone missing.'

'Yeah,' said Krish with a little sigh. 'Hated leaving them in the lurch like that but I was sort of given no choice, I had instructions from on high and stuff.'

'You said Executives "blew up your phone",' said Grace.

'I don't know *what* they were. All us ghost hunters know none of the main religions got any of this stuff entirely right or wrong, so I dunno what to call 'em. Gods? Aliens? You call them Executives? I call them Angels.'

'"Angels" is *not* the preferred term,' said Janusz loudly, just as Darryl approached the group, bearing drinks.

'Oh, I beg your pardon then,' replied Krish, pleasantly. 'But they really did blow up my phone.'

Charity chewed her tapioca with wonder. This was the sort of point in the great narrative of their team-up-slash-romance where there would be a flashback. As he told the family how he'd come to end up in Rutherford's haunted shopping centre at the arse end of the year, she pictured it cinematically – in a faded palette, obviously, because this was before he'd met Charity and his life had changed for the awesomer.

The Executives, or Angels or whatever you wanted to call the beings running the universe and trying to end the world, had indeed blown up his phone in the most literal sense. Krish showed them the mobile, which he now kept wrapped in one of those little red blankets Janusz had installed in their flat's kitchen in case a chip pan went up in flames. When the Executives called him, Krish explained, the phone wouldn't ring, rather, it would ignite like a seventies nightie on a three-bar heater. And it would stay on fire until they had finished talking to him, at which point, the fire would vanish, leaving the phone room temperature to the touch and completely undamaged.

During the same call in which they'd offered him the post of Death, they'd told him to go to the UK. Afterwards, he had found a one-way plane ticket sitting next to him. Krish had spent too many years dealing with ghosts, Demons and other matters beyond the usual remit of the mortal world to just ignore orders from beings from beyond. Besides, he'd never been to England before. He wanted to see Big Ben. Meet one of *Monty Python* – living or dead, he didn't mind.

He hadn't gotten to see Big Ben, yet – let alone any surviving or ghostly members of a seventies comedy troupe. When he'd landed, he'd found in his pocket a train ticket to a place called Skegness. It had taken him some time wandering around the cold, east coast seaside town to realise what was wrong about it. There were several strange residual psychic remains a few miles up the coast from it. Something had been there – something big, something powerful. There was a sense that something had been... devoured, there. The dead in that whole area had been extremely agitated, and more numerous than he'd usually expect next to a largely uninhabited stretch of coastline. He had helped the ghosts, sent them along to the next plane of existence – a place that Krish like to think was paradise, and the Executives told him was called 'Waste'. It wasn't a nice name, but Krish held hope and faith that the other plane was at least peaceful. More peaceful than wandering lost and confused around the crashing sea and the psychic aftershocks of a mysterious calamity.

Once the stretch of coast had been cleared, he'd found another train ticket – again, not for London, but for a rural village in Lancashire. As before, it had taken Krish a while to pinpoint the problem. He'd spent Christmas in a B&B in the windswept middle of nowhere, before following his psychic instinct away from the village to a completely abandoned and ruined gas station on a nearby stretch of highway. Again, Krish had been struck with the sensation that something large had recently been devoured, but this time it had been different. For starters, there had been no ghosts for him to help. Not even along the stretch of highway, where ghosts were usually plentiful. It was as if something had just eaten everything up, including all the dead. Or at least, so he'd initially thought. He'd also found a lot of confusion from the locals over when exactly the large gas station had been abandoned. Many remembered it being there, some had stories about a knife attack there, or a boy's death by overdose, or a ghost which was sometimes on the footbridge, and sometimes in the car park. But none could say when or why the gas station had shut.

When he'd gone out for his daily almond latte, he'd got chatting to the girl at the cafe, who'd mentioned she'd worked there… *the previous month*. From the rot and ruin, the gas station had been abandoned for years, decades, even. It wasn't right… and that hadn't been the only thing that wasn't right. The more he'd talked to the cheerful girl, about her old 'sucky' job at the gas station, about her new girlfriend and her hopes to start her own business, the more Krish had been struck by the feeling that this girl – this vibrant, very alive girl – had recently been dead. She'd been dead and she'd even existed as a ghost, mournful and lost, for some time. And now here she was – fine and dandy in her body – alive as anything. And she had no recollection of it, the lucky thing. Something had devoured the dead, but also something – either the same something or a different something, had brought other dead souls back to life. And, speaking as the newly appointed Not-So-Grim Reaper, both of those things were very wrong.

A third mysterious train ticket had brought him to Rutherford only this morning. It still wasn't anywhere near Big Ben, but at least it wasn't as derelict as the remains of the motorway services, or the empty stretch of coast. Also, unlike the other two places, he no longer had the sense that something had recently been devoured. This place was full of a growing menace, a pressure, like the hours before a sudden summer storm. Whatever he had missed on the coast and on the highway, it hadn't happened here yet, but it was coming. He could feel it. And he wasn't here to stop it, he was here to help. To ease the process. To numb the pain, to hold the hands, to softly soothe. He wasn't here to save Rutherford, or the world. He was here to be its palliative nurse. He was here to tidy up – gently, kindly – making sure everything was where it ought to be so nothing got lost and left behind in what was coming… whatever that actually was.

His arrival in the haunted shopping centre had largely been accidental. He was aware of the Rooks – like Krish himself, the family were known amongst the ghost hunting community – but he hadn't known that they were based in Rutherford. He had assumed they would live in London. He tended to assume most Brits lived in London, he admitted, this was what came from watching too many Richard Curtis movies. He hadn't gone to Oakpines on purpose, instead he'd become aware of the psychic disturbance there while wandering through the town centre following his one lead.

'What lead?' asked Charity.

Krish's expression twisted handsomely into one of mild embarrassment. 'Don't judge me, OK?'

'What lead?' repeated Janusz, in a tone of voice that suggested her brother-in-law was enjoying Krish's discomfort.

'I… saw a poster saying Aurora Tavistock was bringing her show to town,' admitted Krish. 'I thought maybe that could be what was causing all the disturbances. She's supposed to be doing a signing at the bookstore here.'

'Aurora Tavistock?' Brenda scoffed. Krish might as well have told Brenda that he believed babies came from a magic wishing tree.

Krish shrugged, sheepishly. 'Turned out, she wasn't here, but you guys were. So at least the lead led me to you guys. Eventually.' He took another slurp of his fashionably lumpy tea and gave it a thoughtful chew. 'Because – and I don't know if you're going to take this as good news or not – I don't think any of this disturbance is centred around Aurora after all. I think it's more likely centred around… well. Around you.'

'Yeah,' replied Charity, 'that's not a shock. The attempted end of the world has sort of been following us around. It's obsessed with us.'

'Those events I was too late for – the devourings on the coast and on the road – that was you, wasn't it?' Krish asked. 'I can sense residue from them all over you guys. Sorry if that's a gross way of describing it.'

'It's fine,' said Charity. 'Long story short, those were apocalypses we stopped.'

'I see.' Krish chopsticked a few more noodles. 'And if it happens again here, you'll try to stop it again?'

'Of course. Don't want the world to end, that's where we keep all our stuff. Certainly don't want it to end in our home town. That's making it personal.'

'Yeesh, well that's a real pity,' said Krish. ''Cause you guys seem really nice and all, but… well, I think maybe I was sent here to stop you.'

CHAPTER SIX

The Nice Reaper

'Stop us?' Brenda scoffed. 'Stop *us*??'

'I think so,' replied Krish, apologetically. 'So sorry about that.'

'Ha! I'd like to see you try, young man.'

'I don't think you *would* like to see me try, but I'm afraid you're going to have to.'

'What are you going to do?' Brenda continued. 'There's loads of us. *And* we've got Demons.'

'Dear,' muttered Richard in a warning tone.

'Oh come off it – he'll already know about Murzzzz.'

Krish nodded, solemnly. 'And I see the Demon in Darryl. And there's your ghost…' Krish indicated towards Constance, before turning his head to meet eyes with Grace. 'And then there's the stolen suit of Grace Barry.'

Krish got to his feet, with all the aggression of a kitten. Still, Grace took a defensive step backwards. Even kittens could be threatening, if one were a mouse.

'You shouldn't be here,' he said, gently. 'This isn't your home.' He took a couple of steps towards her.

Grace was not a mouse. Grace was an all-powerful being from beyond, wearing the face of a human, but she was still not at all sure what to do about the young man approaching her. True, this wasn't quite her home, but it was the only place that felt like maybe it could possibly be home, in time. It was the only place, since Coldbay's church had been taken from her, that she *wanted* to be home. More than that – this was where she wanted to be Grace. She wanted to be Grace so badly. Could this human's powers to sort the living from the non-living and to remove those who didn't belong in the mortal realm remove her from Rutherford? From the Rooks? From being Grace?

Krish took another step in her direction, and she instinctively shuffled backwards again and her back hit something hard and hollow. He frowned as he stared past her.

'Do they not have separate food and cardboard recycling here?'

Grace turned to follow his eyeline. He was looking at what she'd backed into – a litter bin. She sidestepped away from it.

'Not in Oakpines,' replied Richard, apologetically. 'The council *were* talking about changing it.'

'I signed a petition,' added Janusz, testily.

Krish sighed and shrugged, binning his lunch carton. 'Too late to bother recycling now anyway, I suppose.'

'This has all been a misunderstanding,' attempted Charity. 'It's fine – you're new as Death. I actually had the job for years before you, so we should just chat about your problematic non-consensual popping habit and any concerns you might have. Maybe over drinks or a romantic walk in the park?'

There was something Grace found oddly menacing about Krish throwing the carton in a non-recycling bin. Like he really meant business. She didn't like any of this, not one bit. She wanted to go home. To the Rooks' home. She wanted to get back to her mug with the ugly cartoon cat on it and the slightly uncomfortable sofa. She wanted to be Grace. Grace wanted to go home.

Krish gasped and clutched at his face. 'Ouch! What *is* that?'

'That's nothing,' lied Brenda, her own eyes watering with the sudden pain in her own face.

'It's coming from the Angel… thingie,' said Krish, wincing. 'Did you guys know she could do this?'

'They don't like being called that,' retorted Janusz through gritted teeth. 'It's reductive.'

Grace wanted to go home. She wasn't an 'Angel'. She was Grace! She was Grace! And she wanted to go home!

'Sorry,' replied Krish, 'I forgot, what with the stress of my face feeling like it's been set on fire.'

Grace wanted to go home! She didn't want to be here with Death! Usually the world does not care about what ordinary people want. But ordinary people are not Ang— Celestial Executives. And this Celestial Executive was feeling trapped. And so, the world did listen to what Grace wanted. Oakpines twisted and folded around her, and then, she was home, in the Rooks' house, with her ugly cartoon cat mug.

'Grace?' asked Charity. 'What did you do?'

'My eyes feel like hot pins,' moaned Janusz, clutching his face.

'I… I wanted to go home,' stammered Grace, unsure about what she *had* actually done, or how. 'He was dangerous.'

'He was cute!' Charity huffed, rubbing her own face. 'I didn't even get his number before you yanked us all out of there. Wait.' She squinted over at Grace. 'You *did* yank all of us, didn't you? Including Constance? Where's Constance?'

'Behind you, dear,' Brenda told her, trying to blink the pain in her own eyes away. 'She's pretty tightly latched on to you. Where you go, she goes.'

'So, nobody's missing?' Charity asked. 'I feel like someone's missing. Wait – where's Dad?'

Brenda gasped, looking around the living room.

'Richard?' She turned a glare on Grace that was so wrathful, Grace almost wished she'd taken her chances with the Reaper. 'What did you do with my husband?'

'I don't know! I don't know what happened. That wasn't... did I really do that?'

'You just left my Demonically possessed husband alone with Death!'

'*My* husband is also missing,' added Janusz. Darryl hadn't been brought back to the house with them either.

'What have you got against husbands?' railed Brenda.

'You left him with that hot guy,' Janusz fretted, anxiously wringing at the hem of his wet Christmas jumper.

'Relax, Janusz, he was into me. And he's out of Darryl's league,' said Charity, ignoring the fact that technically Janusz should have been out of Darryl's league as well.

Grace felt a hot panic rise again, and the Rooks clutched at their faces with pain once more. She tried wanting Richard and Darryl to be with them at the house just as desperately as she'd wanted to go home, but it didn't work this time.

'Why won't it work?' she asked. 'They're going to think I just left them behind.'

Everyone looked to Janusz to say something nice and soothing to Grace.

'No, no,' sighed Janusz, his heart clearly not in it, 'I'm sure they won't.'

'Wow,' said Darryl, looking at the space where the rest of his family had just been. 'So Grace just left us behind, then.'

'It won't be on purpose,' replied Krish, amiably. 'It'll be because she's an Angel – sorry... "Executive" – and you two have too much Demon in you for her will alone to move you.'

Richard sighed softly.

'No,' argued Darryl. 'I'm not doing the Demon thing any more. I made my husband a promise.'

'It's still within you, though,' Krish told him, 'whether you like it or not. Also – does Janusz hate me? It kind of feels like he hates me.' He sighed and cracked his knuckles. 'Oh well. I think maybe you'll all hate me by the time I'm done. Let's get Murzzzz out of here first.'

Richard leaped backwards away from Krish, like a cat who'd spotted a cucumber. As he did so, all the Richard about him shifted out of focus, as if he was one big optical illusion, and Murzzzz emerged into view. By rights, a colossal, ancient, high-ranking Demon, with a muscular, prehensile tail, dripping fangs and huge, horrific claws shouldn't really be able to entirely conceal himself within a small, soft gentleman in his sixties, only becoming visible when he wanted to. But also you wouldn't think two people would be able to look at the same photo of a striped dress and see it in two completely different sets of colours. Human eyes and minds are funny, tricksy things.

Darryl snarled instinctively at the sight of the Demon. He had said he never wanted to see Murzzzz again. Why didn't *any* of his parents ever listen to him?

'Oh hi, Murzzzz,' smiled Krish, as if seeing a huge Demon emerge out of a man in a dilapidated shopping centre was as everyday as greeting your neighbour. 'Let's get you home before we upset any more of these shoppers.'

'**No,**' snarled Murzzzz. '**Leave me and my son alone.**'

Darryl spluttered indignantly. 'I am *not* your son!'

Krish took another step towards Murzzzz and held out his hands. 'It's OK. I understand it's complicated. Darryl's got to stay here. You go home, no questions asked and nobody gets hurt. It's all planned out. I'm sure you can't really be happy all cramped up here in a mortal's life, big fella like you. Just relax and we'll get all of this sorted...'

Murzzzz bounded into the air in one fluid, vertical movement, latched briefly on to the ceiling, then launched himself back down towards the floor again. For a moment as the detested Demon sailed through the air, Darryl thought he was about to land a physical attack on Krish, which definitely felt unnecessary despite Krish's 'I have to stop you preventing the end of the world' rhetoric. In the split second that Murzzzz took to sail back to the ground, however, Darryl realised that the Demon's trajectory was all wrong. He wasn't aiming for Krish at all. He was aiming for Darryl.

'Wh...' was all that Darryl managed to say before Murzzzz scooped him off his feet and leaped back into the air again, now carrying Darryl with him like a horrified, furious damsel in distress.

Before Darryl was able to scream 'Let me go, you're not my dad,' there was the sound of smashing safety glass and a rush of cold air as Murzzzz crashed his way out of Oakpines, via one of the skylights.

'Let me g—' he managed, but had the wind knocked out of him as Murzzzz thundered along the roof of the shopping centre, leaping yet again at the edge and landing heavily on the roof of a nearby charity shop. This was intolerable! Krish was just one guy! There'd been a misunderstanding but he seemed reasonable enough, there was no call to carry him like a dolly above the streets of his home town, where somebody he knew might see. But that was Murzzzz for you. No thought.

'You're not my da— he attempted again, but the rushing December air kept knocking the breath out of him. There was nothing he could do.

Well. There was *something* he could do.

He couldn't get out of Murzzzz's grasp in this form, but he had a fighting chance if he turned into a Demon… No. No! He wasn't going to do that. He'd promised. Besides, that was just giving Murzzzz what he wanted.

Instead, he just scowled with fury and humiliation as Murzzzz made quick work over the rooftops of the short distance between Oakpines and his parents' house. Within only a few seconds, Murzzzz descended from the nearest streetlamp to land and deposit Darryl in his parents' front garden, right as Janusz came running out of the door.

'Oh,' said Janusz, 'we were just going back to get you. Are you OK? We don't know why Grace wasn't able to get you two out.'

'Yeah, you do,' huffed Darryl, still winded. He winced at the way it sounded more like a barb directed at his husband than its intended target of Murzzzz.

'The Demon thing?' asked Janusz, gently, darting a glance at Murzzzz.

Darryl nodded. Janusz responded by wrapping him in a tight embrace. '*Zabko*. It's OK.'

'It's not really that OK if someone's brought the new Grim Reaper here to stop us and end the world, is it?' Brenda came out of the door. 'Hello, Murzzzz.'

'He's not grim,' said Charity, in the doorway. 'He's too Canadian to be grim.'

'Nevertheless,' replied Brenda. 'New plan. Everyone in danger of being "sorted" out of this universe by Krish, stays here where it's safe. That's Grace, Murzzzz and Constance – if you can drag yourself from Charity's side, Constance my dear. The rest of us will go and send this new Death packing back to the land of moose, maples and mild manners.'

'Sounds a little bit racist,' huffed Charity.

Murzzzz sniffed the air. He had a nervousness about him that Darryl wasn't used to. '**Er...**' muttered the Demon.

'Canadian isn't a race! And it's not even the Canadian thing, is it, it's the "bringing about the apocalypse" thing. Now, are you going to come with and save the world again?' Brenda asked.

'He's mortal though, Mum. We're not used to fighting mortal humans. And I'm not going to hit him – he's too pretty.'

Darryl pulled out of his husband's embrace and looked at his sister. 'Charity, do you fancy Death?'

'Er, yeah, I thought I was making that perfectly clear from all the flirting I was doing? I bought him boba *and* soba!'

Murzzzz made a couple of loping movements towards the front door of the house, in spite of the fact that in this form he was far too big to pass through the doorway. '**Er,**' he said again.

'What on Earth is it, Murzzzz?' snapped Brenda. 'You're like a dog at a fireworks display.'

The Demon side of Darryl, buried deep within him, sensed danger a heartbeat before he saw Krish round the street corner and head towards their house at an easy run.

'Hi guys,' he called. 'Hope you don't mind too much. Murzzzz was quite easy to follow, he leaves a bit of a trail, and you're really not far from the mall.' He slowed to a speed walk as he approached, catching his breath. 'Oh, it's nice here, isn't it? All leafy and quaint.'

Brenda stepped forwards. 'You are *not* coming into our house!'

'I might have to, I'm sorry. You're hiding an Angel-Executive *and* a Demon there, and it's just clogging everything up. Causing unnecessary unpleasantness. Also I should help your ghost, there.'

He nodded at Constance, still standing just by Charity's shoulder in the garden and not hiding in the house like she'd been told after all.

'Hey,' Charity said to Krish, as behind her, Murzzzz tried desperately to slink his massive frame through the doorway into the house, 'less of that talk now, handsome.'

'Charity,' warned Brenda, approaching the front garden's gate with her hands outstretched as if that were actually going to do anything, 'I don't care how handsome he is, do not do anything that could be misconstrued as an invitation.'

'He's not a vampire, Mum.'

'And I'm not a threat,' added Krish. He was at the garden gate now, undeterred by Brenda's uselessly outstretched hands. 'I really am here to help, honestly.'

'It's not help if we don't want it,' cried Brenda, making the international sign for 'shoo' at Krish with both hands.

'It is if you need it and don't realise it.' Krish held his own hands out, in a stance worryingly similar to the one Charity would take just before 'popping' a ghost away from the mortal world. 'Murzzzz, come on, you can't be comfortable like that.'

Murzzzz was jammed halfway in the doorway like a cartoon bear who'd eaten too much honey – too big to pass through and too panicked to take Richard's smaller form.

'Let's go,' added Krish. 'I don't want to have to force you – that won't be nice.'

'No,' Brenda declared. 'Stay away from my sanctuary.'

'Again, Mum, he's not a vampire.'

'You shall not pass!'

'And you're not Gandalf.'

Indeed, Brenda had no Gandalf powers, and as much as any homeowner likes to imagine there is an invisible, impassable barrier around one's property, in this case the only barrier to Krish was a short decorative brick wall, easily hopped over by a sprightly, if apologetic, young man such as himself.

'So sorry about this,' he said, ignoring the small gate and clearing the tiny wall in three fluid steps.

'How dare you!' Brenda cried.

'Sorry sorry sorry,' Krish cringed, 'I'll be careful of your flower beds, I promise.'

'Darryl! Janusz! You're men! Protect the family!'

Darryl sighed and stepped towards Krish, his own hands out, in spite of how little that had helped stop Krish up to that point.

'Come on now, mate, you can't do this.'

Krish opened his mouth to reply, then closed it again and, with an apologetic expression, ducked right underneath one of Darryl's outstretched arms and darted past him towards Murzzzz.

'Hey,' shouted Janusz, making a grab for Krish, 'don't ignore my husband!'

Janusz's grab only glanced the sleeve of Krish's coat as the Canadian wove past, apologising all the way in a quiet little mantra of sorries.

'*Sukinsyn!*' cried Janusz.

'I can tell you're upset,' gasped Krish, clearing the last couple of steps to get to Murzzzz, still stuck in the doorway. Darryl recognised that expression of concentration on Krish's face. He'd seen it on his own sister, every time she'd dealt with a clearance of ghosts and Demons alike. And Krish was levelling it straight at Murzzzz, and... wait, maybe that wasn't such a bad thing after all.

Krish reached both hands out towards the stuck Demon, but right before he could touch Murzzzz, Charity appeared behind him and grabbed him by both wrists.

'No you don't,' she grunted. And then, in a much less menacing tone, 'Coo, you're strong.'

'Vegan diet is actually really good for building lean muscle,' replied Krish, struggling against her grip.

'Will you shut up about being vegan,' called Janusz.

'And I'd have thought you wouldn't like Murzzzz. Wouldn't your family be better off without him?' Krish asked the also-surprisingly-strong woman behind him.

'I...' muttered Murzzzz, looking behind him and pulling a sorry expression as he tried to make eye contact with Darryl.

If Murzzzz wanted Darryl to say something nice about him, then he'd have a long wait coming, because Krish did sort of have a point. Wasn't it Murzzzz and his selfish decisions in the past and the present alike that had fractured Darryl's family? Hadn't he and Charity asked for Murzzzz to leave? Wasn't Murzzzz the whole reason they'd moved out?

And yet...

And yet, as angry as he was with Murzzzz, it wasn't really fair just to forcibly send the Demon to his home dimension, possibly to be tortured again. He just wanted Murzzzz to show a bit of decency, care and contrition. Maybe give them some space for a decade or three. Besides which, Murzzzz was physically the only thing standing between Death and Grace and Constance, who were hiding in the house. The ghost of his sister's birth mother, and... and he may as well just mentally refer to Grace as an Angel now, since everyone else was. Grace and Constance hadn't done anything wrong. They were both still in the process of finding themselves and finding peace. Didn't they deserve that?

Besides, Darryl was pretty certain that if Krish *did* manage to send the three non-mortals away from this plane of existence, things were going to start getting apocalypsey again. And he'd already been through two pretty serious attempts at ending the world in the past couple of months.

Darryl ran to his sister, grabbed one of Krish's arms and helped her to physically restrain him from touching Murzzzz.

'Guys,' sighed Krish, still struggling. 'Please!'

'You shut up,' demanded Janusz, helping to pull Krish away from the struggling Demon.

With Krish fully restrained by three people, Murzzzz was able to take a deep, calming breath and shift in focus again. Becoming Richard once more, he freed himself from the doorway.

'Sorry about that,' Richard said. 'Sometimes Murzzzz and I get into panic cycles. Well done, kids.'

'It doesn't have to be like this,' cried Krish, appealing over Richard's head to Grace and Constance, who were lingering together in the hallway beyond the door and watching the scene in the garden with concern. 'You're reasonable people. Please don't make me get out my scythe.'

'Oh, Krish,' sighed Janusz in faux-disappointment. 'You messed up. We know you're bluffing. Our sister was *Śmierć* for years – you don't actually get issued with a scythe!'

Uh oh. Darryl was struck again by a terrible sense of imminent danger. The Demon within him bristled at it. His beloved husband probably shouldn't have said that. The sensation travelled along Darryl's arms, and intensified through his fingertips. Something about Krish's arm felt horribly wrong even as Darryl grasped it. Like it was electrified, or made of fire, or acid, or… or electrical acid on fire. He couldn't help but jerk his hands away, as if Krish were a hot pan. Charity, Darryl noticed, did the same thing.

Something had formed in both of Krish's hands. It was made out of something that wasn't quite the bright light of a blazing inferno, and not quite the deep darkness of a buried coffin, but was also somehow both of these things at the same time. It certainly wasn't made out of any form of matter – at least, not one that belonged in the mortal world. It was long – almost as long as Krish was tall – and one end boasted a huge, curved blade that looked like it could cut the very fabric of reality.

Balls. Krish totally had a scythe.

'Holy moly,' breathed Charity in the same tone of impressed jealousy she used to reserve for Darryl's Castle Greyskull playset. 'You got a scythe?'

'Yeah,' replied Krish, looking at it with mild pride, 'well, they offered me the role and I said "So, do I get a scythe, then?" and they were all "We don't see why not".'

'*I* should've asked for a scythe,' sighed Charity.

'Technically, from my family's religion, I should have asked for a noose and a buffalo. But I'm certainly not claiming to be Yama or any kind of god, more a mortal guide. And the buffalo could get messy and I felt like I'd need to always explain the noose. People could see it as bit lynch mobby... A scythe just seemed like something most folks would recognise and get what I was going for.'

'Will you shut up?' blurted Brenda. 'Charity, do something! He's got a weapon! On my property!'

'The scythe's more metaphysical than a weapon,' said Krish, placatingly.

'I don't care if it's physical or metaphysical or the philosophical concept of the relentlessness of time, young man, I want it off my front garden and away from my family!'

Brenda made a good point. Obviously, it was dangerous – it was a five-foot-long stick with a massive great blade on the end of it. Darryl's senses jangled with the danger the scythe posed to Murzzzz, Grace and Constance. Metaphysical or not, it probably wouldn't do him, Janusz or any of his mortal family any good if they got hit with it, either.

'Yeah,' muttered Darryl. 'That's enough, now. Get that scythe away from my family.'

'I'm so sorry.' Krish took a few steps into the doorway of the house, brandishing his scythe. 'I did warn you.'

'Darryl, he's intruding,' shouted Brenda. 'You're too mortal to pop, even as a Demon! Stop him!'

Darryl absolutely was not going to turn into a Demon. Not even for this. A promise was a promise. He darted towards Krish, who was making a beeline for Grace inside the house. Grace squeaked in panic, closed her eyes and disappeared. She must have willed herself away again. Darryl couldn't help but think, with annoyance, that it would be more helpful if, as an all-powerful otherworldly being who could bend the rules of physics to her will, Grace had sent Krish away from the situation rather than removing herself from imminent harm and leaving others behind.

Krish skidded to a halt in the patch of hallway where Grace had just been.

'Oh, she's going to be a tricky one, eh?'

Darryl, still chasing him, barrelled into Krish from behind in something akin to a rugby tackle. Darryl yelped with the pain of touching Krish – which still felt like touching a hot surface or a live wire – as Krish let out a similarly undignified sound at the shock of being tackled from behind. Both men fell to their knees in a tangled heap inside the door, knocking over the shoe rack and sending the welcome mat flying all the way out into the front garden. Krish dropped the scythe and, instead of clattering to the floor as a normal, physical reaping implement would do, it hovered upsettingly over the spot where it had been dropped, silently fizzling with sparks of light and dark. Krish tried to recover quickly, pushing himself to his feet and grabbing the floating scythe. Darryl, back on his feet too, grabbed for Krish's wrist right as Krish tried to turn around, causing Krish to very nearly hit Darryl with the scythe. Krish flinched back immediately, holding the scythe over his head, away from Darryl.

'Woah. Careful, there!'

Darryl recognised the fear in Krish's expression – a terror of accidentally hurting somebody with his new-found psychic powers, and a determination not to do so. Yeah. Same, Death. Same. This was why he was valiantly trying to hold back the Grim Reaper while retaining the form of a gangly man in his mid-thirties instead of that of the ferocious Demon that resided inside him.

Grace may have vanished, but Richard and Constance were still in the house, and in danger from Krish's scythe and misplaced sense of duty. Darryl could see his father backing away from Krish in the kitchen beyond the hallway, and Constance watching with silent concern on the stairs. Krish followed Darryl's eye line to the ghost on the stairs and set his face resolutely.

'No,' warned Darryl, as Krish turned and started heading towards the stairs. Because it hurt to touch Krish, Darryl did the only thing that his panicking brain told him was a viable option – he grabbed hold of the belt loops on Krish's trousers and made himself go as limp and heavy as possible.

'Dude,' protested Krish, 'are you trying to pull my pants down?'

'I'm trying to *stop* you,' Darryl mumbled from his heavy heap at Krish's feet.

Even with Darryl's weight slowing him, Krish managed to take a difficult step forwards.

'Little help, guys?' Darryl called.

In the kitchen, there was an almighty smash. Darryl glanced beyond Krish's struggling legs and saw that Murzzzz had reappeared and the sudden emergence of a huge Demon had caused a considerable number of plates to get broken in the process.

'**Sorry**,' said the Demon.

'No going Demon indoors, Murzzzz,' shouted Brenda from the open doorway.

There was another smash.

'Was that my good gin?' Brenda called.

'**Sorry**,' repeated the Demon.

Krish managed another step towards the stairs. Darryl tried reaching out a foot to get purchase on something but ended up hooking the standing lamp in the hallway. Krish was now dragging Darryl and the lamp in his wake.

'Guys!'

'You *can* go Demon indoors, Darryl,' his mother told him, 'just don't smash anything.'

The lamp toppled over and Darryl waited for it to smash, but it didn't. It was grabbed, mid-fall, by Janusz, who set it carefully out of harm's way.

'My Darryl said to stop,' Janusz tried to grab hold of Krish, but yelped with pain at the touch of his skin.

'Yeah, that's why I'm doing this,' Darryl told Janusz.

Darryl could never quite put a finger on the first time he realised he was fully and utterly in love with Janusz, and had moved beyond his initial combination of feeling attracted and incredibly flattered that such a handsome man could reciprocate his attraction. It hadn't been a lightning bolt as such, more a steady stream of moments that had made his chest tighten and his eyes soften. One thing that he did know was that the steady stream had never stopped. Falling in love with Janusz was an ongoing event. The little moments kept coming. The latest little moment was now. Janusz didn't say another word, but got down on the floor with Darryl, grabbed him by the shoulders, jammed his heel into the downstairs toilet doorway and helped with the extremely undignified process of holding back Death by the trousers.

Krish couldn't keep moving forward, not with both husbands weighing him down.

'Why?' he puffed, straining and exasperated.

'You know why!' Janusz told him. 'We tried to speak reasonably to you!'

'Try not to break the toilet door,' called Brenda. 'Darryl, just go Demon!'

'No!'

'What if he scythes you?'

'I'm not going to scythe mortals,' said Krish.

'He's not going to scythe me, Mum,' said Darryl, over him. 'Charity, are you *filming* this?'

In the doorway, Charity put her phone away, sheepishly. 'I mean, you've got it all under control, right?'

'He's after Constance!'

'Yeah, but he's not going to get to her though, is he? She's not bound to one spot like most ghosts are. She can go wherever.'

As if to prove Charity's point, Constance instantly vanished from the stairs and manifested out in the garden by Charity's shoulder.

At the foot of the stairs, encumbered by two men pulling on his trousers, Krish watched the ghost flicker to the new location and sighed, deeply.

'Guys…' he said, wearily.

And that's when Murzzzz landed on his head.

CHAPTER SEVEN

Watch Charry

Several people screamed at once. Murzzzz screamed because he was a Demon, attacking Death who had intruded into the Rook household. Krish screamed because he had a massive Demon clawing at his head. Brenda screamed because, in leaping at Krish, Murzzzz had knocked the big mirror off the wall. Darryl only screamed a little bit, and just because he was surprised.

'**Get out,**' thundered Murzzzz. '**Leave them alone!**'

'I can't! Ow!' Krish tried to swipe his scythe at the Demon on his head, but Murzzzz arched backwards away from it, his back bending at what would be impossible angles for a human being. 'You're hurting me!'

'**Yeah, well, you're hurting me too,**' growled Murzzzz, '**but you're not getting my family!**'

'Murzzzz, stop,' Janusz cried, still holding on to Krish's trousers. 'We have it under control.'

Murzzzz tried swiping at Krish again, and again, had to duck out of the way of his scythe. This time, one of Murzzzz's great arms smashed into the wall, leaving a dent in the plaster.

'You're just making it worse,' called Darryl, 'as usual! Also – we're not actually your famil— argh!'

Murzzzz bent fully backwards, still clutching Krish's shoulders with his clawed feet, and grabbed Darryl and Janusz off the floor. Overpowering a single Canadian man by holding on to his trousers was one thing, but there was no holding out against Murzzzz's strength. Both Darryl and Janusz were unceremoniously yanked away in a fluid movement which, unfortunately, also caused the top of Krish's trousers to rip considerably. As Darryl was hurled back out into the front garden, he did so still holding on to Krish's torn belt loops. The slap of warm leather across his face as Janusz landed heavily half on top of him told him that his husband had taken Krish's whole belt with him. Darryl propped himself onto his elbows, winded, and glared furiously through the doorway at the fight in the hallway. Krish was still making a valiant effort to scythe the Demon on his head, as his torn, beltless trousers made a slow descent down his thighs.

'Dudes, *why*?' asked Krish as he battled.

'Murzzzz, stop,' called Brenda.

'**Go,**' bellowed Murzzzz, his demonic face twisted with pain and rage. '**Save yourselves, find Grace. She'll have gone somewhere safe, she's a sensible Celestial…**'

Grace appeared from nowhere in the middle of the garden, sopping wet and reeking of British sea water.

'What happened to you?' asked Charity.

'Sorry,' gasped Grace, soaked and shivering. 'I was scared, so I wanted to go home, and the only other "home" I could think of was my old parish in Coldbay, and—'

'And you forgot Coldbay doesn't exist and it's just sea now,' completed Brenda.

'I was stressed,' replied Grace. 'Didn't think it through.' She blinked at the fight in the hallway. 'Did someone pull Death's trousers down?'

'Not on purpose,' protested Darryl, ignoring Charity's faintly lewd smirk. 'This is serious. Murzzzz, for the last time, pack it in!'

Murzzzz didn't listen – why break the habit of an infinite lifetime, Darryl supposed. The Demon lashed out at Krish again, and this time managed to catch him on the side of the head. Krish went down like a good-looking, saggy-trousered rag doll.

'Murzzzz!' Brenda sounded furious.

'Hey!' shouted Charity. She pushed past Darryl and Janusz to the front door. 'That's enough!'

Murzzzz wasn't stopping. Krish was lying in a ball on the floor of the hallway, clutching his head. The scythe was still hanging in the air in the middle of the hallway, right next to Murzzzz, and in the way of Charity as she ran to break up the now very one-sided fight. The scythe was also, Darryl realised, right in the path of Constance as she floated diligently by Charity's side.

'Why won't you ever listen?' raged Brenda.

Murzzzz didn't answer. He wasn't listening.

Darryl needed to get up off the ground. He needed to go and help. Janusz clutched his elbow, urgently.

'*Zabko*,' said Janusz with a quiet intensity. 'You need to intervene. The other you.'

Darryl gazed at him in horror. His eyes couldn't help but dart down to the scar on Janusz's wrist.

Janusz tapped his shoulder – a painless proxy slap of admonishment.

'None of that, now. There's no time. Do it!'

'But—'

'Darryl Rook, do not think I can't find time before the world ends to divorce you! Stop being ridiculous! Go! Go!'

Krish was in horrible, horrible pain. His head felt like it had been hit with a five-tonne cactus covered in curses. There was a furious, high-ranking Demon on his shoulders and his pants were falling down. This was his first proper task in the role of Death and he was pretty sure he was screwing it up comprehensively. Was *he* about to die? He might be about to die. Aw, man, that sucked. And the beings in the planes beyond mortal life were *not* going to be happy with him if he died. He wondered what they'd do to him – for eternity.

'Murzzzz, stop!' That was Charity Rook's voice. It was a real shame about Charity. She was cute. And she definitely seemed to have been into him. In better circumstances, he'd have liked to have gotten to know her better. It was a real bummer he'd only met her on the day he was destined to either kickstart the end of the world or die trying. A real kick in the jewels, that was. Well, he may as well die feeling sorry for himself over his ill-timed love life. He braced for the Demon's next blow.

There was another crash, from behind him, and what sounded like an itty-bitty tiger cub trying to do an itty-bitty roar. And the blow to the head Krish was expecting from the Demon on his shoulders didn't come. Instead, the weight of Murzzzz was pushed roughly away from Krish's prone body.

Krish tried to lift his head to see what had happened, but it hurt too much. Hands grabbed him under the armpits and hoisted him up.

'You OK to walk?' Charity asked him.

'Uh…' muttered Krish, jelly-legged, with a pounding head and having to hold on to his pants to keep them from slipping to his knees.

'It's fine,' Charity told him, and hoisted him into a straight-up *Officer And A Gentleman* lift. OK, this British lady was *strong*.

As she lifted him, he saw what had saved him – Murzzzz was being pinned against a wall by a smaller, hairier, more mammalian-looking Demon. The new Demon kind of looked like a pointy Paddington Bear, and everything about it screamed 'Darryl'. So, this was the part-Demon's other form. Even in Demon form, Krish doubted that Darryl was anywhere near as physically strong as Murzzzz. From Murzzzz's expression, he had been stopped mostly by surprise at seeing Darryl take that shape again and to defend Krish.

'**Son…?**' attempted Murzzzz.

Demon Darryl growled furiously.

Murzzzz changed tack. '**Darryl. Don't fight against me. You know this new Reaper is a threat. That's the only reason why… when your sister was going to be the Reaper, well, that's why…**'

Demon Darryl roared again, adorable yet apoplectic.

Krish noticed Constance, floating along right next to Charity. The ghost was inches away. She radiated sadness. She may not have been stuck in one spot, but she was still stuck. Stuck to one person. So sad. Lost, like every ghost.

His scythe was out of reach. But he didn't need a scythe for a single ghost. He wondered if the Rooks had forgotten about that in the hubbub.

Murzzzz gazed at Krish in horror, like he could tell what Krish was thinking.

'**Darryl,**' he roared.

Krish just needed to hold out his hand and…

'**Constance, go,**' shouted Murzzzz.

He just needed to hold out his hand…

Long, furry arms wrapped around Krish even as Charity carried him, pinning his arms in a fuzzy embrace. The bright-eyed, teddy-bear face of Demon Darryl stared at him from over Charity's shoulder.

'Wow,' said Charity. 'Were you seriously thinking of popping my birth mother while I Richard Gered you to safety?'

Krish looked into her eyes, and then at Constance, and then at Darryl, and then at Charity again, still Richard Gereing him. Something hit him in the pit of his stomach. It was the same feeling he'd had when he'd eaten his final rasher of bacon – a terrible tightening of the gut telling him 'I think, Krish my dude, what you're doing now might be a bit Not Good.'

'Sorry,' he said, and was painfully aware that he'd said 'sorry' several times already that day and had just carried on regardless. 'But,' he added with a cringe, 'but Charity… you can't see Constance, right?'

Charity looked faintly troubled. 'I don't need to. I know she's here with me.'

'But you can't see how sad she is.'

Charity frowned some more. 'Of course she's sad, she's dead. All of the dead are. Right, Mum?'

'Yeah,' replied Brenda in the doorway, rather too breezily, and refusing to look at Constance as she did so. 'They live, they die, they mope about. Such is life and death.'

'Because of their unfinished business,' added Krish. 'I mean, most of the time they're just lost – either physically or emotionally… stop me if I'm mansplaining here, I don't want to mansplain.'

'You *are* mansplaining,' grumbled Janusz, even though he was also a man.

'Constance is lost,' Krish told Charity.

Charity shook her head. 'She found me.'

'Maybe…' Man, he felt bad about saying this, but it was too mean just to reap Constance without explaining. 'Maybe it's not actually about you…?'

Charity de-Richard-Gered him, and stood him on the floor. Krish clutched at the top of his broken pants again to stop their attempted decline as gravity kicked in on them once more. Demon Darryl continued to restrain him from reaching for Constance.

'What?' Charity asked in a tone that suggested the concept of something *not* being about her didn't sit easily in her mind.

'I don't think being with you is bringing Constance any peace,' said Krish, apologetically. 'It can't be, because she's still lost. She still has unfinished business. She doesn't have closure.' He looked around at the family. 'None of you do. I should have provided closure before trying to reap her. I apologise. I got too caught up in the Death role and the sense of urgency I got from the burning phone and the "end of the world" thing. Bringing closure and comfort is what Death is supposed to do.'

'Mansplainer,' whispered Janusz, reproachfully.

'Oh no,' sighed Brenda, 'don't tell me you're another airy-fairy ghost hunter, wanting to move the dead on by talking about their feelings? I get enough of that from this lot.'

'As I mentioned before all this unpleasantness,' said Charity, 'we actually think it's better to talk it through with ghosts. It was Janusz's idea.'

Janusz gave Krish a horrible, haughty glare. Seriously, why did that guy hate him so much?

'But,' continued Charity, 'we only managed to talk with Constance once, in a fake tea shop. She won't speak through Darryl like the others do, so we can't—'

'It's me.' Murzzzz stood sheepishly in the hallway near the kitchen, his head brushing the ceiling even as he stooped. **'I'm the unfinished business.'**

'Not everything's necessarily about you, either,' Charity told Murzzzz.

Krish looked over to Constance, watching her expression as it flitted from confusion to a horrible realisation to sadness and back to confusion again.

Oh, no. I think Murzzzz might be right.

'I think,' said Krish, gently, 'that Murzzzz might be right.' He watched Constance some more. 'Just admitting that isn't enough for her, though. *How* are you her unfinished business, Murzzzz?'

'He was supposed to protect her,' Charity told Krish, 'but he prioritised Mum and Dad's safety instead.'

'There's more to it. I… can't talk about it.'

Krish sighed deeply. How was he supposed to end the world today? Just this one ghost was taking forever.

'I can't do it justice with human words,' continued Murzzzz. Goodness, Demons could be melodramatic. **'But there's something that can be done,'** the Demon added, **'with Demon powers, and… and human empathy, combined…'**

Murzzzz trailed off, and looked at Demon Darryl, expectantly. Krish had never seen a part-Demon roll its eyes in irritated frustration before. It was an oddly human sight.

'Wait,' said Janusz, 'what is this? Does my Darryl have *another* power?'

'Hypothetically,' replied Murzzzz. **'The only ones who can do it are Spawn, and there have been very few Spawn created – so I don't know for sure.'**

'My husband already has many powers,' said Janusz, in a gently bragging tone that Krish assumed was aimed at him.

'Please don't call him "Spawn" though, Murzzzz. You've been told about that.'

'**Darryl**,' said Murzzzz, in as soft a tone as his Demon voice could muster, '**you already know you can see the dead, and channel their voices. You should also be able to channel and project their inner hauntings – their painful memories – if the memories are strong enough and you are in close contact. Please. Focus on Constance. Bring what's haunting her into the light.**'

Demon Darryl just glared at Murzzzz, his expression full of hostility.

'**Not for me**,' continued Murzzzz. '**For her – and for your sister. If it helps, this is your chance to make me look as big an arsehole as you think I am.**'

Demon Darryl scowled, and shot a look at Krish, whose arms he was still pinning.

'It's OK,' Krish soothed. 'I won't try to reap anyone until you've tried this new power thingie. Partly because I wouldn't rob someone of closure if they're close to obtaining it, and partially because I'm intrigued to see what powers a half-Demon has. Also, I kinda have to keep a hold of my pants, here.'

Demon Darryl reluctantly let go of him and went back into human form with a grunt. He turned to Constance.

Oh no. Oh no, oh no. It hurts. The memory hurts on the inside. It's not a new hurt. It's been here all this time, like a nagging toothache that seems worse when there's nothing to distract from it, but now the toothache is everywhere, all over my soul and it hurts, it hurts, it hurt for years and it hurts now and it will hurt forever and—

And something about Darryl reaches out to me and asks me where it hurts, and I show him the rotten tooth inside my soul, and gently, gently, he pulls it out.

It still exists. It still hurts. But it's outside of me, now. He will let me put it back in, if that's what I want to do with it.

I don't want to do that. It's been festering for so long. It stinks. It hurts. I want it out of me.

And now it's out. They can all see the rot, smell the stench. My inner haunting. The Longest Night.

The Longest Night was no euphemistic name. It was the 21st of December, when the sun slinks away from its dim, cold trawl across the edge of the sky in the mid-afternoon and doesn't show its face again until the morning rush hour the next day. There was so much dark for the Demons to play in. Humans like to use cheery lights against the long nights. It makes them feel better, I suppose, but every twinkling fairy light, every warmly dancing menorah flame and every other happy light in the dark that night only created shifting shadows through which the Demons could twist and slip.

It started out with what seemed like a normal house clearance – my beloved Brenda and I working together as a tight two-person team – her finding them, me eliminating them. The men were looking after baby Charity and poor little Darryl, who could already see the dead and Demons himself – his frightened little yelps occasionally acting as a helpful failsafe alarm system. And Murzzzz was on standby in case anything went wrong. We expelled the spirit. Cleared the house for… for whoever it was, I forget the clients. I just remember that we saved their Christmas. All good, all good! Season of Goodwill saved, invoice scribbled out in time for chippy tea.

And then, everything went wrong.

Demons had been waiting for us that night. They came for us – so many of them – chasing us through London. We fought them in alleys, tried to outrun them on the tube with two little ones in hand where it was too public for Murzzzz to change. The terror, the utter terror. Darryl's cries. Oh, that little boy's fear has haunted me ever since. A toddler's screams have jangled a rotting pain inside of me, even as I've watched him grow into a man. Watching him progress into adulthood did nothing to lull the ghost of that frightened little boy.

Still the Demons wouldn't stop. We couldn't lose them, so Murzzzz ushered us into a shuttered department store so we could fight them without drawing in innocent bystanders – as if those poor babies weren't innocent bystanders themselves. And Charity was screaming now, as well as Darryl. My baby, my baby! I wanted to hold my baby, to soothe her. My baby was crying.

I couldn't hold my baby, I had to fight. Brenda couldn't hold her baby, she had to fight. But we had Harry to hold the babies. And we had Murzzzz.

We were supposed *to have Murzzzz. We were* supposed *to be a team.*

I *did not have Murzzzz. Murzzzz was not on* my *team. Murzzzz had decided on a team for himself.*

The relentless hoard of Demons separated us, bewildered us. They turned the large, sprawling shop into a labyrinth of moving racks of empty shell suits and blank-faced, perm-wigged manne-quins. I pushed my way through power suits and stonewashed jeans alone. The intolerable sound of the children screaming came from everywhere – every corner, every wall seemed to reverber-ate with the sound of those two babies crying – and I made a mistake. I followed the sound. I knew it could be a trick, but I couldn't help myself, I couldn't ignore the sound, couldn't risk the possibility that little Charity and Darryl might actually be with the Demons, alone and unprotected. Through shrinking tunnels of colourful Benetton sweaters I crawled, following the wails, until they opened up into a large room on a glass mezzanine – a cathedral to commerce with neon strip lights flickering like votive candles in a thin breeze.

The children were there. It hadn't been a trick. But it was a trap.

My Harry found the children at the same time as I did. He grabbed a hold of Darryl's hand at the same time that I scooped Charity up off the floor. Harry must have said something, but his voice has become lost to me in the fog of death. It's just noise now. Just vocal static. Just the wordless honking of a Charlie Brown adult.

*'**Constance.**'*

That voice. Yes, I remember that voice. Murzzzz. I remember the rush of relief. Murzzzz had found us! He would protect us as we got the children to safety.

*'**I'm sorry.**'*

And I remember that relief turning into something else – a feeling that congealed into a thick, heavy ball of horror in my gut as the Demons shifted into view from the fluid shadows of the treacherous flickering lights.

*'**Not the children,**' Murzzzz told the pulsating shadows. '**We need the children for the Termination plans. Leave them with me.**'*

And I remember screaming. Harry must have screamed too, but his scream is gone from my mind. His scream is now the sound of every screaming, weeping man – every man who has thrown the pretence of stoicism to the wind in his anguish and has snapped and allowed the grief to pour out, like the rolling thunder of a long-brewing summer storm. At the same time, he is a silently frozen face, a portrait of an eternal wail, a Munch, a Picasso, contorted in horror for all time.

The glass of the mezzanine exploded. It flew and sliced into Harry, shard after shard. I remember his last act was to shield Darryl with his body. He must have been such a kind, brave man. And the life in those kind, brave eyes just... went. Just spluttered out, as his life blood swiftly drained. I remember at that point realising I was watching the life leave him as I lay next to him on the floor, and then I discovered the glass sticking out of myself, and felt oddly unbothered by that aspect. I was too upset about Harry, and frightened for the babies. Darryl, unhurt but utterly terrified, looking now not at Harry's body, but at the space where he had just been standing. The part of me that understood my Harry had died knew that the psychic boy was looking at Harry's ghost.

'Harry, go now,' said the boy. 'Tans, he say watch Charry, he go now.'

Darryl couldn't say mine or Charity's names yet. Tans and Charry were our names in his clumsy little mouth.

'OK, see you soon. Love you. Bye.' Darryl started crying again – not a scared cry any more, but a sad one.

See you soon. Love you. Bye.

I had been told to look after Charity. She was still in my arms. I had to get up. I had to get up! I had to get my baby away from there, away from the danger and the threat of that traitor Murzzzz... I'd protect Darryl, too – poor little thing. I just had to get up... Had to get up...

The Demons were gone, I remember noticing that as I tried and failed to get up with Charity in my arms. And then came a familiar, fast, clicking sound – Brenda running in her ridiculous, impractical shoes.

Brenda's shriek – genuine horror – strangled in her own throat so as not to further upset the sobbing toddler.

'What happened?'

'Harry gone. Tans hurted.'

'Where's your father? Where's Murzzzz?'

Richard, hurrying on to the scene – Murzzzz must have darted away into another part of the shop to slip back into Richard's form, the bastard.

'Oh no!' Richard's voice sounded genuinely surprised. 'No, no, no!'

Brenda, kneeling next to me, trying briefly to stem the bleeding, but from the look in her eyes, she knew what was coming.

'Where was Murzzzz? Why couldn't he stop this?'

Richard, sounding lost, 'He… he didn't let me see. Must have been too late, and he wanted to spare me the sight. Son? Are you OK? Can you tell me what happened?'

'Harry gone. He say watch Charry.'

Brenda meets my gaze as my vision fades. 'I'll look after her.'

No question about whether I want that. No chance to tell her about the traitor within her family. She just takes Charity from my arms, and that's the last thing my body feels.

But I was told to watch Charity. So, watch Charity I will. Watch Charity I do. Watch Charity I forever shall.

And there it all is. All the rot, out in the open, and I feel strangely freed.

And the whole family looks at Murzzzz.

The vision projected from Darryl faded. The whole family continued to look at Murzzzz, who cringed a cringe that confirmed everything they had just seen was true.

The silence was leaden. It was broken after several seconds by Grace.

'Oh,' said the Angel disguised as the most mild mannered of priests, 'you fucking piece of shit.'

CHAPTER EIGHT

Arse.

Murzzzz continued to look chastened. Brenda, for once, was entirely lost for words. Grace had rather taken them out of her mouth.

'Yeah,' added Charity after a moment, 'I think Grace speaks for everyone, there.'

'**I did it for us—**' began Murzzzz.

'Don't you even dare,' whispered Darryl in a hot, quiet rage.

Murzzzz nodded, meekly. '**I'll just...**' And he faded back into Richard.

Richard didn't look any happier than Murzzzz.

'I didn't know,' he said. 'He has never let me see what really happened.'

'Really?' Darryl asked. 'Never suspected anything? Little baby me never asked any difficult questions about stuff I half-remembered from that night?'

'I swear, I didn't know.' Richard paused. 'It's still no reason to send him back to the Demons' realm.'

'Oh for crying out loud, Dad!'

'They were torturing him! What he did to Constance and Harry doesn't make that all right!'

'And what about Constance?' Charity asked. 'Darryl, is she still here?'

Darryl glanced at the ever present ghost of Constance Xu, and nodded.

'Thought so. Showing us what happened didn't bring her closure. Maybe to get closure she needs justice.'

'It wouldn't be justice,' replied Richard, frantically. 'It wouldn't help!'

'We don't know until we try. Tell him, Mum.'

Charity turned to Brenda. As did Richard.

'Dear…?'

Oh, great. So this was Brenda's Gordian knot to untie now, was it? This wasn't good. And Brenda was still herself processing the whole horrible truth of what she'd seen, what that meant for her family as well as what she'd been accomplice to and the levels of her own complicity. Murzzzz had betrayed her best friend, and hidden the full truth from all of them, but did that undo the decades that he had provided them with protection? Or how much Richard and he loved one another? Or how much Murzzzz declared to love the family? *Did* Murzzzz love them? Any of them? Truly? Even if he didn't, did that mean they should just turn on him? But what about Constance, her dear poor dead friend Constance? Honestly, she didn't know what the answer to this one was. And she was way too sober for a problem like this. She opened her mouth in order to prevaricate with some nonsense or other – buy herself a little thinking time – but she couldn't form the words. Then a rescue came in the surprising form of the Canadian Grim Reaper.

'You guys,' he breathed. 'That was… wow. You guys went through some real messy stuff there. And all of that for… what was it Murzzzz called it? "Termination"? That's... huh.' His face didn't contort with the strain of any sort of ethical dilemma, he simply nodded blandly to himself. 'Well, guess you were right, and I was wrong. About Constance, that is. She deserves to stay until she finds peace. I still think you would all be way better off without Murzzzz, but maybe that should be up to you. I made a bad call. Sorry. I got overexcited because being Death is super cool. But with great power...'

'Comes great responsibility,' breathed Charity.

Krish nodded at her. 'Superman.'

'Spider-Man,' replied Charity, without the usual air of contempt she showed to people who mixed up their superheroes.

'I just wanted to do the job right, you know,' continued Krish. 'Am... I gonna get in trouble for going with my gut here instead of following the orders from my burning cellphone? By the way, my cellphone still keeps setting on fire.'

With difficulty, he pulled the tightly wadded fire blanket from his bag, and carefully unwrapped it on the floor. The mobile phone inside it lit on fire briefly, stopped for a few seconds, and then burst into flames again.

'Yeah,' said Krish, quietly, wrapping the phone up again, 'I'm not gonna answer that.'

'Too right, you're not,' Charity told him. 'Sod the powers that be. You should get your on the job training from the last person to be Death – i.e. Yours Truly.'

'Cool,' smiled Krish. And, gosh, it *was* a handsome smile, noted Brenda, silently. Possibly even a notch above Janusz's handsomeness. Janusz had a level of handsomeness that could model mid-range knitwear. Krish had a handsomeness that could model cars and watches.

'Charity, you can't just train Death,' said Darryl. 'He might be sad for Constance now, but I think he's still very much on the "Let's end the world" side of things.'

'He has just shown willingness to change his mind based on new information,' argued Charity. 'We'll have him saving the world with the rest of us before you can say *Buffy the Vampire Slayer*.'

'I *loved Buffy the Vampire Slayer*,' added Krish.

'*And* he likes Buffy,' continued Charity. 'We've got to team up with him now – it's fate.'

'That doesn't mean anything, Charity – everyone likes Buffy.'

'Not *everyone*,' added Janusz, darkly. '*Some* of us feel that it makes no sense and don't understand why their husband and sister-in-law get so excited about the blond vampire with the bad accent.'

'He was the hot one,' chorused both of Brenda's children.

'The Librarian Dad One was the hot one,' muttered Janusz, grumpily.

'The Librarian *was* the hot one,' agreed Grace placatingly, even though Brenda was sure that the Angel had never actually watched *Buffy the Vampire Slayer*.

'Can we all please stop talking about Bunty the Vampire Killer?' asked Richard. And, even though the whole family were at odds with Richard over the Murzzzz thing, they had to concede that – with the horrible revelations of Constance's death still unresolved and the latest attempt to end the world continuing to loom – he had a point.

Due to the fountain attack in Oakpines and Grace accidentally throwing herself in the North Sea, quite a few of the family needed to either change or at least dry off their jumpers on the radiator. Because of the recent destruction of his trousers and a phone-related singeing issue in his bag affecting his spare pair, Death was offered an old pair of Richard's cords, which didn't fit him. He then tried Brenda's second-best yoga trousers, which did. After that had been dealt with, and with an absence of other ideas concerning what to do about the whole Armageddon situation, Brenda decided to invite Krish for a sit-down chat over a nice glass of wine. The rest of the family swiftly and loudly suggested they change glasses of wine for cups of tea. *Urgh, fine.* Brenda was in no mood to argue.

Krish set his phone on the table, loosely nestled in its fire blanket. The phone went on fire three times just in the time it took Janusz to make the tea.

'The Manager really wants to get hold of me, huh,' muttered Krish, watching his phone combust yet again.

'Do you have some sort of otherworldly answerphone system on that thing?' asked Brenda, wishing she had a glass of wine. 'Text messages scratched in soot?'

Krish shook his head. 'I'm gonna be in trouble with the higher-ups, aren't I?'

Charity shrugged. 'Join the club. We're all in it.'

'Especially Murzzzz,' added Richard, pointedly.

'Change the record, dear,' muttered Brenda. 'We're all in trouble. Especially Grace, probably.'

'What?' asked Grace, nervously.

'Oh yeah, they're really peed off about Grace Barry,' said Krish, cheerfully.

'Oh,' replied Grace with an anxious giggle.

Janusz set an especially lavish tea down with – Brenda noticed – three different kinds of biscuit. He'd even got the teapot out, and although they didn't have matching cups and saucers, everyone's favourite of the mugs that remained in Brenda's kitchen had been washed and were being deployed. One additional mug had been included for their guest – an old one from an accountancy conference Janusz had attended in 2017, so unloved by Brenda's son-in-law that it had stayed at the back of Brenda's mug cupboard ever since. Janusz would have had to have dug past the nice Denby mugs to get to that one. He must, thought Brenda, really *really* dislike Krish.

Krish, for his part, accepted the Make 2017 Count Expo mug of tea with good grace, even though there was no soya milk to be had, and allowed Charity to 'get him up to speed'. This largely involved a version of the events on Coldbay Island and at Helsbury Services in which Charity played a much more heroic part and Darryl was much more whiny and annoying than Brenda recalled. Krish listened, with a faint but growing frown on his handsome brow.

'So, these Hell Holes are bad signs, huh,' he said politely once Charity had finished telling him her 'Charity saves the day' stories.

'Well, they serve as transport hubs to let in Demons,' said Brenda, 'but the Manager also uses them to access our world and rip living souls from their bodies to gain energy from their despair, as well as folding up and consuming the occasional landmass and unleashing devastating waves of entropy to rot entire building complexes when it's annoyed. For those and other reasons, they generally should be viewed as a portent of a new attempt at apocalypse. So, yeah. They're bad news.'

'And they look like a sort of absence of sky where the sky should be?'

'Yes,' replied Brenda, with as much patience as she could muster.

Krish squinted, past Brenda's shoulder, at the conservatory. 'Kinda like that?'

'What?' asked Darryl, turning to try to follow Krish's gaze.

'If this is some childish "look behind you" joke—' began Janusz.

'Wait.' Darryl got up.

Brenda could see from Krish's expression that it wasn't a joke. Oh no.

'Saw a kind of smudgy sky thing in the distance as I was running over here but I wasn't sure what it was. And anyway I was on my way to try to reap a bunch of you folks, and then there was the fight and I lost my pants, so I put it to the back of my mind, and...'

'There's a Hell Hole?' interrupted Charity. 'In town? Here?'

'Well. Over town.' Krish had a little think. 'Actually, judging from its direction from the train station, more like on the outskirts of town.' He squinted at the conservatory again. 'Still kinda smudgey. I don't know. Could be wrong. But whatever it is seems... bigger? Now.'

Oh *no*.

Darryl peered at the conservatory. 'Mum...? You're better than me at seeing these things early...'

Brenda got up, smoothly, took her son's elbow and walked him through the conservatory into the back garden where they would have the best view of the sky to the northeast. Well. *Most* of the sky to the northeast. Moving around a little to peer around the neighbour's holly bush confirmed that a patch of the darkening afternoon sky above the distant blocky buildings of the Sunnyside leisure and retail estate had turned into a malevolent swirling smudge of not-sky.

Arse.

There was totally a Hell Hole over Rutherford.

Yemisi had to knock three times for Aurora Tavistock to answer.

'Come?'

Aurora was sitting quite still in her hotel room's single small armchair, gazing vacantly into the middle distance. She was covered in all the usual bangles and crystals she always wore for public appearances. Yemisi had been surprised, at first, that Aurora never seemed to take them off, even when she was offstage, off camera and supposedly out of the character of Celebrity Psychic Aurora Tavistock. Often, Yemisi wondered whether this was because the public face of Aurora Tavistock wasn't a 'character' after all, and this was the real her. Just as often, she assumed that actually it was just that Aurora retained her character facade in front of Yemisi as much as she did camera crews and the general public and, as a mere tour-manager-and-PA Yemisi was unlikely to get to meet the 'real' Aurora behind the purple make-up and the swirly black tulle.

Yemisi quietly set Aurora's requested cup of tea down next to her on the dressing table and removed the old one that had been left to go cold.

Aurora frowned into the middle distance, and hummed, as if she'd just been told difficult news. Only as Yemisi was halfway back to the door did Aurora even acknowledge she was there.

'How are sales, my love?' Aurora asked.

Yemisi put on her cheerful voice.

'Almost sold out. I've been going through the attendees' Facebooks as per.'

Honestly, early booking by name made cold reading so much easier. The sort of people who booked early to see Aurora were also the type to post a lot on their social media about the dead loved one they were desperate to hear from. Yemisi always made Aurora a spreadsheet of the online dead, even though Aurora only occasionally made use of it. Yemisi supposed that was impressive, really, even if it did mean the task was a massive waste of Yemisi's time.

Aurora didn't stir. She remained in her position, frowning into nothing.

'We're running a little late for the signing event at the shopping centre,' Yemisi reminded her with the constant patience of a PA who had been trying to gently cajole the talent into actually turning up for a well-planned promotional event for a few hours now, 'but we still have time if we leave in the next—'

'That's cancelled,' Aurora announced. 'Something… something…' she trailed off, looking concerned.

'Are you OK?' Yemisi asked, even though she knew there was little point in doing so. Of all the unknowns that still remained about her boss, the one thing she did know for certain was that Aurora almost never told her the truth.

And that was why the candour in Aurora's tone when she spoke next disquieted Yemisi quite a lot.

'No,' said Aurora. 'Something's gone wrong. Arse.'

Darryl scrubbed at his face in frustration and embarrassment. 'Arse!'

The rest of the family joined them in the cold, twilit garden.

'He's right?' asked Janusz. 'There's a Hole?'

Darryl nodded, with a sigh. 'Can just about make it out, over there. I should have spotted it sooner! I was too wrapped up in all of this.' He waved his hands at his family in general.

Janusz squeezed his arm. 'So you didn't see a little Hole in the sky that is still so small that only clairvoyants can make it out. You went to clear the shopping mall. You knew *something* was up.'

'I should have paid it more attention,' moaned Darryl. 'The uptick in hauntings near the Sunnyside estate – the school, the bowling alley… maybe it *wasn't* just balls!'

'Embarrassing, Darryl,' tutted Charity, with a little-sisterish shake of the head. 'In front of New Death and everything.'

'Yes, thank you, Charity!'

'Oh, don't worry about *him*,' grunted Janusz. 'I bet you've done plenty of embarrassing things in your time, right Krish?'

'Um,' replied Krish, diplomatically, 'sure?'

Charity gave Krish's shoulder a little pat. 'Don't be so hard on yourself.'

'If anything, it's *me* who should be embarrassed,' said Grace, quietly.

The whole family broke into a chorus of 'oh no's and 'not *you*, Grace's. Even Krish joined in with politely telling Grace she had nothing to be upset with herself about.

'Guys, I'm supposed to be an A...' she stopped herself from saying the word. 'An all-powerful being,' she said. 'I knew there were problems here, a deep unhappiness, an unease. I've been trying to deal with them piecemeal, like a human would.' She pointed to the black eye she'd received for intervening in a human way, of which up until now she'd seemed so proud. 'I should have looked at the big picture instead – looked at it like a Celestial would.'

'But you didn't want to do it that way,' Richard reminded her, gently.

'Richard, the world is ending! Again! What I want doesn't matter in the grand scheme of things!'

'What you want should *always* matter,' muttered Richard, a little defensively.

'Well then, in that case,' replied Grace, very clearly lying, 'I *want* to close this latest Hell Hole, right now, and before it's too late. I want to go to Sunnyside.'

Everybody knew this to be a rare lie from the Angel, because nobody who'd so much as seen a picture of the Sunnyside retail and leisure estate would actively want to go there, Hell Hole or not. It sat on the northeast edge of town, between Sunnyside School and a string of car dealerships. The estate was essentially three large car parks surrounded by a series of entirely cubical buildings – from the tiny cubes of the coffee stand and the little shop selling phone accessories and keyrings to the giant cubes of the multiplex cinema, the discount furniture warehouses and the Lamada executive hotel and conference centre which was the only place where Brenda would go to while waiting for her husband to buy a new sofa or something, on the grounds that it had a pub attached to it.

To say that Sunnyside was looking eerie now was a bit of a misnomer – there had always been something eerie about it. Ever since it had been built, it had managed to look desolate even when the car parks were all rammed full – which they usually were since there was no safe way to get to the place on foot. A couple of ghosts of young adults who had drunkenly tried and failed to walk home, back when the cubical gym had been a cubical nightclub, still lingered as a testament to how pedestrian-unfriendly the place was. They drifted sadly over blind corners in spectral sequinned minidresses with ghost stilettos in hand. Brenda noticed that these ghosts were moving in the same direction as the family's vehicle – towards the centre of the park. When Grace slowed to take a sharp corner, one in the memory of a pink dress wafted alongside Brenda's window keeping pace with them for a moment. It had an unusual determination to its demeanour. Its face was set on the road ahead as it stumbled along in the permanent drunken stupor death had left it in. It definitely wanted to get... somewhere. If it wanted to go home, it was facing the wrong way. It was moving back towards Sunnyside, poor lost thing. Brenda made a mental note to do something about that poor pink ghost, as she had done every time she'd passed it since its appearance around the turn of the millennium. Although at least this time she could be forgiven for not doing anything about it right at that moment, what with needing to save the world again and all.

Just as Oakpines had been earlier that day, Sunnyside was exhibiting far, far more than its usual background levels of eeriness. The Hell Hole in the sky above it was forming fast, taking a large patch of the darkness that already existed this December early evening, and managing somehow to make it even darker – a nothingness into which everything fell. The speed at which the void was establishing itself was a worry. Hell Holes needed human misery to power them, they were like automatic doors that ran on despair instead of electricity, so when the void over Helsbury services had been created in a hurry, the immortal beings behind it had done so by ripping several hundred innocent souls from their bodies in one go. From the car park, there had to be thousands of people currently in Sunnyside. Only after being told several times by the non-clair-voyant members of the group that they too could see the figures in modern clothes going to and from the various parked cars in the midwinter gloom was Brenda able to put that worry to the back of her mind. If there was to be a mass culling of the living people passing through Sunnyside, it hadn't happened quite yet. This was one of the only upsides to the situation.

There were – like at Oakpines – far, far too many ghosts. Usually, only a few lingered around Sunnyside – few enough for Brenda to be able to conveniently forget for decades despite seeing them every time the kids wanted to watch a movie or Richard wanted to go to Frankie & Benny's. Now, the central car park heaved with them. From their clothes, most of them were older than the estate. Many of them looked older than the whole town. There were Edwardians, Victorians and Georgians. Clothes like those had rarely been worn by the living in this place, because when those clothes had been the norm, this place had been a field. There had been no mass grave here, no plague village and no mass hangings of suspected witches. When one can see the dead and has a young son similarly afflicted with that 'gift', one checks in advance whether there used to be a plague village nearby before signing off on a mortgage. And it wasn't just the number of ghosts. The way they were behaving was all wrong. Ghosts usually lingered aimlessly where they'd died, lost and forgetful smears of sad. Occasionally they retained enough memory of self to obsess over something, like Constance latching herself to Charity. Brenda was certain that these ghosts weren't where they had died. And they weren't aimless at all as they were all walking with purpose. They were walking towards the hotel. As they passed the bowling alley, she saw a ghost leaving it and floating towards the hotel too. A ghost just casually leaving the building it had been haunting? That wasn't right at all. The other thing that wasn't right was that this ghost was clearly much older than the bowling alley. From its clothing, it was once a reasonably well-heeled nineteenth-century woman. It drifted away from the neon signs of the bowling alley, its shadowy long skirts giving it the smoothly moving appearance of a hovercraft. What business did a ghost like that ever have haunting a nineties build bowling alley? Brenda craned her neck back and saw another thin grey smear drift into the bowling alley before emerging from the other side. They were moving *through* it, she realised. They were moving through the bowling alley – and likely through the nearby new-build school and multiple other boxy buildings on the estate – as easily as walking through a wall. The ghosts probably hadn't even realised they were temporarily haunting a building, it was just a shortcut on their journey – on *all* of their journeys… to the hotel.

But ghosts didn't go to hotels. Some of these ghosts shouldn't even know that the hotel existed. The building should be just as meaningless to them as the bowling alley or the Poundstretcher. It didn't make sense.

There were also Demons at Sunnyside already, Brenda noticed. Quite a few of them had made use of the growing void in the sky to slip through into their world, but none of them were attacking the living. None of them were even attacking the Rooks as they passed, and usually Demons just *loved* to attack them, especially considering how the Demons were even more annoyed at Murzzzz still tagging along inside Richard than his family were. But no – these Demons were converging, as if they were waiting. She'd never seen Demons look patient before, but there they were. And they, too, were gathering around the hotel. Brenda watched from the vehicle window, frowning. This wasn't a haunting. It wasn't even an event akin to Coldbay or Helsbury. It looked and felt like something else, but she couldn't quite put her finger on what.

As it turned out it was Darryl who put a name to it, and when he did so it was not him speaking as an expert in all things occult, but as the husband of an accountant.

'Bloody Hell,' he said. 'It's a conference.'

Oh. Oh, yes. It was an out of town business conference for Demons, with hundreds of ghosts drawn in either as unwitting power cells to open the Hell Hole or as some sort of Demonic Misery Buffet. But why? And why at Sunnyside? Was the conference organised so they would watch her and her family try to save the world for a third time? So that they could take notes for the next attempt, or the next cycle of creation and destruction? Were they expecting Murzzzz, or Grace, or Krish, or even her to take some sort of guest speaker slot? Is that why they'd all come to her town? What other draw could there possibly be to Rutherford than to make things personal for the Rooks – to watch them under some terrible otherworldly microscope as they tried to save the world from an apocalypse that was going to begin in their own home town? Was this a conference about them? The nerve! The sheer bloody—

'Oh no.'

'What?' asked Brenda.

Darryl pointed at a sign outside the hotel. 'Look. Look what they're all going towards.'

'Oh.'

Brenda's 'oh' was delivered with a rage so cold it could make your fingers snap off on it. This conference had a guest speaker, all right, and it wasn't Death or the Angel or the disgraced high-ranking Demon in their ranks.

It was Aurora *Bloody* Tavistock.

'Arse.'

CHAPTER NINE

Princess Diana Is Not 'Kinda Racist'

Under normal circumstances, you could be forgiven for assuming it might be a bit of a humiliation to have to pull up outside of your psychic rival's sold-out show in your home town in a clapped-out church minibus. Brenda did not believe it to be a humiliation at all – in fact, the minibus was a source of considerable pride, for several reasons.

Firstly, the minibus was the family's only form of transport since their family car and its subsequent replacement had been completely destroyed by the all-powerful Manager of the universe in a fit of otherworldly rage after the family had put a stop to the apocalypse. Twice. How many apocalypses had Aurora Tavistock prevented recently? Almost certainly none. All Aurora Tavistock ever did was claim to know what Princess Di thought about various post-millennium royal events. And how was that supposed to save anything?

Secondly, when there were now seven of you – eight if you counted Murzzzz – then a minibus was actually a very practical mode of transportation, thank you very much. Even if one of your party was a ghost, and another shared a body with your husband and therefore didn't need his own seat.

Thirdly, it wasn't technically a church minibus. Closer inspection of the vehicle showed that it had no make or model. The number plate seemed legit but came up with no results if you googled it. It appeared to be around fifteen years old, but Brenda knew that it had been made mere weeks ago, when they'd desperately needed a ride and so Grace, out of desperation, had manifested a vehicle for their escape. Just as the Angel had invented a pious, little, do-gooder parish priest of a human persona for herself to hide inside, so she had conceived of the idea that Grace Barry must be the sort of do-gooder parish priest who would drive a community minibus, and lo, the minibus was created – out of pure Angelic willpower. So, it was not a church minibus. It was the Platonic ideal of what a church minibus should be, with faded paint cheerfully advertising her church – which did not exist – and her local parish – which also did not exist. The minibus had a jellybean-shaped air freshener hanging from the rearview mirror, which smelled distinctly of peppermint. Brenda had checked that company online, and they didn't do a peppermint scented air freshener. When Richard had taken a look under the hood he had discovered, to his distress, that the minibus didn't really have an engine but had 'something a layperson could be forgiven for thinking an engine might generally look like'. It seemed to only ever run out of petrol when Grace remembered that minibuses need petrol and even then it would run quite happily on either unleaded or diesel – whichever Grace thought to put in it at the time. Brenda had recently taken to wondering whether the minibus was as much a part of the physical earthly manifestation of the Celestial being that called herself 'Grace Barry' as the human-looking little priest was – even though it did feel a bit weird to consider that while sitting *inside* the minibus, getting crisp dust on the upholstery. So, no, there was no shame at all in pulling up outside Aurora's bewilderingly popular show in a Platonic minibus that may or may not actually be a corporeal extension of Brenda's Angel friend.

The poster – amongst a mess of unnecessary clipart, too many fonts and Aurora's heavily airbrushed headshot – advertised that her show started at 8 p.m. that night. It was a little after 6.30 and, as well as Demons and the clamouring dead, there were already a few of the living hanging around the hotel's main doors, wearing the sort of crystal-and-velvet-festooned fashions that suggested they were big Aurora fans. Brenda sneered at them, as an automatic reaction. Someone with a death wish might have mentioned that Brenda also dabbled in black velvet offcuts and cheap colourful crystals, but she would have been quick to point out that the difference was, she did it to be deliberately cheesy. She *had* to do it, in fact, because of the stereotypes encouraged by the likes of Aurora and her fanbase.

In spite of their frankly offensive get-ups, and their presence being testament to the annoying popularity of Aurora Bloody Tavistock, what really troubled Brenda about the fans was that, even as the shops emptied out for the evening, Sunnyside was still going to be full of living people tonight as the Hell Hole continued to grow. At Coldbay and Helsbury, the family had been the only living souls there – and a good job, too. Both situations had been incredibly dangerous. The family had barely escaped with their lives and there's no way they could have done so while saving a host of innocent, if rather stupid, bystanders from becoming the collateral damage of uncaring all-powerful beings from beyond. The Lamada's conference centre could host an audience of around 500. An obnoxious splash across Aurora's poster boasted that tonight was sold out. All of this life directly beneath a Hell Hole made Brenda feel horribly uneasy... as well as irritated. Oh yes, she was *still* monstrously irritated at these credulous cattle all going to Aurora Bloody Tavistock's silly little show.

'Why are they all going to an Aurora Tavistock show?' Krish asked.

'Because she does popular woo that tells comforting lies about the afterlife,' replied Brenda through gritted teeth. 'Nothing that desperate people love more than a nice warm bath of lies.'

'Oh, I get that she's popular with the living. She was a guest on *The Social* for her North America tour. Kept saying Lady Di had all these kinda racist opinions, the big fraud.'

'She *is* a fraud. Thank you, Krish.'

The rest of the minibus's occupants nodded in agreement, even Grace, who had never even seen Aurora at work.

'I mean the ghosts. They're all flocking to her, too.'

'Ghosts are just even sadder, lonelier, more desperate versions of living people,' Charity told him from her minibus seat right next to his. 'If anything, they're even more susceptible to the warm bath of deception than the living. Almost all of the ghosts at Oakpines wanted to speak to Aurora, didn't they, Mum?'

Brenda clenched her jaw. 'Yes.'

'You know the bookstore at that mall was advertising a signing with her today, right?' asked Krish.

'Of course we knew that,' said Janusz with a defensive grumpiness. 'Obviously, that's why those ghosts were at Oakpines waiting for her.'

Brenda had not known about the signing at Oakpines, and she suspected that this was the first Janusz had heard of it, too.

'And why the Xenomorphs? Why the portal?' Krish gestured at it all as well as he could with so much of his personal space taken up by Charity. 'Do beings from another dimension want to hear nice lies about Lady Di too?'

'I'm sorry,' snorted Janusz, not sounding sorry at all. '"Xenomorphs"? Like off *Alien*?'

'Yeah,' replied Krish. '"Cause some of them look like the chest-burster one out of *Alien*.' He looked to the two other clairvoyants. 'Right, guys?'

'We've always called them Demons,' said Darryl.

'I know, but that, and the "Hell Hole" and Angels...'

'We're not "Angels",' said Grace, quietly, even though she totally was.

'It's all a bit religionny, isn't it?' continued Krish. 'Bearing in mind that actually none of the religions have got it right and it's looking increasingly like we're living in some sort of endlessly repeating pocket universe that multiple more powerful dimensions maintain and share for resources and leisure?'

'Murzzzz uses the term "Demons",' replied Janusz, testily, 'and he should know.'

'Actually,' said Richard, quietly, 'the word Murzzzz has for his kind doesn't translate as "Demon" at all. It's humans that have sighted them who identified them as Demons, or various different monsters. Murzzzz just goes with that because it's easiest for us humans to understand. Like how Krish and Charity have called themselves "Death". I mean, you gave yourself a scythe, Krish. Because it made sense in your mind that you should.'

'I suppose.'

'Also,' added Richard, 'he uses "Demon" because if we humans were to try to use the name he has for himself, our mouths would light on fire. He's thoughtful like that.'

The Nice Reaper admirably masked his alarm at Richard's last comment. 'Well, Demons, Xenomorphs, call them what you will—'

'"Xenomorphs" is stupid,' muttered Janusz.

'Why are *they* being drawn to Aurora if she's just a smoke-and-mirrors phoney?'

Brenda glowered at the scene. It could just all be a coincidence. After all, the location of the two Hell Holes before this one had been a seaside pier and a petrol forecourt, and there had been nothing particularly psychic about either of those. All of this clamour could just be for a Hell Hole that had happened to open up at the same spot where a fake psychic was in town for the night doing her silly little fake show. True, the odds of that happening by accident were ridiculous, and it wouldn't help explain why so many of the Oakpines ghosts were determined to speak to Aurora. But the alternative explanation was even more unacceptable to Brenda – that Aurora was a genuinely powerful psychic, always had been, really *could* channel the ghost of Princess Di, and that the late People's Princess really was, to quote Krish, 'kinda racist'.

Well. There was one way to find out. Brenda sighed, deeply.

'We're going to have to see the show.'

'But it's sold out,' noted Grace. 'How are we supposed to get in?'

'I think, if it's something we needed,' Brenda told her, 'you'd find you had six tickets in the glove compartment the whole time.'

'But I didn't buy tickets,' Grace fretted. 'I didn't know we'd need to go. You said she was a fraud and I can't just magic six ti…'

Grace trailed off under the immense power of Brenda's cocked eyebrow, and opened the glove compartment of the minibus.

'Oh. Would you look at that?' said the fake priest, with a casual innocence. 'I do have tickets after all.'

People, living and dead, as well as Demons, were continuing to quietly gather. Something was definitely up, and Brenda was getting more and more concerned that whatever was going to kick off was going to do so big time, and was likely to start as Aurora's show did. That was eighty minutes away. There were already so many people around that Brenda didn't want to do anything rash, but maybe they could have a quiet poke around before the show started.

'I am going to need a bunch of carbs for this,' Charity said, 'I can feel it.'

'Oh, you need to carb-load before using your powers, too?' Krish asked.

'Every time,' Charity told Krish. 'Do you get nosebleeds as well?'

'Yes,' replied Krish, 'and in my mouth, and sometimes I bleed...'

'...from the eyes,' they both finished in a joyful unison.

They should probably, thought Brenda, come up with a plan. Maybe, she thought, they could sneak into Aurora's green room, confront her on what she knew in relative privacy.

'So,' said Charity, twirling her hair around her fingers a little, 'were you waiting 'til after we've stopped the end of the world again to ask me out, or are you just being too Canadian to take the initiative?'

'Charity, not now,' sighed Darryl. 'We're saving the world. You're not out on the pull.'

'Er, hypocrite, *you* pulled Janusz while we were clearing a ghost pirate from his flat, and if I don't try to get a date before this latest apocalypse, when *is* a girl to get a date?' Charity turned to Krish. 'Cutting to the chase because potential end of the world and all that – I'm a hot psychic, you're a hot psychic, let's date... you *are* straight, right?'

'Um,' replied Krish, shyly. 'Pan, actually.'

Janusz heaved a sigh. '*Niewymuszenie.*'

Charity's eyes lit up. 'Friggin' jackpot!' She jerked her thumb at Janusz. 'This one here's a Bi.'

'I've got a T-shirt about it,' Janusz mumbled, tugging down the neck of his still damp, horrible Christmas jumper to show a T-shirt in pink, purple and blue stripes.

'Ooh, twinsies.' Krish pulled up his own, much more stylish, jumper to reveal a very similar T-shirt, only in much brighter shades of magenta, yellow and cyan. 'I used to think I was Bi, but I just decided Pan was a better term for it.'

'*Zamknij się, kurwa*,' muttered Janusz, barely audible through gritted teeth.

'As long as you're anything that includes thirty-one-year-old women who are extremely into comics it's all good,' continued Charity, happily.

Krish laughed a little, happily flustered. 'Yeah, um. I think maybe it does include very confident British ladies who know what they like?'

'We should discuss this further over dinner,' continued Charity. 'Cheeky Nando's?'

'I don't know what that is,' admitted Krish.

Charity gasped, horrified.

'Come to think of it,' added Grace, 'I don't think I've ever had Nando's either.'

Charity gasped again.

Maybe Aurora was in cahoots with the Demons, thought Brenda as she plotted their next steps, maybe that was why she was so good at tricking people. Maybe she even had a symbiotic Demon of her own, like Murzzzz. Yes, thought Brenda, they should use this time wisely.

'Mum,' announced Charity, opening the minibus door, 'we're having a cheeky Nando's before the world ends.'

Or they could just go to Nando's. Brenda unbuckled her seat and prepared to follow the others. Because Charity and Krish needed carbs. And definitely not because she'd just remembered Nando's served wine.

The restaurant was fairly full with people choosing to kick off their New Year's Eve with some mid-range spicy chicken – or, as in Krish, Janusz and Darryl's case, some vegan wraps. As a result of this, and Charity and Krish's heroic appetites, they were only just done eating by curtain call time… or, since there was no 'curtain' in the Lamada conference suite, the time they were expected to be in their interlocking conference suite chairs for the show.

'We should have left enough time to go backstage,' hissed Brenda as they sat.

'Dear,' whispered Richard 'you're the one who made us wait while you finished off your third wine.'

'Nonsense,' whispered Brenda. 'Charity was still eating.'

'Shush,' said Charity, who had not yet finished eating. 'And where are the lads? I'm very nearly out of pocket cashews.'

'Pocket cashews?' asked Krish.

'Yeah.' She showed him. 'Little bag of cashews for my pocket. Highly recommend them, for the ghost hunter on the go. They were Janusz's idea. Where *is* he with my foyer snacks?'

Darryl and Janusz still weren't at their seats. They were only getting Pringles from a vending machine. It couldn't take that long, could it?

'Hope nothing's happened to them,' muttered Charity. 'I want my tube o' snacks.'

Nothing had 'happened' to Darryl and Janusz. They were just having a small, quiet, married argument by the crisp machine.

'Because you know I love you,' said Darryl, 'and we made vows to stay together until one of us dies and probably for a while after that, since we both know how ghosts work. So it makes me feel crappy when you get all arsey around good-looking men because it's like you don't trust me.'

'So you agree he's good-looking, then?'

'Oh for pity's sake, babe. Even if he hadn't been bagsied by my sister – and believe me, he really has been bagsied by my sister…' Janusz rolled his eyes, bitterly. '*I've* already been bagsied by *you*.'

'You can't compare marriage and affairs to the rules of bagsy.'

'I absolutely can, and not all men are your dad, Janusz. Your dad seems to be – no offense – a dick.'

'None taken. I'm the one who told you he was a dick.'

'And I'm… a bit of a dick, but in a different way. I'm not going to give our kids a crap time because of whatever their sexuality is and I'm not going to run off because a good-looking person of the gender I fancy smiled at me.'

'This isn't even about my dad!'

'Isn't it?'

'Krish just…' Janusz irritably jabbed the buttons for E-12 to release yet another tube of Pringles, '…thinks he's so much better than me.'

'I don't think he does! I think he just swans around being all handsome and not really thinking about it, like someone else I could mention.' Darryl watched the vending machine's spiral arm push more snacks towards the precipice. 'I don't get jealous about how much better looking you are than me.'

'I'm not.'

'You are. It's the gorgeous elephant in every room. But I'm OK with it, because most of the time when people see us together – with your face and your charm – they assume it must be because I'm really good in bed.'

The Pringles fell off the edge off their shelf and made a noisy descent to the collection tray. Darryl stooped to fetch them while keeping a careful eye on Janusz for the smile that was going to break this impasse.

Janusz couldn't help but smile a very teeny tiny bit.

'But if you're going to be an arse to Krish, it doesn't just make everything all awkward and horrible. It makes him think you had to settle for me because you're mean and jealous and insecure, and not that you used your incredible looks to win me over because I'm an amazing clairvoyant who's terrific at sexytimes.'

Janusz jabbed E-12 again. 'And why do you want him to think you're that good in bed?'

Darryl sighed, wearily. 'Babe.'

Janusz knew his husband had a point, but he felt like he couldn't help it. It was like an instinct for him. Like he was a cat and Krish was another cat. Lovely and friendly on their own, but get them in the same territory and it was all hiss and teeth.

Only, Krish hadn't been all hiss and teeth with Janusz at all. Probably he thought he didn't need to, because he was better. *Co za dupek.*

He was so annoyed that a glaring element of their argument only hit him as they silently carried five tubes of Pringles back to their seats. It was something big. Something Janusz had tried to talk about before, and had been told that it wasn't the right time. Now they were facing their third apocalypse in under two months, it definitely wasn't the right time either. But it had definitely happened. He hadn't imagined it.

Darryl had brought up the concept of them having kids.

Darryl sat with his family, next to Janusz, and passed all of the Pringles over to Charity and Krish. Since it wasn't a stage as such, there was no dimming of the house lights. Instead, there came an introduction over the sound system by a young woman with a middle-class London accent, who Darryl assumed was

Aurora's PA. Any mystic intrigue to Aurora's introduction was rather skewered by the fact that the PA had to first explain phone etiquette and fire safety procedures. Still, the voice tried her best to really inflate Aurora's psychic credentials, promising 'a night like no other and surprises from the realms beyond', like a P.T. Barnum for the twenty-first century. The troubling irony was, when P.T. Barnum had done his own huckstering, his audience weren't actually in danger of having their lives ended by a genuinely dangerous otherworldly bearded lady that they knew nothing about. Darryl was very aware that with the Hell Hole growing above them and Demons skulking in every shadow of the large conference hall, there truly was a horrible chance that this could be 'a night like no other', with 'surprises from the realms beyond' that the audience very definitely did not want at all.

With the Barnum-spiel over, some New Age music faded up to herald Aurora's short walk to the area that had been designated the 'stage'. The audience exploded into rapturous applause. Darryl looked around and saw that many of the ghosts that had drifted into the hall were also politely, silently clapping as they stood around in the aisles – in direct contravention of the fire safety rules. Darryl couldn't exactly blame them for blocking the aisles though. They had nowhere else to go, the dead rarely bothered with the health and safety of the living since they were incorporeal and, besides, nobody ever listened to the fire safety bit at the start of a show.

Still, it remained very odd that so many dead had come to watch Aurora. A desire to hear comforting lies notwithstanding, this much interest in a living person they had no personal connection to was not standard ghost behaviour at all, and leaving the places of their deaths to find her was even more uncommon. How had the dead even known she was in town? It's not like the ghosts had Facebook.

Darryl gave Janusz's hand a little squeeze. His husband squeezed back, but Darryl could tell from his expression that Janusz was still very annoyed about Krish's continued presence. Darryl honestly didn't know what else to say to his husband, right now. It gave him a horrible, sick feeling to think of his Janusz's insecurities, especially with him looking all handsome in that particularly nice Christmas jumper he'd bought him. They turned their phones on to silent, except for Krish, who pulled his out briefly, chewed his lip worriedly as it continued to burn merrily, re-wrapped it, and put it away in his bag again.

The show started, and Aurora began with a cold reading. Darryl sat back in his uncomfortable conference chair with a weary huff, and tried not to get too distracted by Constance hovering irritably nearby.

Oh. Here we go.
Cold reading, on the off chance you don't know, is a parlour trick used by those who pretend to channel the dead. If you're doing a show, your audience will largely be made up of people desperate to hear from a dead loved one, so if you start off with 'I'm getting something from an Albert? Alfred? Algernon…?' If you run through enough old man names, in a room of 500 you're bound to find someone with a dead husband or dad or grandad with one of those names. It's not clairvoyance, it's just gaming probability. And this is Aurora's opening play. Weak.

I stand in the aisle next to my Charity, as unimpressed as the rest of the family. Aurora reels one sucker in straight away, with 'Albert'. It's a woman's father she confirms. Aurora claims Albert is right next to her and speaking to her. He most certainly is not. Aurora offers the woman warm, wet lies. Then the woman asks about Princess Diana. Princess Diana, the audience is told, is not with Aurora just yet. This is, at least, a truth of sorts. The late Diana Spencer is not with her. There are no ghosts on stage with her at all. The many actual ghosts in the hall are lingering around and amongst the audience, meekly. When they were alive they wouldn't rush the stage or call out without express permission from the act performing, and so they are behaving with the same polite reverence now. There are certainly no famous faces amongst the ghostly audience – and definitely not the doe-eyed British Princess who, honestly, I only today found out was dead. Don't judge me, I died in '92, and I've been a little too preoccupied to pay attention to the royals. And anyway, she was so young and full of life – who would have expected she would die? It's a shame. Those poor boys.

Albert's daughter is dismissed, to applause, and now here comes another cold reading – another warm lie. 'Jean'. Of course someone here has lost a Jean. The mourner is another woman – well, most of the audience are. This time, it's Jean's long-term girlfriend Deb. Had Jean lived a little longer to see the time when it was allowed, she might have been Deb's wife. I know all of this from Deb, poor, sad Deb who was robbed of a spouse in more ways than one. Deb is told that Jean considers them married and loves her desperately still. Deb weeps at this nice lie, this obscene fake kindness. There are lots of ghosts present but no Jean. Jean is not there. Jean is not saying those things. Aurora is mining a dead woman's love and devotion and putting words of affection into the mouth of a woman she never knew, who is not there. She is debasing a genuine love, tacking a false happy ending on to their relationship with no genuine care for the actual women in question. All to make it about Aurora. All to make her look—

'Constance Xu, could you please shush? You are being incredibly off-putting right now, my love.'

What…?

'I will get to you and your party when I can. Just because you've all decided to be rude it doesn't mean you can completely disrupt the evening for everyone. A lot of people paid good money to attend tonight.'

The family look as shocked as I do. Brenda, for once, meets my gaze, staring at me in disbelief. For a moment, it's like the good old days, when we loved one another. Or, at least, when I believed we loved each oth—

'I have just asked you to shush, Constance!'

Aurora looks right at me.

'Yes, of course, I'm looking right at you. I can see and hear you. Coo-ee! Do they know you're narrating everything they do? I mean, I know some ghosts do whatever they can to keep their minds intact, but it's a bit weird, wouldn't you say?'

... Er...

Darryl was aware that his mouth was agape. The rest of his party looked cartoonishly flabbergasted – even Grace. Even Krish. Certainly Constance. He'd seen the ghost of Constance's mouth moving so he had always known she was talking a lot, but he assumed she was trying to talk to Charity, or just muttering to herself. He was never able to hear her. That couldn't actually be true about her narrating their lives... could it? He tried to mentally shake himself out of it. It was just another cold reading, right? The Rooks were fairly well known in psychic circles – even to the showboaters. Aurora must have known that if she came to the Rooks' home town they'd show up, and a little research would have thrown up details about Charity's birth mother – Brenda's former working partner. Aurora could just be bluffing, using information she'd found in advance, and reading Brenda's body language to gauge where to look.

None of this accounted for Constance's reaction though. The ghost looked as if Aurora really had caught her out.

Aurora sighed. 'I've lost my train of thought now,' she complained. 'I may as well just get to it. Look, Brenda, I've never held anything against any of you guys. You think it's about you but it's not. It's not even about Krish Patel – hello, Krish my love, how are you enjoying the new job?'

Krish waved a little at her, self-consciously, before Charity grabbed his sleeve and stopped him.

'I'm sure you're going to do a smashing job once you've worked this little bit of uncertainty out of your system,' continued Aurora, 'and on that note would you *please* answer your phone? It is really quite urgent that you do so.'

Krish looked a bit guilty, but still didn't reach for his burning phone.

'Now, Murzzzz will be sitting in hiding thinking this is about him as usual,' added Aurora, 'but it's not. Although, Murzzzz, you *do* need to leave. Face it, my love, you're still as much a tourist as any of your kind. You're just one who's stayed too long and made too much of an impact. I'm sure it's become clear to you by now that you've outstayed any welcome you ever had with that family. But that's none of my business, I'm sure. No, the one I need to speak with is calling themself Grace Barry. Is Grace Barry here?'

Grace seemed to be trying to make her chair absorb her, like a sponge.

'There you are,' said Aurora, resting her gaze on Grace. 'Grace Barry is wanted back. It's very overdue. You are to exit Grace Barry, and return it to the Suit Suite.' She paused, as if listening to someone. It wasn't anybody Darryl could hear, and Constance's lips weren't moving. 'It's not a "Silly name",' she continued moving her gaze away from Grace. 'I think it sounds quite good. It's alliterative.' She paused again. 'Well, it was called that long, long before *Chitty Chitty Bang Bang* came out, so it's not the Suit Suite's fault.' Aurora turned her attention back to Grace. 'Nobody wants to start project termination without you and risk damage to the suit. It took a *lot* of energy and effort to make that suit. But, if you refuse to comply, I'm afraid that's what'll happen, and I'm not sure what will become of you. Nobody does. So. You know. Suit Suite, tout suite…' she trailed off, again. 'No, it doesn't sound silly even when I put it like that.'

She paused again, and Darryl finally noticed a patch of haze next to Aurora. It was around the size of a woman, and swiftly thickened and began to take a human form.

'*Thank* you,' said Aurora in a warm, friendly, faintly reverential tone. 'I knew you'd see it my way.' She turned to the audience with a smile – her annoyance with Constance and the apocalyptic message she'd just delivered to the Angel seemingly forgotten. 'She's here, everybody. The People's Princess has graced us.'

The audience shot to its collective feet in delighted applause, and Darryl found himself standing along with them, along with the rest of the family. He craned to see what the patch of haze really was as it continued to clarify. A slim woman, mid-thirties… oh no. A nice late nineties suit. Oh no, a blonde bob and big blue eyes – no, no, no, no, it couldn't be her. Aurora couldn't have *her*. The ghost tilted her head down and smiled upwards through her big lashes – a well-rehearsed demureness. Oh no, no, no.

'Shit,' he whispered. 'I think that might be Princess Diana.'
'What?' whispered Janusz. 'But you said Aurora was a fraud.'
'Shh,' said a woman behind them.

'I know what I said,' whispered Darryl, 'but there's very clearly something going on. I think she can maybe hear ghosts that I can't even see. She knows about Grace and Murzzzz and there's a ghost talking to her now who absolutely looks like Dodi Era Princess Diana, and now I don't know what to do about anything.'

'Because this means Aurora is for real after all?'

'Because all that stuff she's claimed Diana has told her was kinda racist and I'm not sure I want to save a world where Diana hangs out with Aurora Tavistock and is kinda racist!'

'Shh,' said the woman again.

'What do you even care about Lady Di?' Janusz hissed. 'You don't like the royals. You said they should be abolished.'

'I don't like the royals. Just her.'

'But why? You're a *Guardian* reader. You have that "No war but the class war" sticker on your jogging bottle.'

'You wouldn't understand,' whispered Darryl huffily, against yet another shushing from the woman behind her. 'You weren't there, man. You weren't on this island during the '97 grieftastrophe.'

'Oh no, we Poles can't empathise with national trauma, nothing ever happened to us during the whole of the twentieth century.'

'You *had* to bring the whole Nazis and USSR thing back into it, didn't you?'

'Still rankles a little, yeah.'

If Aurora could hear the husbands' only slightly muted argument, she ignored it. Instead, she concentrated on her one-sided conversation with the Diana ghost. The living audience watched Aurora, enraptured. Many of the ghosts in the aisles did so, too. The Demons continued to lurk – seeming not that interested in the show, but strangely docile, as if they were waiting for something else.

For a brief moment, none of these things mattered to Darryl. Aurora had one of his favourite celebrities next to her. And she was speaking for her, telling the audience her answers to their questions and saying things that were hateful to Darryl's ears. He had faced down a lot of horrors in the past few months, but this was his breaking point. This was utterly unacceptable. Aurora may as well have wheeled out the late Freddie Mercury and told everyone that he was into far-right podcasts. Furthering his frustration was that apparently Aurora could hear the ghost. Maybe she could hear them all – maybe Albert and Jean had really spoken after all and he just hadn't seen them. This was a world turned on its head. He'd never known anyone who could hear the ghosts as well as see them.

Well. There was one way they could hear them. He could offer himself up as a vessel to Diana. This was an incredibly dangerous thing to do at a seance that had attracted hundreds of ghosts. He would be opening himself up as a conduit to all of them, knowing they'd swarm to him like wasps to a bin full of ice cream. He weighed this risk up with his rage at Aurora attributing those words to one of his heroes. He had to know. He had to know what the ghost was really saying and if Aurora was telling the truth. If she was… well, he'd have to process that along with the rest of the crap that the universe had thrown at him recently.

Aurora had to be lying. She *had* to be!

Darryl focused on the blonde ghost, and noticed the ghostly princess turn her head a little as her mouth moved silently. She had noticed him. He tried psychically moving his own consciousness back just a smidge, like shuffling to one side on a sofa and patting a nice warm patch of cushion next to him as a personal invitation. He desperately hoped that none of the many, many other ghosts in the room would misread it as an invitation to them, or not care that they hadn't been invited. Diana stared at him with huge, Disney-mournful eyes. Psychically, he again patted the bit of his mind where he'd scooched over for her. And, suddenly, she was there. On the sofa inside his mind.

'…because you know me, not a racist bone in my body,' came a woman's voice from his mouth. 'She could be purple with green polka dots for all I care because I don't judge colour, I judge vibes and she just gives off bad vibes if you ask me, that's all.'

The part of him that was still him was aware that none of the other ghosts were trying to use him, yet. He wasn't sure how long that would last. They might cotton on fast. He was also aware that Aurora's show had very suddenly ground to a halt and that all of the living in the room – Aurora and his family included – were watching him with various reactions of shock and horror with the exception of his sister and husband who were watching with amusement.

'Darryl Rook,' Aurora cried, 'you are being incredibly rude!'

'Now, Kate,' continued the voice, 'Kate's *classy*. You can't quantify it or explain it, she just has classy vibes, you know what I mean, don't you?'

'I…' Krish frowned. 'I don't remember Lady Di sounding like that. Didn't she sound more "lah-dee-dah"? Not… what *is* that accent?'

'Cardiff, I think,' said Charity.

'Swansea,' said the ghost voice in its high-pitched, thick Welsh accent. From the ghost's tone, she had only just remembered that there was a place called Swansea, and that her accent was from there.

'*Was* she from Swansea?' asked Krish, still bewildered.

'She was the Princess of Wales,' Aurora called from her makeshift stage area.

'That doesn't mean…' Brenda trailed off, her face taking on the expression she usually saved for terrible drivers and ignorant radio phone-in-show callers. 'I'm sorry, Aurora Tavistock, do you not actually know who Diana Spencer was, or how the whole Prince and Princess of Wales thing works?'

'That's not Lady Di,' crowed Janusz, pointing triumphantly at Darryl.

'No, Janusz Wozniak, that is your husband, who has hijacked Princess Diana, and should give her back,' Aurora commanded.

'I used to go to parties,' said the voice in her Swansea accent, with that same tone, as if she were just starting to remember something important. 'I used to open fetes. I was Diana. The best Diana this side of Wrexham. Wales's favourite Princess of Wales. I made them so happy.'

'She's a Diana look-alike, you absolute flat battery,' Charity shouted, delighted. 'Aurora Tavistock got fooled by a look-alike who sounds like she's playing a bit part on *Torchwood*.'

'I was told to come to see Aurora,' said a new voice from within Darryl. He had not invited this new voice. Uh-oh. 'She's not a fraud, is she? I was told to see her! It was so difficult getting here.'

The living audience began to murmur, disquieted.

'This is a cheap trick,' sighed Aurora.

'*You're* a cheap trick,' retorted Brenda, loudly, clearly revelling in the way the mood in the room was beginning to sour.

'They said Aurora had the answers,' said yet another voice from Darryl. Oh, no. The dead were beginning to crowd into him, and they were all worried. They were like a mass of commuters who'd been told that their delayed train was definitely ready to depart from platform eleven, only to find that the train doors weren't opening. And he was the only person in a hi-vis vest to be found in the station. He was overwhelmed by their anxiousness and their sense of abandonment. He could feel his body beginning to sag.

Physically, he was grabbed and safely held by Janusz. Psychically, the fake Diana continued to press up against him, still in the spot in his consciousness where he'd invited her to sit. He felt her distress keenly. She must have fallen into the role of professional Diana post-death and started to think she really was the celebrity she'd been impersonating. The ghost had lost her whole sense of self in an instant. She had no real name any more and no idea of her real family, just opinions about the famous wives of two famous men who were not her sons. Darryl was filled with her bewildered sadness. He felt it keenly, even though none of it made it OK that the fake Diana was still kinda racist. The fake Diana's consciousness clung to his, lost, as they were both pushed back by the other ghosts. He knew that he was beginning to choke and shake. He was about to pass out entirely, which would mean he would no longer be a useful host to all the clamouring dead, and they would leave him.

Then, at the edge of consciousness, he felt the ghost of the fake Diana let go and drift off into the swirling multitude of the dead, all scared, all angry, all driven now by one primary thought – they'd been told to go to Aurora because she had the answers, and now it seemed that Aurora was not what they'd hoped. Maybe she was not a fraud when it came to her psychic abilities, but she was certainly not what she seemed. Aurora was not what was advertised. She was a fraud on a whole other level, thought the very tiny bit of Darryl that was still capable of thought. Because thinking a look-alike was the real Diana didn't make sense unless Aurora was really stupid. There was something else going on. Aurora hadn't even seemed that surprised by the revelation. She hadn't seemed that surprised by anything – just annoyed. Annoyed and huffy at little people wasting her time.

Who did that remind Darryl of?

The darkness closed in.

Oh well, thought the last spark of him. At least this meant the real Princess of Hearts wasn't 'kinda racist' after all.

CHAPTER TEN
And I Feel Fine

Darryl slumped entirely into Janusz's arms and the many worried, angry voices pouring from him were finally silenced. For a second, the whole hall watched the two men wordlessly. Most of the audience looked stunned. Krish looked troubled. Charity and her family weren't too concerned, they'd seen this happen before and Darryl had been fine. Aurora, Charity noticed, just looked annoyed. After a moment, Darryl gasped, opened his eyes, coughed up a mouthful of phlegm and pulled a face.

'Fake Diana,' he croaked.

'Yes, well,' snapped Aurora, irritably. 'Can I carry on now? Is that OK with you?'

'Even though your Diana is fake?' asked Brenda.

'It's not about the Diana,' replied Aurora.

'Yes, it is,' managed Darryl, through a sore throat. 'She thought she was real, because you thought she was real. How could you? Listening to her, feeling her spirit... she was just some lost woman from Swansea who clearly used to read too much *Daily Mail*. She hadn't even been dead that long, I could sense that the moment she spoke through me. Any decent psychic would have known, and either sent her along or helped her find her true self.'

'I am more than a "decent psychic", Darryl Rook.'

'Yeah. Yeah, you know a *lot*, don't you?'

'Yes, I do,' replied Aurora. 'Now, can I please get on with the evening?'

'And it's clearly not all down to cold reading but there are no ghosts on stage with you most of the time so it isn't even down to the dead,' continued Darryl. 'You know all this stuff, apparently from nowhere… but you don't *care* about it.'

'So?'

'I'm not saying it's fundamentally human to care,' Darryl rasped. 'I've met a lot of humans who don't care. And not everyone who cares is a human.'

Charity noticed her brother give Grace a little smile at that. The Angel, for her part, gave Darryl a shy little nod of appreciation back. Absolutely nobody gave Richard, and by extension the buried form of Murzzzz, a little smile.

'But,' continued Darryl, 'you thought that was the real Diana.'

'Will you stop going on about Diana? So, I was fooled. I hold my hands up to it. Nobody's perfect.'

'No, but you are. You're too perfect. You always seem to know what you *need* to know. And I think the Diana mistake happened because you never *needed* to know who Diana was.'

Charity scrunched up her face. Darryl wasn't making much sense, but then he had just been possessed by like a hundred ghosts or something. Maybe he needed a sit-down and a sweet drink.

'Maybe we should go,' mumbled Richard.

'It's like,' said Darryl, desperately, 'it's like… when you're signing in to a website and they make you click the squares with a tractor in to show you're human, because for some reason a bot or whatever isn't going to be able to take the word 'tractor' and apply it to the pictures in the squares. It's like you saw a ghost that looked like it could be a tractor and went "that'll do".'

'Why are we talking about tractors?' Grace asked. 'Janusz, maybe we should help Darryl get some air, or…'

Darryl pointed weakly at Grace. 'Did you know, from her voice, that that wasn't the real Diana?'

'Yes…' replied Grace, defensively, sounding unsure of herself. 'No. I… actually don't think I've ever really heard her voice. She's just an abstract idea to me, like *Dirty Dancing* or Eurovision.'

'Exactly.' Darryl turned his trembling finger to Aurora. 'An abstract idea. An implanted concept of the world to help you pass, to hide the fact that you're not real. Aurora Tavistock, you are a Suit.'

The family were the only ones who gasped, since they were the only ones who understood what Aurora had just been accused of.

'A Suit?' asked Aurora, archly.

'That's the term you prefer, isn't it?' asked Darryl. 'I know you people don't like the A-word.'

'What's going on?' whispered a woman in front of them.

'I think that man's calling her an arsehole,' whispered her friend. 'Rude.'

Aurora's expression changed. It was sort of a smile. 'And you got all of that from me not knowing Diana's accent?'

'You don't falsely invoke that woman's name in front of me and get away with it,' said Darryl, still trembling. 'I… wait. Was I *right*? Are you actually a… you know, like Grace?'

'I'm not like Grace, my love,' replied Aurora, and suddenly the hall felt all wrong. It felt as if its own dimensions didn't fit it any more, as if it was simultaneously too big and too small, like a badly cut blazer. 'I am so much more than the being calling themself Grace Barry.'

Darryl let out a weird little victory noise, like he'd just beaten Charity at *Street Fighter*. 'Nailed it!'

Brenda practically yelped with joy. 'I *knewwwww* you were a fraud!'

Darryl and Brenda aside, none of the other people in the hall seemed even vaguely happy about this turn of events.

Meanwhile, the space around Aurora was continuing to warp. It made Charity's stomach lurch, and not in a pleasant, rollercoaster kind of way. Around her, audience members clutched their seats and one another nervously, and muttered about what psychic power or stage trickery could be responsible for the sensation of everything both folding inwards and outwards at the same time. Charity nudged Grace.

'Can *you* do that?' she asked their Angel.

Grace shook her head.

'Can you... stop *her* from doing that?'

'I really don't think so,' whispered Grace.

'Didn't I always say?' continued Brenda loudly, seemingly oblivious to any terrible tummy tumescence. 'And now you're not even just a fake psychic, you're a fake *person*! Oh, Aurora. Aurora, Aurora, Aurora! After all that sneering from your lot about us little mortals, you still came down here in your fake psychic suit to get some attention? To get on *Loose Women* and do a tour of Home Counties conference halls?' Brenda was breathless with exhilaration, now. 'That's *pathetic*!'

'That's enough!' Another woman hurried on stage. She had the dark clothes and harried expression of a PA, stagehand and all-round general dogsbody. She gestured to Charity's party. 'You lot – out.' Then, she turned to Aurora. 'Do you want to stop? Is this...? What *is* all of this?'

Aurora Tavistock just straight up ignored her assistant, which was frankly very rude, but absolutely standard for the behaviour of the 'Suits' Charity had met besides Grace.

'None of this was about this little world,' replied Aurora, and although she spoke at a normal volume, her voice travelled and jangled painfully inside Charity's head. 'All of it was leading towards this. You can't possibly believe I came here because I like this place? Or the attention? If I wanted mortal attention I'd have gone further back in time, allowed a religion to form around me. Sparked a few Holy Wars or something funny like that. I came here out of necessity – slotted myself only a couple of decades into the past. Made myself more successful than you Rooks or Patel, in order to push you, to give you something to strive towards. To try to make you better versions of yourselves.'

'Arse gravy,' shouted Brenda, 'there's nothing about a big fraud like you that could possibly change what sort of people we are!'

'No, I know,' replied Aurora. 'That did *not* work, all of you little people are just as chaotic and petty and blah as you ever were. I even drew big crowds of the dead to my shows for you lot to practice doing your little clear-up jobs on.'

'You did that on purpose?' called Brenda.

'You're welcome, my love, not that it improved your abilities much. But all of it was leading here. To tonight. It took far too many wrong turns, but all of the outstanding issues are now here in the same place. And, Death is here.'

The audience, already murmuring with disquiet throughout this whole odd and upsetting turn in what they'd hoped would be a New Year's Eve of psychic entertainment, raised the volume and urgency of their troubled mutterings.

'Is this still part of the show?' asked the woman in front of Charity. 'It's gone a bit dark, hasn't it?'

'I mean Krish Patel,' continued Aurora, in that uncanny jangling voice. 'You remember Krish from earlier? Give the nice people a wave, Krish my love. Krish has a scythe and everything. Sounds very fancy. Nice and traditional for what's coming.'

The audience turned to look at the Nice Reaper sitting next to Charity, who gave a tiny, self-conscious wave. 'I'm just here for the show,' he managed. 'Not really participating. And the scythe's packed away nice and safe.'

'Well, we'll see how long that lasts, my love,' replied Aurora.

The women in front of Charity gave Krish a critical stare before turning back to one another.

'That lot's part of the show, then,' whispered one of the women, jabbing a thumb at Charity's party.

'Didn't I say?' hissed the other. 'Didn't I say them two foreign-sounding ones were too good-looking, and had to be actors?'

'Oh, shut up, Carol,' whispered her friend.

Aurora held out her hand, with the expression of a parent who had decided it was time for her pre-school child to leave a birthday party.

'Grace Barry?' said Aurora in a gentle voice that made Charity's whole skull ache.

Grace met Aurora's gaze, and shook her head.

'I came all this way for you, Grace Barry. You've had your fun.'

'I'm not leaving them,' replied Grace. 'I know what'll happen if I do.'

'Nothing bad will happen to you, Grace Barry. You'll be debriefed at Head Office, then given the time you need to decompress. Couple of reality cycles should do it.'

'Not to me,' said Grace, 'to *them*. To this world.'

'This world is broken. And it's the mortals who broke it, just like they do every time. Time to reset.'

'But all these people! My friends! The strangers here, and everywhere else in this world. I don't want you to hurt them.'

Aurora quirked a brow. 'Even the one who gave you that black eye?'

Grace brushed a finger gently over the shiner. 'Even him. Even the tyrants and the bullies and the polluters. Even Murzzzz.'

Aurora rolled her eyes. 'Murzzzz is a dick. Everyone thinks so – this dimension, his dimension, even his own family.'

None of the family said anything to disagree with this. Richard frowned.

'Yeah,' replied Grace, 'well... even dicks have redeeming features. And even dicks deserve a chance.'

'Listen to yourself! Talking absolute nonsense! What's happened to you, my love?'

'I've lived,' Grace told her. 'I've lived in this world. And it's flawed and it's short and it's violent, and... it's beautiful. It has so much love in it, Aurora, and so much care. And yeah, it's broken – really, really broken – but I honestly believe it can be fixed. So many people want to fix it, they just need more of a chance. Maybe if you lived here too—'

Aurora snorted. 'I have lived here for longer than you, Grace Barry. I've been in this suit for years, and I haven't let it wreck my mind.'

Grace glared at her, as the hall continued to lurch inwards and outwards like a terrible kaleidoscope. 'What's your assistant's name?'

Aurora wrinkled her brow. 'I don't understand.'

Grace addressed the PA in black. 'How long have you been working for Aurora, dear?'

The PA winced. Her face was hurting.

'About a year,' replied the PA. 'And Aurora knows my name, of course she does!'

She squinted at Aurora, who just shrugged.

'It's Yemisi!' the PA, whose name apparently was Yemisi, looked hurt, both physically and emotionally. She clutched at her head. 'You really didn't...? After a year? Oh my days, Aurora.'

Grace pointed, accusingly at Aurora. 'You're not living here. Not really. Because you're not letting yourself care.'

'Of course I'm not. I don't want to end up like you.'

'If you're not letting yourself live properly, you're not going to get it.'

'I don't want to "get it"!' Aurora's only very slightly raised voice left Charity's ears ringing. 'You think you're so high and mighty, but what you're doing is horrible! You're just a tourist, latching on to this rubbish little mortal family like Murzzzz did! You really are no better than him! You've brought them nothing but upset and pain. You physically hurt them. Only just now, you hurt poor Whatshername...'

'Yemisi,' growled Yemisi, still clutching her forehead. 'And I'm fine. Whatever that was, it's passing and I've stopped seeing stars.'

Grace pulled a guilty expression at Yemisi trying to rub the pain from her head.

'We have made several attempts to bring you home without a fuss, Grace Barry,' continued Aurora, 'and every time you've made things difficult, for us and for this family you claim to care about. My love, I'm afraid this time I really must insist. And this time, I've built in a few assurances regarding your cooperation.'

'Such as?'

Aurora gestured around the hall.

'Oh, no,' breathed Grace. 'This audience. It's... They're hostages, aren't they?'

'What?' asked one of the women in front of Charity.

The other woman in front of her shook her head, calmly. 'Part of the show, innit? Actors, like you said.'

'I wish I knew how they're making me feel all sick and drunk,' added the first woman in a whisper.

'We shared a whole bottle of pinot beforehand,' hissed the second woman.

'You filled a room with the living and invited a load of Demons to hold them hostage, you maniac,' shouted Grace.

'And the beings you call "Demons" are terribly bored, my love' replied Aurora with a bland smile. 'They usually get to do world-ending stuff themselves. And it gets very messy, so that's why we *tried* to do it more mercifully this time, but if you're going to be difficult about it... I really don't think you want to see what the "Demons" are capable of doing to a few hundred mortal bodies.'

'What are you doing?' Yemisi hissed to Aurora. 'Why are you threatening the audience? Don't do that please. You're not the one who has to deal with all the refund demands.'

'Aurora Tavistock, you sly sod,' piped Brenda. 'This whole show was just to give the Demons time to assemble, wasn't it?'

'And to give these people an entertaining show,' Aurora told her. 'Least I could do, considering what's coming.'

A few of the audience gave her a quiet, confused smattering of applause.

'So why did you collect the dead here too?' asked Brenda. 'Are they hostages or another threat against the living?'

'Oh, they're just to power the door,' replied Aurora. 'I've been gathering them all afternoon. Surely, you must know the doors need ghostly misery to open, by now?'

'Yes, this is the third one we've closed down in two months,' replied Brenda, primly.

'Well, my love,' replied Aurora with a cold, fake politeness to mirror Brenda's, 'third time's the charm. Come along, Grace Barry. Everything's in place. Whether it's painless or not is down to you, but it really is time to end this nonsense.'

Grace looked around herself at the full conference hall, with a troubled expression. Charity's heart sank – she knew what Grace must be thinking. Could the family fight off a hall full of Demons? Possibly. Could they do so without any collateral damage to all the living trapped in here with them? Definitely not. Grace looked at Charity, and her family. She looked at Krish. She turned to her side, and looked Brenda dead in the eye.

'Grace,' warned Brenda, quietly.

'Aurora's right, isn't she?' said Grace. 'I hurt you sometimes, don't I? I don't really belong here, and sometimes it gets you hurt.'

'Grace.'

'I won't let you get hurt,' said Grace. 'I think the end is inevitable, now, but I won't let you get hurt. I had such a lovely time, being me. Being small, and full of love. Thank you so much for having me.'

'Grace, no,' hissed Brenda.

'I think I love you,' said Grace. 'All of you. I think maybe you were my family. Krish, I don't know you well enough yet to say that of you, but you seem like a lovely young man. Murzzzz… well, I suppose your heart was in the right place. Mostly.'

And she stood up, in spite of the family's growing protestations. Charity already knew that there was nothing any of them could do that would overturn Grace's will. Grace nodded at Aurora.

Aurora smirked.

'The End,' she said.

Bewildered, the audience broke into another round of polite applause.

145

CHAPTER ELEVEN
The End

'No,' warned Brenda over the applause. 'No.'

More of the Rook family chimed in with ineffective 'no's.

But Krish could see what was at stake. He could see the Demons skulking and slithering in every shadow and behind every pillar. There had to be a hundred at least. Maybe more. It was likely that Brenda and Darryl could see the full extent of the number of Demons, too, but they seemed to really love Grace so it was understandable they didn't want her to give up and leave Earth just like that.

'Sorry, I'm not sure this is fair, Aurora,' he protested, meekly. 'You're abusing Grace's better nature.'

'Well, it's hardly my fault she's got a "better nature" to abuse, is it,' replied Aurora. 'Don't worry, Grace Barry, we'll get that out of you soon enough.'

Grace gave a small, sad little glance over her shoulder, a silent goodbye.

'Grace, you're dooming this world,' warned Krish. 'I don't know you very well, but you don't seem the doomy type.'

As soon as he said it, he wished he hadn't. Her miserable expression was one of someone who knew all too well what she was doing, and saw it as the lesser of two evils. Krish had seen for himself what Demons could do to people. Given the straight choice of that happening to hundreds – perhaps thousands, depending on how long this massive horde of Demons would be allowed to rampage – and simply switching the living world quickly and painlessly off and on again, he'd seriously consider the latter, too.

'Grace, we can fight these guys,' called Darryl in unsure tones. 'We saved hostages before, we can do it again. Every last one, right?'

Darryl glanced at his mother for reassurance and backup. Brenda had the sort of expression a mother would pull if a small child had just announced that all their financial woes were over because they'd just found a dollar in the street, and intended to invest it in a winning lottery ticket.

It was over, thought Krish. All those civilisations, all those lives, the Pyramids, the coral reefs, that bento place he really liked back in Winnipeg – they would soon all be gone. And not with a bang, but with an Angel's surrender in a leisure estate conference hall. And here he was – Death, the Reaper himself, with his own scythe and everything – and he wasn't doing anything. *Shouldn't* he be doing something?

Around him, the dead began to scream, silently. They threw back their heads, screwed up their eyes and stretched open their mouths in noiseless howls of misery. They did it as one, with no warning. Hundreds of them, no longer watching the show with curiosity and vague unease, but now, in an instant, consumed by some terrible internal horror. No. No! He *should* be doing something. Allowing the lingering dead to suffer was the opposite of what he was meant to be doing!

In the high-ceilinged space above where Aurora Tavistock was standing, a… a 'nothing' opened up, splitting the air. The 'door', or the Hell Hole, or whatever one called that proto-portal that had been festering above the hotel, had suddenly ballooned in size and power as if someone had grabbed hold of a threadbare patch of fabric and pulled. The rip in the air was so big and so close that Krish could now make out something behind the nothingness. It appeared to be an office. One of those really modern offices where everything's brightly coloured and chrome and glass and very sleek-looking and yet nothing actually quite works properly. One of those offices that's full of 'breakout spaces' with tables that are either too low for you to work at your laptop or too high so people have to perch precariously on tall bar stools, and acoustics that mean nobody can make out what anyone else is saying. One of those offices where great attention has been paid to choosing thematic wall decals but where there aren't enough desks or working plug sockets. Krish had seen a lot of those offices in Winnipeg. Half the time with psychic call-outs to places like that, they weren't actually haunted, but the design of the place would so subtly 'off' that it gave the living a severe case of the heebie-jeebies. It made a weird sort of sense to Krish that the appearance of that sort of office space in an otherworldly dimension would be heralded by the sudden suffering of hundreds of souls. It made sense, and he didn't like it.

He discovered that his scythe was in his hands. Unfortunately, the main thing that alerted him to this was a collective panicked shriek from some of the audience around him. The audience had, up until this point, been on board with all of the interruptions believing them to be a part of the show, but a young man standing amongst them with a large bladed weapon probably was a bit too out-there to be a plausible encore piece.

'He's got a machete,' panicked one of the women in front of him, even though the scythe looked nothing like a machete.

'And he's got women's leggings on,' added her companion in an equally disturbed tone. Oh yeah, he was still wearing Brenda's yoga pants. He wasn't sure how that made the situation any worse, but it certainly didn't seem to make things any better.

He couldn't exactly do anything about the pants, but he could do something about the fright his scythe was giving the living. He put his reaping weapon away again into whatever metaphysical pocket he always pulled it from. It vanished as instantly as it appeared and, at the sight of something that looked like a magic trick, the panicking crowd relaxed. They could explain it away as all part of the show now. Some of them even clapped again although the woman in front still regarded his yoga pants with suspicion.

'Krish.' Grace had stopped moving through the crowd, and had turned to look at the hubbub in the audience. She stood, halfway between the Rooks and Aurora and not quite underneath the great rip in reality. She met eyes with Krish and he saw that she was crying. Krish's heart leapt – had the Angel changed her mind?

She smiled sadly, and gave him a thumbs up. 'That's a really cool trick. Um. Good luck.'

Oh. No, she definitely hadn't had her mind changed by him accidentally manifesting and then un-manifesting a symbolic agricultural tool.

'Grace,' attempted Brenda, 'listen…'

But Grace had done all of her listening. She'd been convinced that to stay would be to directly cause harm, and from what little Krish knew of the Angel, he could tell that knowingly causing harm was something she couldn't bear to do. As he watched Grace his face started to hurt. From the reaction of others around the room, all of the living members of the audience were feeling a similar effect. It was possible that Grace was hurting the dead too, but there was no way for Krish to tell since the ghosts were still mutely wailing in anguish as they had been just before the tearing open of the Hell Hole. As the ghosts continued to scream, and many of the living winced, sucked sharply through their teeth and covered their faces with their hands it all added to the whole 'Grace was hurting people while she stayed on Earth' argument.

Krish found that, as much as it hurt, he couldn't look away from Grace. There was a light emanating from her – a terrible light. Krish couldn't have said what colour the light was, unless 'Ow' was a colour. It was something well beyond the usual human visual register. It was like looking at the sun only it was worse because at least the sun was of the solar system, of the universe – this was the light of something beyond. And still he couldn't look away.

'Grace, stop,' shouted Brenda. 'If one of you Celestials takes off your suit in front of mortals, the sight of the real you will kill us, remember?'

'Is that what they told you?' asked Aurora in mocking tones. 'And you believed them? Oh, my loves. Our true forms are painful to mortals' silly little monkey brains, but hardly fatal. Probably. There's a slight chance of the risk of long-term neural damage but it's not as if it matters – they'll all be dead soon anyway.'

Brenda groaned. 'Helpful to the end, Aurora.'

'You're doing great, Grace Barry,' trilled Aurora. 'You're making the right choice. The ethical choice.'

Krish watched as the light became brighter at the centre of Grace's forehead and spread downwards, creating a line down the Angel's face, her neck, her chest, her belly… like a zip being undone down the front of her entire body. The line of light grew thicker, and even more painful to those watching, and then everything about Grace peeled away. Not just her clothes, not just her skin – as if that wouldn't be upsetting enough – but everything. Everything human about Grace, everything that fitted into Krish's world was pulled off her like a onesie. Briefly, her split skull and chest turned inside out, wet and meaty and – goodness – Krish was struck by how disgusting mortal life must seem if it was just something you had to put on for work. The squishy inside-out flesh suit continued to peel away until it was nothing – lost in the horrible light. And then, the light wasn't in the conference hall any more, it was in the slightly-off, colourful office beyond the rip in reality. And then, the light was gone.

His face didn't hurt any more.

Grace was gone.

Grace is gone.

Grace is gone, and it isn't fair.

I am struck with a fresh grief – a sensation that I haven't felt for a long time. I can feel the Hell Hole suck at the grief like a leech – like a hungry cuckoo chick in a starling's nest – trying to steal my misery, to feed off it as it is doing the rest of the dead. I am able to hold on to my grief, keep it from the Hell Hole. My pain is mine. It belongs to me. All of it, including this new grief that gusts through the stagnant mist of all the sadness and loss and hurt that I've been carrying around since my death. This is not the grief I usually feel, this is a mourning for the loss of Grace.

It's probably a trick, right? An Angel trick? Grace isn't real. She's a Suit, deliberately designed to make humans like her – to make humans find her sweet, and there's enough of the human left in me to fall for it. I shouldn't fall for it. I should concentrate on Charity.

Charity will mourn the loss of Grace. Sweet little Grace. I stood helplessly and watched her go. Of course I stood helplessly, I'm dead,

I'm mostly just here to linger and watch the family taking part in this story.

But I liked Grace. I wish I could have protected her. Of course I do, that was what she was designed to make me feel. We were meant to find her pleasant and a bit pathetic and want to protect her. I know this. I know all of this, dammit! But, it... hurts, somehow.

She didn't want to go, just like Harry didn't want to go and just like I don't want to go. Why does this have to keep happening? Why do beings who call themselves 'merciful' keep ripping my family apart?

No. No. No, Grace wasn't family, she was an interloper. A tourist. Like Murzzzz. She wasn't my family.

And yet...

I think Charity saw her as family.

Family doesn't even matter any more. Nothing matters. They're going to end the world, and all of this will be oblivion. So it won't matter who my family were and who was a part of it and who was not.

Was I even really a part of this family? My own family was torn apart. Harry was taken from me. Charity was taken from my arms. And I've been following her around, unable to touch her or to speak to her. That was my family.

How would I feel if Murzzzz hadn't had his way? If Brenda and Richard had been the ones who were killed. If Harry and I had been the ones to live. If Darryl were my adopted son. If I had been the one to find Grace, wouldn't I have welcomed her into my home and my family? Even if the world was ending, wouldn't I want to be with my family right up until the last atom of the universe disappeared?

Perhaps it won't matter once the universe has ended but I think that, until that happens, this family still matters, and perhaps those of us who linger at the edges of it, non-mortals looking in, matter as much as the humans and mostly-humans at its core.

I have lingered, and watched, and told myself the story of this family for so many years. I've watched them add members, lose members, get members back. I've watched them fall out, make up and hold an uneasy truce. Watched them fight Demons, and fight against the end of the world, and fight their own self-destructiveness, and an awful lot of ghosts. And what have I learned from the things I've watched? The Rooks are a mess, full of secrets and deception, and Harry and I would probably have done a much better job of raising those kids had Murzzzz gone along with the original plan to let us live. But with all of that said and done, after everything they've been through together, they deserve the chance to see that final atom of the universe together, arm in arm. All of them. Including Grace.

They love each other.

I love them.

Yes. Yes! I love them. I can feel it – a painful kernel at the centre of the hurt and the grief. It's love. Even after everything, even with my resentment unswayed, I still love all of them.

Most of them. Murzzzz can still piss off.

Charity is crying. So is Darryl.

The babies! The babies are crying! I have to do something!

Death is still with us. A soft, sweet, kindly-eyed Death. The Nice Reaper. He can't hear me. None of them can hear me. Perhaps he shouldn't have to. Perhaps Death should just know when a dead person has come to a decision.

And I have come to a decision.

Death turns his head, and meets my eye.

Hello, Death. I think I can help them. And for that, I need to go with Grace.

'Um,' said Krish, 'I know this might not be the time, but—'

'Whatever it is, it's very much *not* the time, you gorgeous idiot!' Brenda was frozen to a spot a little way from her seat where she had made an attempt to follow Grace before the Angel had unpeeled herself and disappeared. Her hands were clawed in her hair in distress. 'She's gone. She's gone! See, this is why I don't make friends – every time I try, something like *this* happens!'

'Yeah,' continued Krish, with a sheepish cringe, 'about that... Constance wants to go, too.'

Brenda's expression didn't change. 'What do you mean "go"?'

'She wants to move on,' murmured Charity, and, oh, Charity was really crying now. Krish didn't like that. 'Can't blame her. It's over.'

Charity was right. The Demons were still hiding in corners and shadows and they weren't attacking quite yet, but all of the ghosts bar Constance were still screaming silently, and the void was continuing to grow. Yeah. This was the end.

'Goodbye,' sobbed Charity, looking into the vague direction of Constance, 'it was nice getting to know you, if only a little bit.'

'No! Why now?' Brenda jabbed a finger towards Constance's ghost. 'She's up to something. Some heroic nonsense.'

'Maybe,' replied Krish. 'She wants to follow Grace to Head Office.'

'I knew it!' Brenda continued to wave her finger at Constance. 'You want to try to fetch Grace. How are you going to change her mind if we couldn't, eh? How will you even find her? How will you get back? What's your plan? Hm?'

'Brenda, you know she can't reply.'

'Yeah, cause she's got no answer, no plan, no nothing!'

Krish sighed, and gently stretched his hands out towards Constance's ghost until he felt that little bit of pressure – that little biting point – that told him he was about to send a spirit away. 'If a ghost wants to leave, I have to help them.'

'No no no!' Brenda clambered past her son and son-in-law to get to Krish.

'Hope you find what you're looking for, Constance,' Krish told her, and pushed.

'No, no, no...'

And the tension gave way. There was that little suck-pop sensation as usual, like pushing your fingers into Jell-O, and Constance became unrooted from the living world. She began to float away into the bright office on the other side of the portal, as if sinking through a viscous liquid... but something was wrong. Maybe it was due to the power of the Hell Hole, or the general end of the world that was definitely picking up steam right in front of him. Maybe it was Constance's determination to do something about the situation, or maybe it was her proximity to Brenda – a powerful psychic equally determined that whatever Constance was going to try to do, she shouldn't try to do it alone. The metaphysical Jell-O – or whatever it actually was that the fabric between realities was made of – kept on sucking even after he'd pushed Constance through. He couldn't pull his hands out. Even as he struggled to free himself, Brenda leaned over the chair in front of her, pushed both hands through the Jell-O walls of reality and somehow grabbed a hold of Constance's leg as the dead woman drifted towards Head Office. This didn't stop or slow Constance's journey towards the Hell Hole, instead it began to pull Brenda in as well. She was caught in Constance's wake, or... no. Krish realised, looking at Brenda, that she wasn't helplessly caught in any sort of ghostly undertow, she was accompanying Constance on purpose.

Brenda definitely wasn't dead so, as the Reaper, Krish was pretty sure that this was against the rules. There was a good chance that just trying to go into Head Office would kill a mortal. Krish had no idea what would happen but he knew, at his core, that it was a place that living mortals should not go. Even Constance was trying to kick Brenda away, but to no avail. The clairvoyant held fast, with an angry, determined grin. And Krish still couldn't free his hands.

'Dear…?' managed Richard. Murzzzz flickered briefly across Richard's face, aghast, incapable of helping, before sinking back into Richard, both occupants of his body equally horrified and unsure of what to do.

Darryl made half a step towards Brenda but was blocked by Janusz.

'Absolutely not,' Janusz told his husband, which was enough to stop Darryl.

'Nope,' said Charity, in a tone that suggested she was speaking to herself. 'Not both mums. Not today, bitches.'

Krish kept fighting to free his hands. Brenda had, Krish noticed, clambered along Constance's body and now had the protesting ghost in a tight, furious embrace. Constance and Brenda's forms had both lengthened in the uncanny viscous Jell-O between planes – their heads were almost at the Hell Hole by the makeshift stage, but their feet were still right by Krish in the audience.

Charity looked at Krish's eyeline as he helplessly watched the scene, then at her brother's as he did the same, as she clearly made a mental calculation to work out the locations of Constance and Brenda. Then she pushed out both hands through the suck-pop tension of the fabric of the universe, and took a hold of both women's legs.

'Pri…' managed Richard, just before all three women disappeared through the Hell Hole. 'ncess…' he finished saying to the spot where Charity had just been.

Janusz glared daggers at Krish. 'Did you just send my mother-in-law *and* sister-in-law into the void?'

'Not on purpose!' Krish protested, at long last managing to pull his hands out of the sticky substance between worlds. 'They both wanted to go.'

'You can get them back, though?' asked Richard, with all the pathetic hopefulness of any desperate loved one who already knows that the answer will be no. 'Right...?'

Krish knew he couldn't get them back. He sent people through to the other side. He didn't bring them back. He'd heard of it working – he had heard that Charity had managed to do it a handful of times, but he wasn't Charity, and Charity wasn't here. And Charity would most likely not be coming back.

Rats.

Rats! He'd really liked her, too. Talk about sucky timing.

The Hell Hole was still growing. Charity and Brenda were gone and, because Grace was also gone, that meant that the world was going to end. In his satchel, Krish felt the now familiar vibrations of his phone lighting on fire inside its blanket. Krish was clearly still expected to act as the Grim Reaper for the apocalypse, and he was expected to do it alone – as if today hadn't happened, as if the connections he'd made with his predecessor and her family counted for nothing. Rats, rats, rats!

Aurora was still on the makeshift stage, beneath the rapidly expanding Hell Hole. She cut a beatific figure, smiling gently as she stood at the centre of this trap, this sacrificial temple stuffed with the living and the dead and an awful lot of Demons. To one side of her, the fake Diana screamed along with the rest of the ghosts. To the other side Yemisi was frozen in shock, terror and a growing anger. Aurora didn't look at either of them. She gazed placidly out at Krish as a line of bright, painful light vertically split along her forehead, her face, her throat, her chest. Like Grace, she peeled inside-out from the centre until she was formless light that vanished swiftly into the shining colourful lines within the Hell Hole.

Yemisi screamed. Several of the audience screamed although many more of them applauded even harder – even getting to their feet – still convinced that this was some sort of brilliant ending to her show.

A lot of the screams were coming from the sides of the conference hall, Krish noted. From shady areas close to dark corners and pillars. Places where the Demons had been lurking. The Hell Hole's sudden explosion of power must have finally made the prowling Demons visible to non-clairvoyants. The others noticed it too. Richard peered into the shadows and, with a snarl, gave control of his form to Murzzzz. Darryl bristled silently and tried to see what was going on, past the crowds of people – many of them now, understandably, freaking out about the appearance of Murzzzz. Krish turned back to look at what was left of the stage.

On the high ceiling above the still-petrified Yemisi, a patch of malevolence drew itself together, like a huge polyp, or some pulsating mollusc the size of a bear. Its base still attached to the ceiling, it stretched itself downwards – a terrible, slimy, silly putty thing – and grabbed Yemisi by the head.

The poor ghosts were still screaming. Rats. He should probably concentrate on that, right? And the Demons were attacking anyway. Aurora had gone back on Grace's deal, after all of that.

Rats. Grace was gone. Brenda was gone. Charity was gone. The world was ending, the dead were suffering and the Demons were going to rip the living apart. Rats.

And what could he do about it? What *could* he do about it? Probably something, right? Because he was Death, right? Charity had been Death, and she was pretty awesome. She'd definitely try to do something.

Screw it.

He pushed past a couple of terrified audience members and vaulted a chair to reach the aisle, manifesting the scythe again as he went. Yeah, that would probably alarm people, but these people were really very alarmed by now so he may as well. He was Death, harbinger of the apocalypse, chosen – well, second choice, but second choice out of a few billion was OK – to usher all of humanity into their final resting places as the world ended. That was what he had been chosen to do but, after what he'd seen today, he didn't wanna. And he wasn't gonna. And it wasn't just because of a cute girl in a *Star Wars* hoodie, although it also *was* kind of about a cute girl in a *Star Wars* hoodie. It was also because there had been a deal.

He pulled the blanket swaddling his burning cellphone out of his satchel, and shook it so that the phone fell onto the floor. When the impact of falling onto thin carpet tile failed to smash or extinguish the flames, he stamped on it, crushing glass and electronics beneath his heel. The fire died along with his poor cellphone. There had been a deal, but it hadn't been him, or the Rooks, or humanity in general who had gone back on it – it had been the jerks who had chosen him. And, Celestials or not, if the other side was going to renege on that deal, then he wasn't going to play nice.

Well… he wasn't going to do as he'd been told, at least. Obviously he'd 'play nice'. He was *always* nice.

Death swung his scythe.

CHAPTER TWELVE

Suit Suite, Suit Suite, The Wearable Shareable Suits

'Well.'

Charity was on the shiny, shiny floor of a lobby. It was a beautiful lobby – very modern with lots of chrome, glass, pine and block colours, but there was something wrong about it. She'd seen this dimension before, on the other side of the previous Hell Holes. She'd likened it in her mind to a duck – smooth and calm on the surface, but underneath something was desperately, ungainly paddling away against a current. Everything about this dimension felt uncomfortable and 'off'. She tried to put into the back of her mind the notion that there was a chance she could be stuck here forever. She decided instead to be grateful for the upsides of her situation. Being pulled through the Hell Hole hadn't caused her to explode or shrivel away to nothing or anything like that. She couldn't breathe, she realised, but that was OK because wherever she was, she didn't need to breathe.

She was still holding two ankles. She let go of them, swiftly. 'Um.'

The owners of the ankles propped themselves up, awkwardly.

'Landing on a marble floor like that really should have hurt at least a bit,' said her mum.

'Not when you're dead,' replied Constance.

Constance!

'Constance!' Charity beamed.

'You can hear me again,' noted Constance.

'Yes,' Brenda told her.

'Like in that place the Angels took us before they blew up Helsbury,' said Constance.

'No, it's different this time,' Charity said. 'That time, those two Angel-Hotties had total control over everything. That place they took us to wasn't really there and it was like… like you were only half there – like you were only there as much as they were allowing you to be. This time is different. I don't know if anyone's in control here. I don't even know if anyone knows we're here yet. But you seem more like you're… you're just here, with us. Nobody's stuck a barrier between us.' Charity reached out and poked the dead woman on the ankle again. It felt as solid as it had done when she'd grabbed it before being pulled into the rift. 'See? I can touch you.' She paused. 'Sorry I called you both "bitches" earlier, it was in the heat of the moment.'

Constance lunged forwards and tackled her in a hug so tight and so forceful that it knocked her back down onto the floor. But it didn't wind her. It didn't hurt her at all.

'I can *touch* you,' cried Constance, with delight. 'And I heard what else you called us both in the heat of the moment.'

Charity hugged her dead mother back.

'My mums,' replied Charity from within the tight squeeze. She made eye contact with Brenda. 'Is… that OK?'

'I mean, it's true,' said Brenda, getting to her feet. 'Might get confusing, though.'

'Yeah. Is it OK if I keep calling you "Constance"? Just for clarity's sake? Also, you're, what, four years younger than me? So "Mum" might be weird.'

Constance pulled out of the hug, nodding happily. Tears were streaming down her face.

'You all right?' Charity asked her.

Constance shook her head. 'I'm *happy*,' she sobbed. 'I haven't been happy in thirty years and it's a lot.'

'Ah, you'll get used to it.'

'I'm a little concerned that we can touch Constance and body slamming the floor does us no harm,' said Brenda, reaching a hand down to Charity to help her up. 'Doesn't mean we're dead, does it?'

'I don't know.' Constance took the helping hand while Charity stood up by herself.

'Well, surely you're the expert in being dead, Constance.'

'But I feel different here,' Constance told them. 'Not alive, as such, but not a ghost, either. Maybe this place makes us all the same. Maybe it's a state of death, maybe it's something else.' She paused. 'Do you think… this might be… Heaven?'

No. No, that felt wrong. Even if there were a Heaven – and with what Charity had seen in her years of ghost hunting and unknowingly being the Grim Reaper, it seemed unlikely – this place was just slightly too off to be Heaven. She couldn't quite put her finger on what it was that was wrong. Luckily, before she had to, her mum butted in.

'No it can't be. Heaven would never have a breakout meeting space with standing desks.' She clacked towards a beautiful-looking spiral staircase in the middle of the lobby. 'Come on, then. Whatever this place is, we need to get Grace back from it. Or at least give her the option. Right?'

Charity nodded, and so did Constance, wiping her streaming eyes on her sleeve.

'Right. Let's go and save an Angel from this… "Hell Hole" feels like the wrong word, too,' said Charity.

'I mean, we did literally go through a Hell Hole to get here, princess.'

'Yeah, but it's quite nice once you get here.'

Constance set her newly dried face. 'Let's go and save an Angel who doesn't like being called an Angel, from a surprisingly nice Hell Hole.'

On the other side of the Hell Hole in the mortal world it was decidedly not nice and it was getting more not-nice with every passing moment. Screams – both audible and unhearable – filled the conference hall. Three silently howling ghosts were struck by Death's scythe in a single swing. It pushed them, almost effortlessly, from the living world into whatever dimension it was the dead needed to go to. Krish felt bad about doing it so unceremoniously and without their say-so. Each of them had been a person once – somebody's beloved. They had been someone who had worked and dreamed and struggled and cared. He wished he had the chance to talk to them and hold their hands as they went. But there wasn't time. They were in agony. All he could do was to end their suffering as swiftly as he could. This was, he realised unhappily, how all his reaping was destined to go if he really was the Death consigned to oversee the apocalypse. Well, nuts to that. He was going to try to be a better Death than that. He just needed to get through this itty-bitty Armageddon first. It'd be OK, right? Hadn't the rest of the Rooks already stopped two of those? Easy breezy, right?

He glanced at the remainder of the Rook family. They did not look at all easy or remotely breezy. Richard had let Murzzzz take over, while Darryl backed Janusz away from several Demons who were approaching them. Oh, there were many

Demons. So very many. It seemed an insurmountable number to Krish. Even as he watched Murzzzz leap at them, Krish knew that it wouldn't be enough. Murzzzz couldn't keep all of them from tearing any innocent onlookers apart.

'*Zabko,*' Janusz said to his husband, urgently.

'No...' whined Darryl in a tone that suggested capitulation was seconds away.

'Look at this.' Janusz squeezed Darryl's shoulder and gestured at the conference room. 'You must.'

'But—'

'You did it this afternoon and it was fine.'

And I hated having to do it! It's a slippery slope!'

'It's the end of the world, *zabko*! No time to argue. Come on.'

Darryl gazed at Janusz with a sad, pained expression, then pushed him away.

'Stay away from me.'

'You're not going to hurt me,' Janusz told him. 'You didn't earlier today. I trust you.'

'*I* still don't trust me, though. Krish!'

Krish had to pretend that he hadn't been surreptitiously watching the whole scene. He blinked at Darryl, innocently. 'Mm?'

Darryl pointed at Janusz. 'Keep this one safe for me, yeah?'

Krish nodded, and grabbed Janusz's arm with his scythe-free hand.

'Hey!' Janusz shouted. 'Ow, that hurts. Darryl!'

Darryl didn't say anything else. A look of concentration flickered over his face, and then... it wasn't Darryl's usual face. He was back in Demon form, or demi-Demon, or whatever was the best term to describe the cute, little, spiky teddy bear of a being that Darryl was able to turn into. Demon Darryl leaped away to help the humans under attack.

Touching another human's skin while he was holding his scythe seemed to hurt them, so Krish shifted his grip on Janusz so he was just clutching the accountant by his penguin sweater on one hand and wielded the weightless scythe with the other, which frankly made him feel kinda badass. He reaped another two wailing ghosts with it, which didn't make him feel badass at all – just sad.

Around him, members of the audience screamed and scurried. Most of them had now been persuaded that this wasn't a part of the show at all, and were clambering over one another through the conference hall – whose dimensions were constantly and maddeningly shifting like the inside of a kaleidoscope – trying to get away from the shadowy Demons emerging from corners and pillars. Krish noticed one audience member manage to make a grab for the handle of an emergency exit, only for the door to disappear and reappear a metre to the left. The audience member tried chasing it, but it was like trying to swat a fly – the door always moved *just* as a human got to it. Just because *most* of the audience believed they truly were in danger and this hadn't all been part of the show, didn't mean *all* of them were on the same page. Three people were still sat at the front with an air of eerie calm – even after Aurora had peeled herself into nothing, and the walls shifted and shadows lunged – holding out like the last hardliners in the cinema sitting through movie credits in hope of a cut scene.

Murzzzz leaped over the heads of the mortal humans – panicking and unpanicked alike – sinking his claws into his fellow Demons. Demon Darryl kind of did the same, but with sweet little hops instead of mighty bounds and, when he sank his fangs into a Demon, it looked like a kitten attacking a squishy ball.

Beyond the void, the clean, bright colours of whatever lay beyond shone at Krish with a cold, insincere cheer – a passive aggressive smile of a dimension. He couldn't see anybody through the hole. He swung his scythe against another screaming ghost, and hoped that whatever was going to happen to that poor soul now, it would be more tolerable than the state they'd just been in. And he hoped Charity would be OK, wherever she was.

Charity was not, right at that point, OK. She was climbing the large, open spiral staircase that rose from the centre of the lobby of the vast, shining architecture of Head Office. By rights – in a dimension that was supposed to be off-limits to humans and which Charity had only ever seen a floating mass of burning eyeballs inhabit before – there shouldn't have been any stairs at all. No stairs would have made sense. Yet there were, bafflingly, stairs… and desks and beanbags. Everything in Head Office seemed to echo the mortal world in a way that was faintly wrong, and this unnerved her. Just like everything else she could see in this dimension, every aspect of the stairs was counterintuitive in ways that were too small to take note of by themselves, but added up to make the experience of climbing them even more unpleasant than that of climbing a normal staircase. It was far too long – the high ceilings meant it was a hike up to each level, with no landings halfway to catch your breath. It was also too wide, so to hold the railings you either had the choice of taking the much longer trek along the far edge or the dizzying tight corners of the centre. At both of these bannistered edges, the stairs were not spaced out in a way that a human could easily climb. At the centre of the spiral you had to angle your feet or even use tiptoes on the narrow, curving steps. On the outside, the steps were two and an awkward half of a pace apart. Charity had first tried climbing at the centre, but it had started making her feel sick, so now she was at the outside edge, huffing and puffing and tripping over the not-quite-right distance between steps. Her mum, never a fan of walking anywhere she didn't have to and not in the least bit sensibly shod, was taking in the experience with her usual Brenda-ish flair and complaining bitterly under her breath with every step. The only one who seemed to be even remotely enjoying herself was Constance, but this was the first time in over thirty years she'd had something like a corporeal body, so she was probably just happy to use her legs.

They reached another floor. It was, like almost all of the floors they'd passed, painted purple. Etched in really quite small lettering on a clear perspex plaque on the wall, in a language that Charity couldn't read but could, for some reason, understand, was the word 'Amethyst'. They had realised, after the first couple of floors, that none of the levels of this office or whatever-it-was were numbered – instead, they were coloured, and almost all were subtly different shades of purple. There seemed to be no rhyme or reason to the ordering of these colours – they weren't getting lighter or darker, nor were they moving towards the red or blue ends of the purple spectrum. Also, occasionally the purple would get broken by a chartreuse floor, or the startling marigold floor they'd passed two levels down. These non-purple floors seemed no different to the others, save for the distinct lack of purple to them. Upon reaching the first couple of floors, Charity and her party had jumped out, expecting to surprise whoever or whatever it was that actually dwelled in this world, but after a few awkward moments, it dawned on them that these floors were all deserted. They would check each one, wander around a bit, find nothing there but countless breakout spaces and kitchenettes with no kettles or microwaves, and then, after a while, wander back to the staircase.

'They must all be in a meeting or something,' murmured Constance, not for the first time, as they poked around Amethyst floor.

'About what?' asked Charity. 'About Grace? Do you reckon Grace is in the meeting?'

'And who's "they"?' Brenda added. 'Angels, or... or more of The Manager?'

'I don't know,' replied Constance. 'I don't know any more about this world than you do. I know the dead are supposed to be all wise about what lies beyond and all, but honestly, I just hung around you guys for decades.' She pulled an odd, unsure face. 'Which was fine. I mean, I'm pretty sure I wouldn't have been able to gallivant around dimensions even if I wanted to. Not that I wanted to. I wouldn't have known how. I didn't... waste my afterlife or anything.'

'Nobody said you did, Constance,' Brenda told her.

'Just, from what you said of the old me, when I was alive, I sounded pretty brave. Heroic, you know?'

'I wouldn't go as far as that,' said Brenda with a small smile. 'You were a good ghost hunter, though. It's a shame you can't remember so much of how you were. But it's OK. Death changes people, that's one thing I know for sure. Makes human souls all small and sad. Comparatively, you coped pretty well.'

'Would I have moped, when I was alive? Or tried to take on Head Office single-handed?'

'Probably tried a messy mishmash of both,' replied Brenda. 'Just like you've done after death.'

A short silence descended and, as Charity looked fruitlessly around yet another purple floor of beanbags and confusing-looking drinks machines, she enjoyed the fact that, now that they could communicate properly, Brenda and Constance seemed to be getting on. They were talking as friends, as if all the hurt of The Longest Night had been forgiven – or if not forgiven, at least pushed to the side enough to allow room for something warmer and softer between them in the way families and old friends so often do with old wounds.

'I've got proper legs again here,' added Constance with a hint of pride.

'Yes,' replied Brenda, pleasantly, 'I saw.'

'Forgot how much I missed walking.'

They reached the next floor.

'Woah,' Charity interjected, stopping suddenly.

The other women stopped with her, lowering their voices to whispers.

'What is it?' Brenda asked. 'Is someone there?'

Not someone. Some*thing*. A glass box of a room in the office that had seemed, at first glance, to just be yet another empty conference space was, on closer inspection, very different to the office's many, many glass boxes. There was a glowing circle in the middle of the floor, with a similar one directly above it on the high ceiling. On the wall just next to the door was a sign, again etched in small letters in some material akin to perspex, and in a mysterious yet comprehensible language.

'"Suit Suite",' read Charity. 'Oh, that's fun to say out loud.'

'Vastly superior life forms apparently,' muttered Brenda, 'and *that's* the best name they could come up with.'

Charity stepped cautiously into the glass room. Like all the others, it was empty, and even though the glowing circles suggested it was operational, there seemed to be no imminent danger from the device in the centre of it.

'The Suit Suite's where Aurora wanted Grace to bring... well, Grace,' Charity noted. 'The bits of Grace that looked human, that is. This must be the place where Angels put on their people cosplay.' She glanced over her shoulder at the other two women, who were lingering by the door. 'You know – where they dress up as human beings.'

'We've both been around you and your silly nerd obsessions for over thirty years, princess,' replied Brenda. 'We know what "cosplay" is.'

'Dressing up as Sailor Moon and then pretending to be Sailor Moon at a nerd convention,' added Constance, 'and then punching that guy when he tried to see up your skirt.'

'That was in character. Probably. I should start going back to conventions, I shouldn't have let the creepos stop me. Sod it, I'll go next year. In a mini-dress. I deserve it.' She had a thought that delighted her. 'Me and Krish can have a couple's costume!'

'If there *is* another convention,' muttered Brenda. 'If there is a next year.'

'There'd better be, now I've had my couple's costume idea.'

'Even if we're able to get back to the mortal world, which is debatable, are you and Krish even a couple, yet?' Brenda asked.

'Yeah, I don't remember you guys actually having that conversation,' added Constance.

Charity ignored her mothers, and touched a finger against the glowing circle on the floor. It felt warm, but managed to do so in a vaguely unpleasant way. It wasn't 'warm bath' warm, it was 'warm toilet seat' warm. Eurgh.

'Wonder if all the human suits come out of some sort of celestial storage somewhere, or whether they can be made bespoke?' she wondered.

Charity knew that there were basic, samey suits that Angels could throw on for a quick visit to the mortal world. She'd seen two of them when they'd been accosted by Celestials at Helsbury services before Christmas. They'd been identically good-looking, of indeterminate race and gender. They had reminded Charity of the first, bog standard character-skin a video game might give her before customisation. She supposed that, to an Angel, that particular human suit design was their version of a mass-produced plain T-shirt and jeans. Just something to bung on before nipping out to the shop. Then there was the Grace Barry suit. The being that her family knew as Grace hadn't custom-made that suit, but it had been much more unique and complex than the standard good-looking androgynous suit. 'Grace' had seemed like such a real human that she had fooled not only the family, but the very Angel who was wearing the suit. The Angel had completely forgotten that she wasn't actually a small, anxious Anglican priest with a love of Fairtrade tapestries and acoustic guitar. The Angels had seemed very keen to get that suit back, so it must be one of their best suits, but still it hadn't been custom-made for Grace. The being they knew as Grace had shaped herself to fit the suit, not that other way around.

Now Charity – Charity enjoyed cosplay and so she'd understood where Grace was coming from. Losing herself inside the person she'd dressed as was easy to do when you were suited up and in character. But part of the joy and the skill of cosplay was making and customising the costume yourself.

'How do you think it works?' she asked, still standing over the circle.

'You probably have to be an Angel for starters...' Brenda broke off in horror. 'Don't stand on it!'

But Charity was already standing on the warm, glowing circle. She gazed up at the ceiling circle. 'What's the harm? If I have to be an Angel for it to work, it just won't activate, right? Unless...'

'Unless what?'

'Well, I mean, I'm special, aren't I? The Angels *said* I was special. And they warped history to feed me hero stories all my life so I would easily accept my specialness.'

'You quit!' Brenda replied.

'As Death, not as being special. Look at us – we've already stopped two apocalypses, we're best mates with an Angel and we managed to sneak into this dimension and all the way up to the Suit Suite without any alarms going off or anything.'

'We're still not Angels, princess!'

Charity beamed brightly at Brenda. 'Maybe we're better. How have we saved the world the last two times? Stubbornness. Stubbornness and being annoying.'

Constance shrugged a 'Yeah, good point' sort of a shrug. 'How would that make the Suit Suite think you're better than an Angel, though?'

'Because stubbornness is just another form of willpower. And I'm starting to think that maybe willpower might be the biggest superpower of all – at least to the Angels.'

Brenda and Constance exchanged sceptical glances.

'We came here because we were determined to follow Grace,' Charity continued. 'Grace became Grace – became so like a human that she fooled even herself – because that was what she wanted to be. What if Angels can make stuff happen just by willing it? What if, in this dimension, we can do the same?' She grinned again. 'Worth a try, right?'

'No, princess, not worth a try.' Brenda took a step towards her. 'We are a very long way from home, we don't know the rules of this realm and we're trying to find our friend. You can't just stumble around guessing things…'

'Stumbling around guessing things is all we have right now, Mum.'

'But what if you get hurt?'

'We're not in a place of mortality, right now. And besides – I've got my mums with me.'

She could see the face journeys of both women as they again turned the pluralisation of 'mum' around in their heads, getting used to the idea.

She used the moment of distraction in order to concentrate. They weren't in a place where mortality applied, but they *were* in a place of incredibly powerful immortal beings and, just because they hadn't encountered any yet, it certainly didn't mean it would stay that way – especially if her party intended to find

Grace and persuade her to come back to help save their world. If this device could spirit up something that could help out with that, it would be nice. A suit to disguise them, maybe, so they could sneak past the immortal beings. But Grace and Aurora had both taken their suits *off* before coming here, so three suits walking around could look just as out of place as two living mortals and one dead mortal. However, there was something else about the suits. They didn't just affect how one looked. They affected one's physicality as well. The Grace Barry suit had made Grace so like a mortal that she could be hurt – she would get a black eye if she were punched. So… what if a mortal were to make themselves a suit that worked the other way? What if a squishy sack of meat and ape DNA were to make a suit that could overpower Angels?

Could it be done? She had no idea how much it took to overpower an Angel, nor did she know how many Angels could try to stop them reaching Grace. She didn't even know for sure if a mortal could wear one of their suits, or even work the device.

She mentally put on Brenda's best 'Don't you know who I am' attitude. She concentrated and willed it to work. It *would* work for *her*! She was the former Grim Reaper! The only one to officially be too good for the job! They'd given Krish a scythe, for pity's sake and – while he was very handsome and charming and a very good Reaper she was sure – he was still a last-minute second choice. Had the scythe been manifested from here? Maybe. Maybe it could manifest accessories for special mortals. And if it could create a scythe for Krish, well…

The warm circle beneath her feet crackled, emanating a bothersome level of pins and needles. Not painful as such, but also definitely not pleasant. The glowing circle above her did the same, and there was the sensation of something very thin being put on her, like a clammy layer of grease, like make-up that's slightly too heavy so you feel it all day.

Brenda and Constance shrieked. Charity looked down at herself and saw tatty black robes that floated as if they were submerged in water and skeletal hands clutching a large scythe.

'I'm suited up as the OG Grim Reaper, aren't I?'

Constance nodded, her face a picture of horror.

'Oh, it's really not nice hearing your voice coming out of that skull, princess,' said Brenda.

'So I *can* use this thing, then.' Charity mentally rejected the skeletal appearance and, with more unpleasant pins and needles, the bleached bones and dark robes peeled off from her, leaving her looking just as she had when she stepped into the Suit Suite.

'You're not going with the massive terrifying scythe-wielding skeleton to rescue Grace, then?' asked Constance.

'I'd have thought that would be right up your street, princess,' added Brenda. 'Looked like something out of one of your cartoons.'

'I ain't turning up to this party dressed as someone else's idea of a job I already quit,' Charity explained. 'That is absolutely not my style. What matters is that I willed this thing to show how it could kit out a Grim Reaper, and it did this. That's the standard setting. I never go with the standard setting. I customise.'

'So what, princess? You're going to build your own Grim Reaper?'

'I'm not the Grim Reaper, Mum, and that's a good thing. We've gone to a boss fight level to rescue an Angel so we don't need a Grim Reaper. We need an ultimate hero.' She looked up at the circle on the ceiling again, and let her favourite stories fill her mind. Simple stories: a single determined do-gooder or, at best, a tiny band, taking on a horde set on ending the world. Black and white drawings, brightly coloured TV series and movies. Chosen ones and scrappy outsiders facing horrific odds and punching them in the face. *Blam. Kapow.* Protagonists who could swallow down those inner voices telling them that they were too small, too insignificant, and that they couldn't do it in order to stand up against armies, against gods, against titans. Those stories, simple as they were, had always made her feel like she could do anything. They were her talismans. They were her faith. They made her feel good inside. They made her feel certain. And that certainty hadn't been swayed by the recently revealed fact that she'd been deliberately exposed to those very stories by Angelic powers in order to condition her to do their dirty work for them. No. That was just a part of the Hero's journey. The secretive sponsor turning out, in the third act, to have been an antagonist all along? Standard superhero stuff. The Angels ensuring Charity was exposed to all those hero stories was, by Charity's logic, an example of the hubris that would turn around and bite them on the bums in the end – or whatever it was Angels had instead of bums.

'Oh,' Brenda sighed to Constance. 'She's going to turn herself into Batman or something.'

'Not Batman,' replied Charity.

'Then which of your cartoon superheroes are you going to get that thing to make you a suit out of?'

Charity looked down from the ceiling circle and smiled, as pins and needles spread from the soles of her feet and the top of her head to jangle down every nerve in her body.

'All of them.'

CHAPTER THIRTEEN

Spock, The Rock, Doc Ock And Hulk Hogan

'Hate' was, Janusz had always said, a very strong word. He couldn't even bring himself to hate his father, who had been – and, as far as Janusz knew, remained – a terrible person. He didn't hate Murzzzz, in spite of the damage the Demon had done to his family. He didn't hate the stupid, gorgeous Canadian, vegan *Śmierć* currently clutching him by the Christmas jumper and waving his silly little scythe around, even though Krish was very annoying with his smug handsome face. But Janusz *hated* this situation.

He had never been a big fan of the end of the world. It was very stressful to keep having to go through it again and again. And his husband's pain at having to take Demon form again – that was another thing that Janusz hated. Since the day he'd met his Darryl, he had recognised a man with an awkward relationship with his own body and his own powers. Always hunching, always slouching, always making little comments disparaging his looks compared to other men, including Janusz. Always bitterly self-conscious about the fact that his clairvoyance was less potent than his mother's – an insecurity that was never helped by Brenda's manner, bless her. And now that he'd found out about his part-Demon lineage and the latent powers that came with it, Darryl was scared of himself. It didn't matter that Darryl had already saved Krish in that form, saved Janusz in that form and saved the day multiple times in that form. The rot of self-doubt was too deep. Darryl was too certain that he was rubbish to even entertain the thought that perhaps he could be magnificent, and it hurt Janusz's heart. Yes, Janusz had a scar on his wrist from when his husband had once caught him while in Demon form. His claws had accidentally cut Janusz, but Darryl catching him in that state of enhanced physical strength had saved Janusz from falling – and saved his life. Janusz kept trying to tell Darryl that he'd made the right call, but because of a slight scarring on Janusz's arm, Darryl couldn't forgive himself. Darryl knew that Janusz had a past that had been filled with pain, both emotional and physical. The newly discoloured marks on Janusz's arm were not his only scars and so Janusz could understand why Darryl was so ashamed of the injury he'd caused by saving him. But Janusz didn't mind the new scars at all. They were a trade-off for his life. They were marks made when Darryl switched forms, without even thinking, and plucked him out of the air as he fell. But Darryl couldn't see the difference between them and scars caused by the sadism of others. And Janusz hated that Darryl could possibly think that, in any form, he could be as bad for his husband as the tormentors of his teenage years.

He also really didn't like that he was currently trapped in a constantly shifting, kaleidoscopic nightmare of a leisure estate conference hall filled with Demons who were lunging at screaming hostages. Both Murzzzz and Darryl leaped from shadowy shape to shadowy shape, but with that many Demons to fight and so many humans to protect, it was like some sort of terrible whack-a-mole. Janusz could barely see what was going on in all the chaos. He tried to pull himself free of Krish's grip to go to Darryl, but another annoying thing about that horrible, handsome man was how strong he was.

'Hey,' puffed Krish, one-handedly swinging his scythe against invisible ghosts once more, 'so this is all looking pretty bad, huh? Pretty terminal.'

'You tell me,' grunted Janusz irritably, 'you're the horseman of the apocalypse'.

'Aww man, I totally should've asked for a horse, too,' muttered Krish. He swung again. 'But yeah, it looks bad to me. So, I think before it gets any worse, we should talk.'

'What?'

'Well, I'm already kinda facing the prospect I left it too late to have a proper talk with Charity, but I still have time with you. And if the end of the world happens, we'd have left things on a bum note, and I don't like doing that.' He swung again. 'Why d'ya hate me, bro?'

'I'm not your "bro". And I don't hate you. Hate's a strong word.'

'Then, why d'ya dislike me so much?' Another swing. 'I'm not gonna get between you and your guy. Even if I wanted to – and, no offence, but I don't want to – I wouldn't be able to. I see a lot of relationships in this job – between the living, and the dead – and I know absolute love when I see it. Your family has it in shovels and, my goodness, the shovel full of love your husband has for you could dam a river.'

'Don't patronise me. I know my husband loves me.'

'I hope you do. And I know it's not just because you're good-looking—'

'I'm not that good-looking…'

'Oh, come *on*.' Another swing of his scythe. 'It's OK to be OK with your ad model looks, just like it's OK for him to be OK with all those super psychic powers he seems weirdly downbeat about.' Another swing. 'Everyone in this family has a power.'

'And you're saying mine is just my face?'

'Charm goes a very long way, even in this business.' He swung again. 'Had to develop plenty of charm of my own, since up 'til now I worked by myself. But – no shade on Brenda – I kind of feel that with your group you might have had to work harder, to overcome a bit of a charm deficit.' Another swing. 'I'm not trying to be better than you. I just think in this line of work, you need at least one person with people skills, or else you end up like Aurora Tavistock.'

'Aurora Tavistock was not human.'

'True, but a lot of human psychics saw her success, tried to be like her and crashed and burned. Because they had no Janusz about them. I think we're kinda similar because I had to be my own Janusz.'

Another swing, and a little smile.

'You *are* patronising me,' grumped Janusz. 'Or, you're... trying to come on to *me*?'

'For the last time, you big, handsome, jealous idiot, I like the sister! She's very flirty and she has big *Star Trek* and *Pokémon* vibes and I like *Star Trek* and *Pokemon* so that's two things we have to talk about if she comes back from the afterlife before the end of the world – which is unlikely, but still! I like the sister!'

Janusz had never seen or heard Krish lose his cool before. Something about him snapping and getting all flustered, flicked some deeply buried, hidden switch inside of Janusz. Krish wasn't perfect. He wasn't perfect! He was getting all flushed and frustrated over Charity of all people – his silly, childish sister-in-law who was the biggest dork Janusz knew. This man was getting worked up over a grown woman who collected Funko Pops. And he was upset that Janusz didn't immediately love him. Krish was insecure! What an idiot. What an endearing idiot. Oh, and his collar was all askew, and his hair was ruffled. This wasn't a rival at all! Krish was a nerdy, annoying, vegan little brother-in-law in waiting – that was all.

Janusz sighed a little. 'How do I help you?'

'I don't think I need help getting with Charity if she comes back, thanks. She seemed very into me, I think we pencilled in a date.'

'With this.' Janusz gestured to the chaos all around.

'Oh! Well, I could do with my hand back. Can I let you go?'

Of course Krish could let Janusz go. He wasn't a little baby. He wasn't going to go running to Darryl as soon as Krish released his jumper. Janusz rolled his eyes. Krish let go and gripped the scythe with both hands. Janusz heard the Demon Darryl snap and snarl in the fight beyond, and Janusz was struck by a need to go to his husband. Obviously, he couldn't because then he'd look stupid in front of Krish.

'Just stay close, OK?' asked Krish, swinging his scythe. 'Maybe if we can get closer to the portal we can do something to help Charity and the others.'

Janusz stayed close, and found that he was OK with this. At least he wasn't getting in the way. Maybe there was someone who might need to be charmed, and he was more likely to run into that person paired up with Krish than trying to help Darryl.

Slowly, Krish pushed his way towards the Hell Hole. Janusz followed close behind, and didn't allow himself to wonder whether Krish might have just Januszed Janusz.

Beyond the Hell Hole, there was no great battle with Demons and tormented ghosts. There was another long climb up the poorly designed spiral staircase though which, to Brenda's mind, was probably as bad. Constance was still enjoying having a corporeal form and was leading the way up the staircase in a fairly sprightly fashion. Even Charity was finding the stairs much easier now, and was keeping pace with the dead woman, fuelled by whatever new powers she'd put into her celestial "suit". Brenda struggled to keep up.

Charity had spent quite some time in the Suit Suite, looking up at the glowing circle on the ceiling as layers and layers of celestial 'something' had been placed around her. Every now and again, she'd paused, had a think, and announced 'Oh wait, and *this*.' And then the Suit Suite had piled more 'something' upon her. Saying that any one element of the final result was 'the weird thing' was moot because they were far beyond weird, now. But the element that was most striking about all of this to Brenda was that every new celestial suit that got placed over Charity looked exactly like Charity. Charity had sworn blind she was giving herself a suit of fictional superheroes and so Brenda had been expecting something that looked like Charity's bedroom – some awful mess of mishmashed comic book references – but apparently every one of Charity's ideal superheroes just looked like Charity. And, honestly, Brenda really wasn't all that surprised, when she really thought about it. Charity was now wearing, by Brenda's count, well over fifty suits on top of one another, all of which looked exactly like Charity – silly Princess Leia hoodie, neon-coloured 'cats in space' leggings and all.

'And you're quite all right under all of that, princess?' she asked.

'Yeah, it's not like wearing clothes,' Charity replied. 'No wonder Grace forgot she even had one on. Feels like wearing nothing at all!'

'You are still wearing your clothes though,' Brenda said.

'Why did you put on an American accent and stick your bum out when you said that?' Constance asked Charity.

'I was quoting *Simpsons*!'

Constance's eyes lit up. She put on a terrible American accent of her own. 'Eat my shorts!'

'Oh yeah,' said Charity. 'You died during *The Simpsons* early seasons, didn't you?'

'The nineties, princess,' said Brenda. 'Most people just call those days the nineties.'

Constance stopped suddenly, holding her hand out to indicate to the others to do the same and hush up for a bit.

'Anyone else hear voices?' whispered Constance.

Yes. Brenda could hear voices. They were low, and distant, and had a forced politeness to their tone that suggested they were having some sort of meeting. And there was another upsetting detail about the voices.

'Anyone else's face hurt?' asked Charity.

Yep. The sound of the voices really hurt Brenda's face. Her eyes burned. Her ears rang. Her sinuses stung like she'd just accidentally inhaled vodka.

'Oh, *that's* what that feeling is,' whispered Constance, her voice low with wonder. 'Physical pain! I'd forgotten what that felt like.' She grinned. 'Oh, it really sucks, doesn't it?'

The other two women nodded in agreement, as they all started silently climbing, following the low, painful sounds.

They exited the staircase again, onto yet another purple floor. There were no breakout spaces or impractically positioned open-plan desks on this floor. Instead, there was rather a narrow corridor and a clear sign on which was etched, in very small lettering and in a language both unfamiliar and yet understandable to Brenda, 'Debriefing Room'.

Charity gently pushed past Constance, and led the way along the corridor. The one floor where lots of people or Angels or whatever-they-were would have to convene at the same time, and it was the one with hardly any space to move, thought Brenda to herself. While she was only too aware that the beings that used this place were nothing like humans, none of it seemed well designed for anyone to use. Why did Angels need desks and breakout spaces in the first place? Why did they need beanbags? Why would *any* being of *any* species need beanbags? This dimension had so many beanbags. It was all wrong.

The voices grew louder, and the pain in Brenda's face grew sharper. Not since her last really bad hangover had she been so acutely aware of every single cavity in her skull. Everything jangled and skrieked, like hearing a neighbour playing bad jazz on a Sunday morning.

The left-hand wall of the corridor looked different. It wasn't just purple like the other wall. Brenda could make out lights and shifting shadows beyond it, and very faint, back-to-front patterns. In fact, it wasn't a wall, it was a large window that had been covered in a huge purple decal so that it was almost entirely opaque, but not quite totally. Brenda grabbed Constance's arm and signalled for the other two to stop. She pointed at the window.

'We might be able to see through,' she told them, in as low a whisper as could still be heard by the other women.

Charity squinted at it and shook her head.

'Hang on,' whispered Constance, and leaned in towards the window.

The dead woman moved swiftly, so Brenda didn't have the time to register what she was trying to do and warn her that it wouldn't work here. She was only able to form the 'n' of 'no' before Constance smacked her forehead on the glass with a loud, dull clonk.

'Ow,' murmured Constance.

'You're not incorporeal here, genius.'

'Yep, remembered that a moment too late,' whispered Constance, rubbing her head. 'In my defence, I just spent thirty years poking my head through walls to watch what was happening... oh no.'

Oh no.

The purple suddenly faded away from the window. The decal or privacy screen or whatever-it-was dissolved, leaving the whole huge window completely transparent. Beyond it was a giant meeting room with walls covered in display screens showing what seemed to be stills taken from very high-res security footage of Grace's few weeks in the mortal realm. Also in the room were around a hundred smears of sunlight. Brenda recognised the bright shapes of the Angels from the moments Grace and Aurora had unpeeled their meaty human suits, just as she recognised the pain in her face from looking at them. They hurt Brenda's eyes so much that she could only look at them by squinting and looking through her lashes. From what she could make out, they were around eight foot tall, thin columns that were tapered at the top, brushing the floor at the bottom, and constantly vibrating at a register which made Brenda feel a little bit sick. Perhaps it was an instinct of Brenda's mortal monkey brain to see human shapes in the abstract, but the basic silhouettes of them seemed to her as if they could be extremely tall, thin men, standing with their arms at their sides. They actually reminded her of ghosts but, where the remnants of the dead were often little more than vaguely human-shaped smears of haze, these beings were smears of painfully bright light of indeterminate colour.

There was something else in the room with them – a huge, impossible puzzle of countless spinning, interlocking rings of fire, all covered in eyes. It was the being that called itself the Manager – the being that kept trying to end Brenda's world, and was absolutely furious with her family that it had failed to do so thus far. It was the being that had the power to make an island fold itself away into nothing, and a sprawling motorway service station succumb to a century of entropy in a handful of minutes – and had the mind to do so, when annoyed.

Of course the Manager was here. Brenda was fairly sure that this place was the Manager's realm. Whenever she had seen it through a Hell Hole before, the Manager had always been in Head Office. Brenda had no idea whether all of the Celestial streaks of light were also native to this realm, or whether they were interlopers like her and her party. There was one thing Brenda did know and that was that her party had definitely been spotted. The streaks of light had stopped speaking. They had no faces, but Brenda could tell from the feel of them that they were all glaring out of the window at Brenda's group. They were all very still, just for a moment. The only being that moved in those couple of seconds was the Manager, who drifted a little closer to the window, every one of its multitude of terrible eyes turned towards Brenda. She could feel the irritation coming off the Manager in waves.

'Sorry to disturb your meeting,' she smirked.

On reflection, she probably shouldn't have smirked.

The columns of light began to move, horribly fast, towards a door that was really quite far along the narrow corridor. This place really was terribly designed, wasn't it?

They began to pile out of the door, but had to approach Brenda and her group in single file due to the narrowness of the corridor. They didn't scream or shout, but their calm, sweet voices hurt Brenda's face so much it made her nose want to invert itself up her skull and strangle her brain.

'Intruders,' they said, in agonisingly nice tones, 'you're not supposed to be here. Did you come for the one you called Grace Barry? They're not one of you. They don't belong with you, we're helping them understand that. It's very selfish of you to try to get in the way of helping them find peace.'

'Stay back,' Charity said to the other women – quite needlessly, since she was already in front. 'I've got this.'

As cocky as Charity's words were, she too was having to avert her eyes from the approaching smears of painful light, and had the crook of her arm raised to attempt to block out the searing pain of seeing them even in her peripheral vision. Charity turned slightly to grin at her mums behind her. Brenda could see that her eyes were squeezed tightly shut. She was, Brenda supposed, well used to fighting supernatural beings that she couldn't see, but this was different. The Angels were so much more powerful than ghosts, and this time she wouldn't have any help from a clairvoyant.

'You're not going to fight them?' asked Constance, incredulously.

'All the superheroes, remember?' replied Charity. 'It'll work. Probably.'

The first Angel was only seconds away.

'But how can you fight something you can't look at?' Brenda added.

Charity snorted, reached down, and pulled her right sock and trainer off in one fluid movement. She flung the footwear at the Angel. The scuffed, colourful trainer hit the being in the spot where, if they were humanoid, their chest would be. The vibrations of the being changed a little in the spot where it was hit, and the figure slowed very slightly, but that was the only effect. The shoe bounced harmlessly onto the floor and the Angel continued their approach. Charity pulled off the other sock and shoe, brandishing it as a weapon in spite of the minimal effect that the first shoe had had. She planted herself barefoot, head bowed, aping some hero stance she must have seen in one of her cartoons or children's movies.

'*All* the superheroes,' muttered Charity.

The Angel dashed to attack her. Just as they got into range, Charity, her eyes still screwed shut, did something she'd never done before. She breathed out a plume of fire. The sudden heat did something to the Angel's vibrations that the being clearly did not care for, and they shrank back, radiating heat and alarm.

'Who programmed the mortal produce to be able to breathe fire?' asked the Angel in a sweet voice that made all of Brenda's fillings buzz painfully against her dental nerves. 'Did the Manager do that?'

Charity laughed a low, dangerous laugh, and did something else she had definitely never done before. She extended her tongue a good three metres at one of the Angels coming up from behind, before throwing them against a wall with it; then flung her remaining shoe like a dagger at a third Angel, pinning them to the window with a spike heel that the trainer had instantly, impossibly grown; then somersaulted over the first Angel, who was still on fire and complaining bitterly, only to land perfectly on her bare feet between two more Angels where she pulsed out a wave of bright white energy from her whole body that hurled them to the ground.

'Produce *definitely* shouldn't be able to do that,' wailed the Angel who was still on fire.

'Where's the Manager??' called the one still stuck to the wall.

Brenda risked another little glance through the window into the meeting room. The being of interlocking rings of fire and eyeballs was no longer in there.

'What are you doing over there?' shouted another Angel voice from far back along the corridor. 'We're vastly superior beings – that's just a mortal in a suit, don't let it—'

Charity vanished.

'Ow,' said the Angel, far along the corridor, 'how did it get to me so f— It's gone again! Manager!' Charity reappeared in the spot she'd just been in, eyes still tightly shut.

Pained, outraged celestial queries and demands began to flood the corridor as Charity continued, gleefully and blindly to pick off the Angels as they stood trapped in a narrow line.

'Who left the Suit Suite unattended?'

Charity ducked away from one Angel and used some sort of newfound telekenesis energy to pull a chunk out of the purple wall and fling it at another Angel.

'What kind of suit even *is* this?'

Charity turned briefly into a lion and clawed at the Angel she'd ducked away from.

'This is the Manager's fault! Where's the Manager??'

'*Hadouken*!' screamed Charity, which was not an answer to the Angel's question, but did launch a fireball from her fists.

'More fire?' wailed the very first Angel who'd attacked and was still trying to extinguish the flames engulfing them.

Charity launched a whip-like material from each hand – one was an old-bra shade of grey and one was sparkling gold. The grey one wrapped around an Angel like a cocoon, the gold one caught an Angel around its tapered top.

'I like to wear a mortal suit and put the feet in custard,' said the gold-entangled Angel, hurriedly.

'What?' asked the grey entangled Angel, muffled. 'I should be able to get out of this, why can't I get out of this?'

The gold entangled Angel didn't say any more, it just radiated embarrassment instead.

Charity used a gust of air to propel herself up and along the window, where she seamlessly pulled her shoe out of the Angel it was still trapping. As she took a hold of the shoe again, it was no longer a trainer with a stylistically jarring stiletto heel, but a sharpened boomerang, which she hurled along the corridor before landing back down on the ground.

'Someone set the power parameters of the Suit Suite far too high,' complained a struggling Angel.

A small storm cloud manifested about the struggling Angel's head, cartoonishly mocking their frustration, and hit them with a thunderbolt.

'And whose idea was it to make this corridor so narrow?' called another.

Charity somersaulted again, backwards, shooting sticky balls of white webbing along the corridor.

'Manager!' called an Angelic voice from really quite far down the corridor. 'Where's the Manager? This space is all wrong! Change it, immediately!'

Charity breathed deeply, raised her arms above her head and took three running steps towards one of the Angels that still remained upright and unfettered.

'Smash!' She leaped, and brought her fists down onto the tall pillar of light.

'No,' replied the Angel. It didn't sound scared, or worried. Brenda recognised that tone. It sounded annoyed.

Charity smashed with her fists, but the blow didn't affect the Angel she was launching herself at – the Angel managed to deflect the energy of it outwards into the claustrophobic space around them. The wall and the window and the meeting room beyond crashed down to lie flat on either side of them, and then somehow kept on going, vanishing into the floor, which was no longer purple, but green. The Angel had somehow made Charity punch Head Office onto a different floor. This green floor was very open plan, and had plenty of room for Charity, Brenda and Constance to be surrounded, Brenda thought. The handful of Angels that Charity had managed to trap or fell or set on fire were still out of action, but around two dozen Angels still remained. As Brenda predicted, the Angels immediately started spreading out, encircling the three women.

'Charity Xu, I commend you on your willpower,' said the Angel in that same, recognisably irritable tone, 'but you are not the only one who has it. Willpower is not unique to mortals. We are *Executives*. Our will overrules all.'

'Yes,' added another Angel, 'it does! These are just mortals with a suit – we can just melt them or something.'

'Have you not been trying to melt them from the start?' asked a third Angel. 'I've been trying to melt them, and they simply will not melt.'

'Head Office has a strict No Melting policy,' said the first Angel. 'Not my idea, believe me.' The first Angel turned their attention back to the three women. 'In your realm, on the other hand, we can melt as much as we wish now. The end of your world has been signed off on, and that's the end to it. Can't go against our willpower in your world.'

'You're Aurora Tavistock,' said Brenda, 'aren't you?'

'No,' replied the Angel in Aurora's coldly annoyed tones. 'That was a suit, that's not what I am, my love. There is no Aurora Tavistock, as there is no Grace Barry. The Executive you came for is not your concern and not your friend. They will be fine. You're not welcome in this realm. You are merely causing chaos, as mortals always do. Now, speaking of things mortals always do, it's time for you to go back and die.'

'Oh, so you guys and the Demons are allowed to come to our world and cause all sorts of suffering –' asked Constance, 'hurt people, kill people, rip families apart – but we're not allowed to come here to speak to our friend?'

'Demons are bored tourists in your realm,' replied the Angel who claimed not to be Aurora. '*We* are benevolent guides and instructors. *You* are just troublesome interlopers.'

'Double standards,' muttered Brenda. 'Or... triple standards, I suppose.'

'And,' continued the Angel Formerly Known As Aurora, 'the one you called Grace Barry is *not* your friend. Don't you ever *listen*??'

'Pardon?' asked Constance with a sarcastic grin that was so very Charity that it hurt Brenda's heart a little.

'That suit Charity wears may be powerful, but nothing any mortal can do is enough to seriously threaten us,' continued the Angel, 'you will not change our will. All you can do is buzz around annoying us, like little flies.'

The other Angels had completely surrounded the women now, and were closing in.

'See this as your open window, my loves,' continued the Angel, 'and buzz away out of here, before we swat you.'

The circle of Angels was almost on them, now. Honestly, Brenda had managed to get this far just by being annoying. She'd halted two apocalypses already by being annoying to the right beings in the right way, and she wasn't going to stop now. She opened her mouth to say something else annoying, but Charity spoke over her.

'Why are you talking like I didn't just kick your Angel arses in a corridor while looking really cool?'

'We're not "Angels",' said the Angel, 'and we don't have arses. And you didn't "look cool". And we're not in a corridor any more.'

'Yeah, I know,' replied Charity. 'Now I can really go to town. So why don't you let us find Grace before I go full *Ready Player One* with this suit?'

'Do you know what she's talking about?' asked the Former Aurora to Brenda and Constance.

Brenda shook her head, truthfully. If she tried keeping up with all of Charity's silly references, she was certain she would go quite mad.

The Angels continued to approach. They had formed a tight circle of light around the women now and, even if Brenda wanted to leave Head Office, she doubted she'd be able to – certainly not while they were being kettled by celestial beings. The circle of light tightened and tightened. Brenda glanced across at Charity, to see what she *did* mean by 'full *Ready Player One*'. Charity just stood there, her eyes closed, her fists raised and her head slightly bowed in yet another cartoonish pose of heroic readiness. The circle tightened more and Brenda wondered why Charity hadn't actually done anything yet. But then she noticed that Charity wore a small anticipatory smile that suggested all she was waiting for was the perfect moment – not in terms of the fight as such, but in terms of looking cool.

The circle closed in by a few more centimetres, and Charity decided that that moment had come. She raised her fists a little higher, and then bit the heel of her own hand.

'Why did…?' started Constance.

'Cartoon,' explained Brenda with a sigh.

There was a suitably dramatic explosion of harmless steam from Charity's body and, in the blinding confusion, Brenda felt something push against her side. It felt like a leg. A very big leg, that was getting progressively bigger, really quite fast, and was, on closer inspection, clothed in neon-coloured cats in space leggings. Oh. Charity had made herself go all big.

The steam cleared, and Charity unfolded out of a crouch, her head and torso rising and rising to eight, nine, ten metres. A dozen arms unfurled, like an enormous butterfly opening its wings. The sharpened boomerang took this moment to fly back towards her and be caught in the top two of her multitude of hands, where it glowed bright as it changed form – in a manner that Brenda could only really describe to herself as 'Nineties Saturday Morning Cartoon' – and became a dozen weapons, one for each huge hand. Two giant gauntlets, twin pistols, two broadswords – one set with a red and black stone, the other set with a blue stone – a katana, a giant mallet, a bo staff, a metal fan, a ray gun and a lightsaber. Charity herself finally stopped growing when her head brushed the high ceiling. She stood, towering over all of them, even the Angels – a colossal, twelve-armed creature brandishing a mishmash of cartoonish weaponry, like some terrible destructor god dreamed up by a sect of religiously nostalgic thirty and forty somethings.

'Ah ha ha ha,' boomed the giant Charity. 'I did it! This feels amazing! I am violating *so* many copyrights right now!'

'Is that the Sword of Omens?' asked Constance, pointing to one of the broadswords.

'Yep,' replied the giant cheerfully, bringing two gauntletted fists down on the surrounding Angels. 'Other one's from *She-Ra*.'

The Former Aurora tried to deflect the blow again but, on the open plan green floor, the energy had no nearby walls or windows to blast into. It did make an impressively large circular indent in the floor, though.

'Ohhh,' breathed Constance. 'Yes. I remember that. I remember cartoons!'

Honestly, thought Brenda, she was surrounded by nerds.

'We used to watch the Saturday morning shows,' said Constance, dreamily, as Charity swung with swords and shot with pistols and lasers into the complaining but apparently unkillable circle of Angels. 'Me and Harry. We didn't have brunch or do crosswords at all – nothing that sophisticated. We had a little telly opposite the bed and we'd watch the cartoons, even though we were too old. And when you were born we'd watch them as we fed you, even though you were too young to watch them yourself. I remember! It wasn't all sunshiney and grown-up like an advert for a kitchen suite. Our flat was small and dark because we were poor. Ghost hunting hardly brought in any money. And we weren't all perfect and dreamy, we were silly. I can remember being silly!'

Brenda pulled her friend back and away from Charity's dangerous-looking metal fan as she used it to waft away a deeply annoyed Angel.

'You *were* quite silly. The apple certainly didn't fall far from the tree when it comes to Charity. But the Angels at Helsbury said that all those cartoon hero stories were deliberately fed to Charity to prepare her to be Death. Maybe your silliness was all just a part of their plan.'

Constance shot her an offended glare. 'Or maybe we just liked *Thundercats*. Anyway, if they did feed those stories to Charity, look what chaos it brought them.'

Charity threw herself forward into yet another somersault – one which took up the whole of the space from floor to ceiling – swords, lasers and bullets whirling. It looked ridiculous.

'You look ridiculous,' called the Angel Formerly Known As Aurora.

'I look,' boomed Charity, 'magnificent.'

'Yes,' shouted Brenda, 'she looks magnificent. Shut your face, Aurora, or whoever you really are. You didn't even know who Princess Di was.'

Many of the Angels were dissipating, muttering that this was no way to be treated in Head Office, and calling for the still-absent Manager. Charity focused on the Former Aurora, pointing her twin pistols at the being.

'Where's Grace?'

The Former Aurora snorted with derision. 'There is no such thing as Grace.'

Charity pointed both broadswords at the Former Aurora. 'We just want to talk to Grace. Where's Grace?'

'Are you threatening me? You can't actually do me any harm.'

'Good. I don't want to. I just want to talk to my friend.'

'They're not your friend!'

'Yes they are! And while I can't hurt you, what I *can* do is annoy you. Really, really annoy you.' The giant Charity glanced down at Brenda, and gave her a little smile. 'I learned from the best.'

The Former Aurora snorted again. 'You people barely bothered me when I was walking the mortal world so what makes you think you could bother me now, my loves?'

'Don't underestimate them,' came a voice. 'They really are horribly annoying. Trust me.'

It was a familiar voice to Brenda. Not that she ever enjoyed hearing it. It was the voice that kept trying to end the world. It was the voice that had angrily collapsed an island and blown up a petrol station while she and her family were still in them. She looked in the direction of the sound, and saw a terrible, impossible shape of interlocking fire and eyes. The Manager. Next to it was a smear of light. It looked like all the other smears of light she'd seen – around eight feet tall, thin and vibrating unpleasantly. And yet, there was something very familiar about this other being, too. Looking at the Angel hurt Brenda's face, but in a recognisable way. It was a very specific sting that was almost comforting.

It was Grace.

CHAPTER FOURTEEN

What A Sad Little Life, Brenda

'What have you done?' asked the shimmer of light that was Grace.

That had once been Grace.

That *still* was Grace, thought Brenda, until Grace herself – or themself – said otherwise.

'Look at this mess,' complained the Manager. 'You're not allowed in here, you're certainly not allowed to fight here and you are *definitely* not allowed to break my floors.'

'Aurora broke the floor, though,' muttered Charity. 'Smash deflection – it looked pretty cool.'

'Every *time*!' the Manager interrupted. '*Every* time, with you people!'

'Charity, why are you huge?' asked Grace. 'Did you steal a suit?'

'Of course they've been stealing suits,' snapped the Manager. 'Look at her, she's wearing fifty-six of them at the same time! And you know where she got that idea, don't you?'

'I didn't "steal" the Grace Barry suit,' sighed Grace. 'I just got lost in it.' Something about Grace made them look slightly smaller to Brenda than they had been just moments before.

'A likely story,' replied the Former Aurora, wafting over to them. 'Hello, Manager. Nice to see you finally decided to show up to deal with your latest shambles.'

The Manager's fiery rings dimmed a little at getting berated. 'Blaming me,' muttered the Manager, 'of course.'

'Of course I am,' retorted the Former Aurora. 'Your whole project is a disgrace. I had to start project termination for you, because you keep failing—'

'I was working on it,' replied the Manager, in the weary tones Brenda was well used to hearing from complaints department staff. 'I did ask for a little patience...'

'It's not good enough! The whole thing's falling apart!'

'The mortal world always falls apart sooner or later, it's the humans, they're too destructive—'

'Which is why we outsourced it to *you* to terminate the project when the time was ready. And instead there's the huge energy waste of two failed attempts, one of our executives has lost their mind and still thinks they're a friend to the mortal produce and, if that's not enough, you allowed three of the mortals to slip into your *horribly* designed Head Office, steal fifty-six suits and attack us during a meeting!'

'Well, they got in through the door that *you* opened up, in the wake of returning the Executive *you* lost. And I can't help but notice you were fighting too...' muttered the Manager.

The Former Aurora glowed with rage, with such an intensity that Brenda's vision turned red and she had to screw shut her suddenly streaming eyes.

'I am trying to solve your problems. Don't you *dare* speak back to me!'

Ohhh, Brenda was really enjoying this argument between the Manager and the Former Aurora. It was always so lovely when two beings that she hated started fighting and making one another miserable. It was even better when she was aware that she was the catalyst for their argument and their unhappiness. She wiped her stinging eyes and noticed that her tear ducts weren't streaming tears as a result of the Former Aurora's rage, but blood. Oh well. Still worth it.

'Guys,' said Grace, ever the peacemaker, 'should we maybe have a sit and a chat about this?'

'No!' chorused the Manager and the Former Aurora.

'For the last time, my love, try to at least remember your true form,' continued the Former Aurora. 'We can't sit! Only mortals can sit!'

The shaft of light that made up Grace bent slightly at the top and, through the stinging blood-tears, it looked to Brenda like the thoughtful tilting of a head. And... was Grace even shorter than they were a second ago?

'Then why are there so many beanbags?' Grace asked, in their usual, gentle tone.

'I don't know!' the Former Aurora shouted, and – oh – now Brenda's ears were bleeding too, but she wasn't going to miss a second of this. 'It doesn't make any sense! None of this Manager's designs make any sense!'

'It's the Ethereal Ideal,' retorted the Manager, sounding more than a little cowed.

'What is ideal about *any* of this?' asked the Former Aurora.

'It's... Head Office,' replied the Manager, in a tone that suggested it was making this argument out loud for the first time, and was only now struck by quite how pathetic it sounded.

Charity, who had been standing around all huge and brandishing a dozen weapons in a dozen mighty hands, was now looking really rather awkward about being a giant, battle-ready juggernaut sidelined by an argument about project management and interior design. The cartoonish, many-limbed goliath form peeled away from her in multiple meaty layers, revealing the usual, human-sized Charity within – like a brightly painted doll at the centre of a matryoshka.

'I think the fight's over,' muttered Charity to the other women.

'Yeah, this fight's much better,' replied Brenda, fishing blood out of her ear with a fingertip. With the Former Aurora and Manager still at one another's – not throats because they didn't have throats – whatever they had instead of throats, Brenda beckoned to Grace.

'Hey. Psst. Hey. Grace.'

Grace started wafting over towards them, then seemed to find a sort of solidness in the bottom end of their streak-of-light form. Grace pressed into the battle-damaged green floor of Head Office as if with a human foot affected by gravity and physics and so on. And then, seemingly automatically, the bottom half of Grace's form split in two, like legs, and they planted another shimmering 'foot' on the floor. Grace was no longer drifting, but walking like a human.

'Why did you come here?' Grace asked Brenda. 'I made my choice. I couldn't let innocent people get...' Grace trailed off under the look on Brenda's face. 'They let innocent people get hurt anyway, didn't they?'

'The menfolk are doing their best back there, but yeah,' replied Brenda.

Grace shifted slightly. Grace was almost as short now as they had been in human form, and as they turned, Brenda could make out the vague shape of a face. It looked like Grace's human face – the old face, the face of the suit. It reminded Brenda of ghosts – no longer human, but retaining the human forms they had around the point of their deaths like a memory of being human. The face of the little priest became clearer as they turned it towards the Former Aurora. 'Did you go back on your word? After forcing me to have a disciplinary meeting?'

199

The Former Aurora stopped arguing with the Manager and seemed, just for a moment, to be speechless.

'Why are you talking to the mortals?' demanded the Former Aurora after their brief, awkward silence. 'You're confused enough already, they'll only make it worse.' The Former Aurora addressed the Manager. 'Tell them!'

'N…' Grace stumbled over the word. 'No! No, sorry but no.' Brenda was sure she could make out arms on the Angel's form, pulled up against their chest, defensively. She could even just about see the stripes of Grace's favourite cardigan from back on Earth, and the little white rectangle of Grace's dog collar. 'And,' continued Grace, nervously, 'I think I'm a "her", actually, and I think I really am still "Grace", and…'

The Former Aurora vibrated with rage again, and Brenda did her best to catch the blood dripping from her eyes and ears.

'See the damage you've caused??' The Former Aurora barked at the Manager. 'And, I can't help but notice, the mortal world *still* hasn't been terminated!

'Ugh.' Charity wiped the blood from her own face and neck. 'Well, this hoodie's ruined, now.'

'You just said *you* wanted to take over termination,' argued the Manager.

'I should not have to do your job for you,' the Former Aurora raged. 'Fix. This. And then, you are *fired*. And you can take your horrible designs and your horrible Head Office and your horrible beanbags with you!'

The burning rings of eyeballs pulsated for a moment.

'Get out,' said The Manager. It didn't sound angry any more. Just tired.

'Who?' asked Grace, timidly. 'Me, or… or my friends, or…?'

'All of you. I don't care. Just get out. I put millions of years of hard work into a reality, into supplying my client dimensions with the energy they need, into doing it ethically and to an ideal, and then I try to end it nicely and I get nothing but grief from all sides and both sets of clients treating *my* mortal universe as some sort of adventure playground and then shouting at *me* when one of *their* lot goes AWOL and decides to stay with the mortals. And now you're smashing up *my* Head Office in direct disregard of my rules and insulting *my* ethereally ideal décor. Get out! Fire me. Fine, whatever. But I am doing the best I can with an impossible brief, and these deeply annoying mortals are making everything worse. But you Celestials and the Demons *really* aren't helping either. So, all of you, Just. Get. Out.'

'So, we can take Grace with us?' asked Charity, cheerfully. 'Honestly, that's all we wanted.'

'No,' replied the Former Aurora.

'Yes!' said the Manager over them. 'Fine! Bravo! You won! You got what you wanted! You get to go back and experience the violent, bloody end of the world together!'

Brenda felt a strange sensation all over. It felt like she was being pushed by some mighty, invisible force – pushed hard against the very fabric of reality – like a hand against cellophane. There was resistance, but also the sensation that at any moment it was going to give way. This was, she realised, what it felt like for ghosts to get 'popped' out of the living world. It wasn't a pleasant sensation.

And... oh yes. The end of the world. That was still going on beyond the Hell Hole. As the invisible will of the Manager pushed harder, she felt the Hell Hole manifest around her and she could hear the screams of the trapped humans in the auditorium, the roar of Murzzzz fighting against the Demons and the cute little baby growl of Demon Darryl doing his very best – bless his cotton socks. Maybe there was still something Brenda could do here in Head Office to stop it, while she was on a roll.

'Now listen here,' she said, but it was too late. The thin fabric of reality gave way. She got popped. Eurgh. It felt horrid. She was never going to be rude to a ghost ever again.

Well. Unless they were annoying. Or she was tired. Or hungover. And she was tired and hungover a lot.

She was never going to be rude to around thirty per cent of ghosts ever again.

Darryl still detested his Demon form – really he did – and he resented having to use it again so soon after swearing off it. But, he supposed, this form was far stronger and more agile. In human form right now he'd be prey like all the other trapped humans. He clung halfway up a concrete pillar, spotted a Demon about to attack a screaming couple, and launched himself at it, claws outstretched. Urgh – his claws really were quite cute and fluffy, weren't they? It was like a kitten attacking a bit of string. Still, with his silly little kitten claws, he was able to scratch at the other Demon until it gave up and left the terrified couple alone. That was something, right?

It would feel like a more useful something if it was actually getting him anywhere – if it was properly getting rid of the Demons and if it was saving lives in a more palpable way. Even if he were buying time for any particular purpose or plan that would be something, but he wasn't. He was just fighting Demon after Demon blindly, with no strategy beyond saving the next life he happened to see in peril, and he had no idea how long he could carry on for or how long he was going to have to *try* to hold out. Probably until the end of the world, which was likely to be very, very soon. His sister was gone. His mother was gone. Grace and Constance were gone. He was aware of a terrible ball of grief, deep in his stomach, that he couldn't spare the time to bring up and process right now. He kept it swallowed down, but it agitated the core of him from inside, like a bad paella. It was going to have to come back up soon, and when it did it was going to be horrific.

There was no time, no time – no anything any more. He couldn't see Krish with his Janusz amongst the trapped, panicking throng. But there was no time to worry. The Hell Hole was still wide open to the strange, shining dimension that Demon Darryl understood was home to the Manager. The end could come through it at any moment but, until then, all he could hope to do was to mitigate the suffering of the living trapped in here, alongside Murzzzz. Urgh. Of *course* his last moments of life would be fighting side by side with Murzzzz, of all beings. Just his bloody luck. Another nearby scream caught his attention – an upsettingly young sounding scream. A child, a girl, probably around five, was cowering in a corner as a Demon bore down on her. Demon Darryl mentally berated whatever adult had thought it was a good idea to take a little kid to a psychic night as he twisted on his heels and leaped. In one movement, he managed to kick the other Demon away from the child and scoop the little girl up. He clutched her to himself, carefully directing his sharp claws away from the kid's skin, and leaped again, up, out of the screaming, swarming melee on the ground. He anchored himself into the wall with his claws, and scanned the conference hall for a relatively safe spot to put the kid down.

The kid gazed up at him, wide-eyed, terrified and bewildered with her face streaked with tears.

'Te... ddy?' she managed to stutter out through the fear.

Yeah, he totally looked like a teddy.

'**Nrerh**,' he managed in reply through his Demon mouth. He hoped it sounded like a vaguely reassuring growl. Damn it, there was nowhere to deposit the kid that would be out the reach of all the Demons. Right, then. He hauled the kid up high onto his back so she could grab the fur on the scruff of his neck, and jumped back into the fight. He'd just have to make sure nothing got close enough to attack him from behind. Maybe he could find this kid's parents, before the end.

He hit the floor on all fours and bounded over to Murzzzz, who was struggling to hold off around a dozen Demons at the same time. He managed to wrestle away the Demon who was trying to rip Murzzzz's head off. His head freed, Murzzzz managed to make eye contact with Demon Darryl.

'**Son…**'

Demon Darryl snarled and growled a warning out at Murzzzz, even as he struggled to free him from more of the Demons.

'**Look. I just wanted to say. If this is the end… I understand why you resent me. Hate me—**'

An attacking Demon bit Murzzzz on the face. Demon Darryl slashed at it with his silly little claws until it squealed and shrank back, thick ooze bubbling from the wound.

'**Ow,**' grumbled Murzzzz, also oozing and bubbling from the bite. '**It's OK,**' he continued. '**I shouldn't have interfered with your family. I thought maybe I could be the one Demon to intervene in mortal lives in a positive way, instead of just causing pain and chaos, but I just caused pain and chaos anyway, in different ways. But, as much as you hate me, I still love you. I always will.**'

Demon Darryl pulled another Demon off him, and growled a growl that he felt best conveyed 'Oh stop being so bloody passive aggressive, would you?'

Murzzzz was freed from enough of the attacking Demons that he managed to fight the others off and get to his feet.

'**Thank you,**' he told Demon Darryl. '**Back to it, then. I, er, I don't think it's going to stop this time. Still. We do what we can.**' He tilted his head a little at the kid on Demon

Darryl's back as he clambered up a concrete column. '**Is that a kid?**' he asked. '**All very *Monsters, Inc.*.**'

And with that, Murzzzz leaped away, to extract another Demon away from screaming humans. Demon Darryl turned and started fighting his way towards the Hell Hole, and wondered whether the last thing he'd ever hear Murzzzz say was that he looked a bit like *Monsters, Inc.*. He could tell from a cluster of Demon screeches that Krish had managed to fight his way quite close to the Hell Hole. As he bounded closer, he saw that there were far fewer silently screaming ghosts now than there had been before, but still plenty of Demons. The Demons well outnumbered the ghosts, now. While Demon Darryl was glad that the ghosts were no longer trapped and in pain, this was still far from ideal. He could see that the Nice Reaper was nearly surrounded, and that Janusz was still at his side. This concerned Demon Darryl – it wasn't exactly what he'd meant when he'd told Krish to keep his perfect darling safe. And besides that, as well as being a perfect darling, Janusz could be a bit of an arse, and if he'd been on his own with Krish all through the fight, Demon Darryl was worried that his bloody husband had been rude to the poor psychopomp again. He introduced himself to the fray around them by landing on a Demon's head, which was fast becoming his Demon form's traditional form of entrance.

'Oh, hey!' Krish gave Demon Darryl a smile that was full of good cheer, in spite of all the *everything* going on around him. 'Thanks for joining! Aww, cute kiddie on your back. Hey kiddie!'

The tension between Krish and Janusz seemed to have evaporated. Maybe the imminent end of the world had helped Janusz get over that weird, needless jealousy that afflicted him every time Darryl even spoke to a cute guy. Well, supposed Demon Darryl, maybe even mushroom clouds could have a silver lining.

'You OK there, little one?' Janusz asked the child. Behind him, Demon Darryl could feel the fur of his neck move as the child nodded, her face still pressed close into his dark brown shoulder floof.

'It's like the, um, the film,' continued Janusz. 'Dan from Roseanne is a monster – real fluffy guy.'

Krish took out another Demon with his scythe. '*Monsters, Inc.*!' he replied. 'Yes, I see it! You ever watched *Monsters, Inc.*, kiddo?'

Demon Darryl felt more movement on his neck as the kid shook her head.

'It'll all be on streaming, see if you can watch it later…' Krish trailed off, struck by the unspoken reality that there likely wasn't going to be a 'later' for watching nice animated movies or doing anything at all, really. He cleared his throat and carried on regardless, still in a tone of child-soothing cheerfulness. 'It's got Steve Buscemi in it. Kids love Steve Buscemi, right?'

'Steve Buscemi's very good,' agreed Janusz.

It was deeply weird seeing Janusz and Krish getting along so suddenly thought Demon Darryl. End times. Literally.

Krish swung his scythe at another Demon as Demon Darryl slashed at one who was trying to lunge at Janusz. Hurt, the attacking Demons squealed and shrank away, clearing a pathway to the makeshift 'stage' area of the conference hall. The Hell Hole loomed overhead, still shining with the chrome and glass of Head Office. In front of it, blocking the aisle, stood the Fake Diana. She was still rooted to the spot, noiselessly scream-ing. Demon Darryl had no way to tell whether the suffering of the ghosts involved physical pain or was merely the emotional anguish of miserable, lost souls – former humans who had lost everything, even their own names. He supposed it didn't matter. They were clearly hurting, either way, and their pain was powering the Hell Hole, which was causing the suffering of the living. Suffering upon suffering.

'Cover me,' muttered Krish, and darted forwards.

Demon Darryl did so, kicking away another Demon before it could get to Krish. Janusz broke into a run to keep up rather than split the group. Death swung his scythe and the Fake Diana disappeared. Goodbye, England's Pretend Rose. Demon Darryl hoped she'd find peace where she was going. Peace, and maybe some less upsetting opinions about the beautiful diversity of human society.

'So,' said the Nice Reaper, conversationally, 'it's not much of a plan, but I'm gonna see if I can shut this portal. Because it turns out that just reaping away the ghosts doesn't stop it.' He waved a hand around at the now largely ghost-free hall. 'Maybe the portal already got all the ghost-suffering juice it needed to open up and now it can just stay open.'

'It's still probably kinder that you reaped them anyway,' added Janusz. 'Considering.'

'Aww, thanks, buddy,' grinned Krish. 'But we still want to try and close this bad boy. So, the closer I can get to it, the better. If I can't close it from this side, well… I mean, no human's tried closing one from the other side yet, right? Could work.'

Demon Darryl grunted with concern. There was one pretty major flaw with the 'close it from the other side' plan.

'Everyone wants to sacrifice themselves in the Hell Hole, today,' sighed Janusz.

'Frankly, it looks nicer on that side than it does on this, right now,' said Krish, 'and half your family already went through – at this point, I'm just going with the flow. I might even find the ladies in there, which would be nice, I certainly owe your sister a date…'

And it was at that moment that the sister in question came tumbling out of the Hell Hole at considerable speed. Demon Darryl saw Krish hold out his arms on instinct to catch her but spotted that he was still holding his scythe, which could have got very messy so he leaped in front of him and caught Charity in both arms. His mother suddenly followed behind her, which meant he had to fumble his sister over to one arm and try to catch Brenda single-handed in the other which caused him to accidentally drop them both onto the conference hall's rather sticky carpet. Constance fell out of the hole as well, but Demon Darryl was all out of arms and there was no point trying to catch a ghost.

'You came back,' said Janusz, happily, helping Brenda up off the floor as Krish gallantly did the same for Charity.

'Darryl, you seem to have a child now,' was Brenda's warm greeting to her son. 'How long were we in there?'

'Maybe half an hour,' replied Janusz as Demon Darryl rolled his eyes a little and, safe in the knowledge that his mother and sister had returned from Head Office unhurt, went back to picking off the Demons trying to surround them. 'She's a rescue child. Doesn't he look cute with a kid, though?'

'Very *Monsters, Inc.*,' agreed Charity.

'That's what I said!'

'How long were you in there from your point of view?' Krish asked.

'Few hours before we got kicked out,' Charity told him, with considerable pride. 'I beat a bunch of them up and they couldn't hack it.'

'So time would be on my side, from that end of the portal,' muttered Krish. 'This could work.'

'What could work?' asked Charity.

'He wants to sacrifice himself,' Janusz explained.

'Oh no you will not, you silly hottie,' Charity told Krish. 'I just did that, *and* went full *Ready Player One*, *and* came back in time for breakfast. *You* get to hear all about it in quiet awe later when you take me to a very nice restaurant.'

Demon Darryl came bounding back from the fight just as another figure came out of the Hell Hole, to his surprise. It was Grace. Not in the shaft of light form he'd last seen her in after all of the humanity had peeled off her like a wet, visceral banana skin, but in a form that looked almost entirely like the old Grace again. She was small, middle-aged, and wore a stripy cardigan, black dog collar shirt and sensible trousers. Still though, there were bits of her that didn't quite look like the old Grace. She looked... 'unfinished' was the best word Demon Darryl's brain could come up with for how Grace looked. Her usually unkempt, salt-and-pepper hair now ended in several inches of shimmering light that floated as if her head were underwater. Her sensible trousers rippled like sunlight on the surface of a lake.

Also, Grace didn't fall out of the Hell Hole in the same way as Charity and Brenda had done. Instead, she floated for a moment, hanging in the air, as light as a dust mote, before glancing down, blinking and then seeming to remember that in this universe, if you found yourself a few feet above the floor, you were supposed to fall. It was like watching Wile E. Coyote step off the edge of a cliff. A very small, very sweet and shining Wile E. Coyote. Even when she did remember to fall, Grace didn't seem to hurt herself at all. She merely picked herself up again, saying 'Ow' in a quiet, distracted voice, almost as an afterthought. Like someone who had gently donked against a streetlamp and not actually done any damage to themselves but felt that it still needed to be acknowledged.

'Grace,' called Krish, delighted. 'They actually found you? They brought you back!'

'I think I just got expelled from Head Office,' muttered Grace. 'Like Adam and Eve... ooh, and like Lucifer. Oh dear.'

'And you're you again,' Krish noted. 'Mostly.'

There was suddenly a hair bobble on Grace's wrist, that hadn't been there a second before. Grace tied back her curls with it, and it transformed into her old Grace hair again.

'And you found your old suit again?' asked Krish.

'Um,' said Grace, frowning down at her hands. 'How did I…? Did the Manager do this…?'

Grace turned to Demon Darryl, who had no idea. He shrugged, as best as he could while still in Demon form, with a kid on his back.

'Aww,' said Grace, 'did you adopt a child?'

Then, yet another figure emerged from the Hell Hole. This one did not have the form of a small, sweet lady priest. And this one didn't fall to the ground like a cartoon coyote. This one was a terrible, eye-aching streak of light that hovered angrily above them all.

Darryl's mother let out an almighty, Brenda-ish 'Cuh!' It was the sort of annoyed 'Cuh!' Brenda usually reserved for when a shop *said* they had an offer on Pinot Grigio, but it had actually just ended the day before.

'Cuh! Aurora, what are *you* doing back here? Haven't you done enough damage without following us around?'

'The Manager threw me out,' said the streak of light, in Aurora's voice. It was said it to themself quietly and with an air of disbelief, as if by saying it out loud, they could find a way in which it made some sort of sense to them. 'The Manager threw *me* out!!' they repeated. And no, it still wasn't making the situation make any more sense to them. In fact, it only served to make them angrier about it. 'Me!! Doesn't it know who I am??'

'Aurora?' called a different voice from the throng of Demons and the living. 'Ms Tavistock?'

Demon Darryl followed the voice and saw the woman who, earlier that evening, had still been working as Aurora's PA. Yemisi was only a few feet away from Demon Darryl, in a sweaty disarray but defending herself admirably by using a chair as a shield. So far, so normal for a celebrity's PA although she was, of course, defending herself from Demons, which was where her usual experience of PA work probably didn't compare.

'Ah,' said the Former Aurora. 'It's you. I doubt you can help with this.'

'Why didn't you tell me?' demanded Yemisi. 'I ran myself ragged for you! I'd go out and get you tea, special fancy tea when the hotel tea making facilities were right in front of you! Did you even drink tea? I gave up my New Year for you! I could've gone out in Clapham! Seen my brothers! Snogged some gorgeous stranger who smelled of Bleu de Chanel and Carling, but no! You just left me to get eaten by Demons.'

'Demons don't actually eat mortals,' the Former Aurora sighed, 'they just rip them up.'

A minor Demon, right on cue, lunged up at Yemisi from behind. She tried to swing the chair at it, but Demon Darryl could see it was going to be too late. He jumped, and kicked at the other Demon's head. He wasn't fast enough to stop the Demon from sending the poor woman flying to the ground, but at least his intervention was fast enough to spare her any other injury. The Demon squealed and hissed, and vanished through the fabric of reality.

'Ow,' Yemisi whined. She glared up at the Former Aurora, hurt and angry. 'You didn't help! Didn't even warn me!'

'It's not *my* job to assist *you*. It *was* your job to assist me, you were paid a reasonable wage for your trouble. Obviously now that position is obsolete so I don't know why you're crying. I don't owe you anything. I could pay you your fees up until the end of the show, but then what would you spend it on?'

'You're firing me?'

'Yes, of course. I think it should be perfectly obvious that your services as an assistant and tour manager are no longer needed here.'

'I'm being attacked by shadow monsters *and* you're an alien and you're firing me???'

'I am not an "alien", mortal, I am a Celestial Executive, one of the highest ranking beings in any dimension. And you are produce. Power cells. Battery chickens. And the chicken coop has become so full of your own filth now that it can no longer be sustained, so we're switching it off and on again.'

'You can't switch a chicken coop off and on again,' cried Yemisi. 'Ugh, you're such a... a fraud, Aurora. You couldn't even tell who the real Diana was! I *knew* Princess Di wouldn't really be kinda racist!'

'How dare you, mortal?'

'Yemisi! My name is Yemisi!! And you can't fire me. I quit!'

'Fine, saves me the bother. You're not even on my list of people to fire today,' replied the Former Aurora, huffily. 'Where is the Manager?'

'I think you annoyed it,' said Grace, meekly.

The Former Aurora vibrated with fury. Demon Darryl shifted his body to shield the child on his back from the pain of looking at their anger.

'Grace Barry, this is all your fault.'

'It really isn't, Aurora.'

'If it wasn't for you...' The Former Aurora trailed off and, in their rage, did something that, for all Darryl had seen in his life – especially over the past couple of months where the world had repeatedly been trying to end – he would never have thought could be possible, even for a Celestial Executive.

The Former Aurora grabbed the conference hall, turned it inside out, and threw it at Grace.

CHAPTER FIFTEEN
Taflu yn Ofalus

One moment they were all trapped within the conference hall. The next moment, there was no 'in' to be trapped inside. All of its inside was on the outside, and Demon Darryl, his family, the kid, all the Demons and mortals and any remaining ghosts, were out in the frost-covered car park. The conference room was still the size of the conference room, but inside out and raised above the streak of light that had once been Aurora. It rained chairs down onto the freezing tarmac, before the Former Aurora lurched swiftly in Grace's direction and the huge, inverted room went crashing towards her.

Demon Darryl knew absolutely nothing about Angel biology, or whether one could easily survive an inside out concrete hall to the face, but he certainly wasn't expecting Grace's counter-move. Grace, seemingly as a natural flight instinct, dodged the colossal missile – but not by moving herself, rather by moving the dimensions of the car park. Suddenly, the car park was impossibly huge, and Grace, the family and all the mortals were in it and far, far away from the launched conference room, which crashed forlornly on the distant horizon. All of the other Demons had been left miles away – if a measurement as normal as miles even still existed as a concept in this impossibly stretched-out car park. Demon Darryl wondered why he'd moved with them this time given he was still in Demon form, before remembering the child on his back. Grace must have automatically moved the child to safety, and the child had dragged him along. Murzzzz took a moment to come bounding over, with a confused expression, as the other Demons in the distance wondered amongst themselves what had just happened to the normally basic physical rules of the mortal realm. The Hell Hole still hung resolutely ahead, although Darryl couldn't make Head Office out behind it any more. It was just a nothingness swirling above them.

'**What just happened?**' Murzzzz demanded of Grace, hurrying up to them. '**In all my millennia, I've never seen anything like that before.**'

'I think… we're fighting,' replied Grace. 'I don't usually do fighting.'

'Aww man,' moaned Charity, 'I just took off my super suit. Should I get it back? I fought loads of them, back there.'

'You're not going back to Head Office, princess,' Brenda told her.

'Listen to your mother,' Grace told her. 'I don't think any of us are going to be allowed back there. And I don't want you humans fighting any Celestials on Earth. Head Office is the Manager's realm, nobody can really cause anyone any proper damage there. You can't even muck up the fabric of reality much in Head Office, that's why the Manager was so upset about the damage to just one floor. Head Office's structure usually stays how the Manager wants it. With its weird stairs and its beanbags and all that purple.'

'Horribly designed place,' Brenda agreed, quietly.

'But here?' Grace continues. 'Anything goes, here. Nobody respects this realm.'

The Former Aurora appeared again, a shaft of terrible, burning sunlight above the cold, dark, glistening car park.

'So, it's going to be like *that,* eh?' demanded the Former Aurora. The furious streak of light plucked the colossal car park up off the ground, flipped all of the mortals off it into frozen mud and scrunched the mile upon mile of tarmac into an enormous sphere. Again, Grace moved not only herself but all of the Rooks and assorted mortals with her away from the path of this latest needlessly huge projectile.

'Er,' muttered Janusz after Grace's latest dodge, 'are we up a mountain?'

'I think this is Mount Snowdon,' said Grace. 'Sorry. I saw one of those documentaries where a comedian goes on holiday with their mum and they walked up here and it was pretty and I thought "I'd love to go with the family some day and get away from it all". Must have lodged in my mind as a place to – you know – get away from it all.'

'Shoulda packed a proper coat,' added Krish, shivering. And, yeah, thought Demon Darryl, the top of Wales's highest mountain wasn't the best place to dump a load of humans dressed for an indoor event, in the middle of the night on New Year's Eve. And even though they were now several hundred miles from the Sunnyside leisure and retail estate, the Hell Hole still swirled frustratingly above. Maybe it was just everywhere, now. Or, at least maybe it was going to be everywhere they went.

'You do realise Aurora will just throw this mountain at you?' Brenda said to Grace.

'They might not,' replied Grace, sounding extremely unsure.

The Former Aurora appeared again and, to Former Aurora's credit, didn't pull the move the Rooks had been expecting. The Former Aurora had something other than a mountain to throw at Grace. It was bigger than a mountain. Much bigger. It was a sphere of crumpled tower blocks, office buildings, houses and streets. Cars and streetlamps tumbled from it and clattered down the mountain.

'Shitting Norah,' breathed Brenda. 'That's Cardiff. Bloody maniac's trying to throw Cardiff at us!'

Yeah, that was Cardiff all right. Darryl could just about make out the stadium, crushed against the Senedd building on the surface of the terrible, impossible ball.

Grace glared up at the wadded-up city, and flared with a bright, painful rage.

'Pack it in,' Grace shouted at the Former Aurora. 'I'm trying to take the pacifist route, here!'

The Former Aurora only shone all the brighter, and then threw Cardiff at them. Grace didn't dodge, this time. Instead, she raised both arms above her head and, from the dark horizon behind her, at an astonishing, physics-defying speed, came a projectile of her own. A colossal ball of land, dotted with buildings and dripping sea water, came sailing over the dark countryside. Demon Darryl was reminded of the Coldbay case, when the Manager had folded up the whole island and thrown bits of it at them, but this was so much bigger. Many times bigger than Coldbay. And around five or six times bigger than the wadded-up city of Cardiff. Darryl, along with his family and the assorted mortals, watched the colossal landmass as it soared over the mountain, over their heads, and kept on going until it smashed into Cardiff and stopped it in its tracks before the furiously hurled city could get within striking distance of them.

'Was that Anglesey?' asked Brenda, after the almighty smash.

'Hmm?' replied Grace, guiltily.

'Did you just pick up the island of Anglesey and use it as a weapon?' Brenda clarified.

'It... it was nearby,' stuttered Grace. 'Fleeing isn't working and so I had to fight back. Sorry.'

'Doesn't Anglesey have a population of a few thousand people?' added Brenda.

'Little over seventy thousand, yeah,' replied Grace, 'but I deposited them all gently in Caernarfon so they'll be fine!' She watched as bits of Wales continued to rain down on the mountains. 'Ooh dear, but what about Cardiff? That's loads and loads of poor people...'

'In a field near Pontypridd,' called the Former Aurora, 'for all the good it'll do them. This is the end of the world after all, but I'm not enough of a monster to throw living humans at you.'

'See, that shows that you do have empathy for the mortals after all,' called Grace. 'Perhaps by living amongst them, you've developed an understanding—'

'Stop trying to reason with me!' the Former Aurora interrupted. 'You're not my counsellor or my negotiator, you're just a pain!'

There was a new sound; from behind the Former Aurora came a terrible rumbling – like rock grinding on rock – growing closer and louder.

'Don't you dare even *think* of throwing Bristol at me!' shouted Grace.

'I'm not throwing Bristol at you,' called the former Aurora. 'You'd only counter by throwing the Isle of Man at me!'

'Blast it,' muttered Grace, 'that *was* my next move.'

The terrible crunching, grinding sound grew louder and louder and finally, in the gloom of the night, Demon Darryl could make out what was approaching them. It was so huge that, as it cleared the horizon, it took up around a quarter of the night sky. A frozen land, clearly once very beautiful before being scooped out of its frozen location and wielded as a massive projectile by a furious otherworldly being.

The others watched it rumble and groan into view with jaws slack at the absolute scale of the thing. As it approached, a look of recognition fluttered over Krish's face, followed swiftly by one of absolute outrage.

'You sick frick!' he shouted. 'That's—'

'Baffin Island??' interrupted Janusz. 'You're using Baffin Island as a weapon?'

'Actually, I prefer to refer to it by its Inuktitut name of Qikiqtaaluk,' Krish informed Janusz.

Janusz rolled his eyes and sighed. '*Dlaczego jesteś taki?*'

'That is a biodiverse, naturally beautiful and culturally important land for the Inuit peoples – heck, for *all* Canadians,' Krish shouted at the Former Aurora. 'And by the way, Janusz,' he continued. 'I'm "like this" because I try to be *respectful*, because I *give* a crap!'

'Keep forgetting you understand Polish,' breathed Janusz, chastened.

Krish turned his attention back to the Former Aurora, pointing a trembling finger. 'So, I don't care if you *are* an alien or a deva or an Angel or whatever it is that is trying to end the world, you frickin' put that back as it was where you found it, or so help me, I'll... I'll be mad!'

'Shut up, mortal.'

'Don't talk to the Grim Reaper like that,' interjected Grace. 'He's not just some mortal, he's the link between the human realm and the Waste dimension... actually, sod it – don't talk to any of the mortals like that! And put Baffin Island back, like he said!'

Darryl's Demon ears picked up yet another ominous sound – not a grinding of rock, this time, but an altogether less earthly sound. It was the distant growls and screeches, and the scrabbling of claws on the mountain's sides – the other Demons had found them. He could hear them climbing the mountain. He braced himself, and gazed over in the direction of the sounds. A lone, huge, powerful Demon cleared the mountainside, leaped into view and began bounding towards them, fast. Luckily, it was the one powerful Demon who was very unlikely to do them any harm. Murzzzz skidded to a stop close to Demon Darryl.

'They're coming,' he growled. '**Is this Snowdon? Got up to some mischief around these parts, long before Richard. Think some of it made it into the *Mabinogion*. Anyway, sorry about that too, I suppose. Urgh, when you start apologising for all your wrongdoings, you do start to realise it's a bit of a list, don't you…?**'

The Angels kept arguing, either unaware of the approaching Demons or too wrapped up in their spat to care.

'But *you* just threw an island at *me*…' whined the Former Aurora.

'I don't care,' replied Grace. 'Put it back! Don't make me get the moon involved in this.'

As the sounds of the approaching Demons grew nearer, Demon Darryl found himself glancing nervously up at the moon. It was still hanging where it was supposed to in the cold night, just about visible between the colossal mass of the wadded-up Arctic island blotting out much of the sky and the also huge swirling void of the Hell Hole that swallowed up another quarter or so of the stars. Grace wouldn't… Would she…?

'You wouldn't,' called the Former Aurora, still holding Baffin Island aloft. 'That would cause much more chaos than flinging a frozen island.'

'You're disrupting the fragile ecosystems of nomadic tribes, arctic foxes and caribou,' shouted Krish, angrily.

'You get the moon involved, that's disrupting far more than that,' warned the Former Aurora. 'I mean, think of the tidal problems alone…'

'I'll do it,' warned Grace.

'You're bluffing.'

'No I'm…' Grace blinked, several times. 'I'm not…'

Darryl rolled his Demon eyes. Why was it that the one Angel on their side had to be *such* a pushover? And so terrible at bluffing?

'Yes you are,' replied the Former Aurora, sounding amused. 'You wouldn't do anything to your precious Earth's precious moon. But I might.'

'No…'

'After I've flattened your mortal friends with this big dead lump of Canada.'

'It's not dead,' screamed Krish, 'it has vibrant fjords!'

'Not any more,' cried the Former Aurora, as the huge sphere of frozen earth began to accelerate towards them. Several of the humans screamed – and as Demon Darryl noticed a moment too late, not all of them were screaming about the rapid approach of Canada's largest island. Some of the nimbler Demons had managed to scale Snowdon, and were scrambling towards the mortals stranded at its peak. He and Murzzzz stepped forwards. There was nothing they could do about getting crushed in the Angel fight, but there was a chance they could hold back the Demonic carnage once more.

And then, in the chaos, there was a word, and the word was 'STOP'.

At the Manager's command, Baffin Island stopped flying towards the mountain, and hung in the sky. Both Angels stopped fighting. The Demons stopped in their tracks. Darryl slid back into human form, the little girl still holding on to his back. Even Murzzzz sheepishly shifted back into Richard. The Manager hung in front of the Hell Hole, and for an innumerable set of interlocking rings of fire and eyes, it looked exhausted. When it spoke, it was with a weariness Brenda could feel in her own bones.

'Just,' sighed the Manager, 'just stop.'

'You heard the Manager,' snapped the Former Aurora.

'All of you,' added the Manager, with millions of years-worth of exhaustion behind it, 'I allow you into Head Office and you cause chaos, you steal, you smash things up, you undermine and criticise me… I send you here and you immediately start crumpling up bits of the world *I carefully made*, and throwing them around.'

'Are… you…?' the former Aurora Tavistock faltered. 'Surely, you're not talking to *me* like that?'

'Yes, I'm talking to you like that! Put Qikiqtaaluk back where you found it, right now! It has polar bears and delightful fjords!'

'Told you so,' muttered Krish.

The Former Aurora flickered with a particularly irritated, disappointed vibration, and above them, the huge island reversed course, slowly uncrumpling as it sailed off northwest.

'Honestly,' said the Former Aurora as it went, 'what difference does it even make now? If the Manager insists we take this disagreement back to our own realm, then fine – that's what I wanted in the first place, Grace Barry. A no-nonsense debrief meeting in the "neutral space" of Head Office, and definitely no more dallying in a mortal realm that is overdue termination.'

'No,' replied Grace, determinedly.

'Grace Barry, do not make me throw Greenland at you!'

'You leave Greenland alone,' cried Krish and the Manager in unison.

'I'm staying here,' added Grace.

'"Here" is the flimsiest, basest, most temporary of realms,' replied the Former Aurora, exasperated, 'and it is hours, if not minutes away from no longer existing, and then what? You might not be able to get back! I am trying to *help* you get over whatever it is about this world that has destroyed your mind.

And I…' The Former Aurora dimmed a little. It was rather like watching an Angel slump, dejectedly. 'I don't get it,' continued the Former Aurora, in a quieter voice. 'I just… I don't understand why you're being so difficult, Grace Barry.'

'I…' Grace fumbled for words. 'I can't explain it. It's not the suit – I'm not wearing the suit any more. I want to be Grace Barry, but it's more than that. I…'

Nearby, Darryl, back in human form, shuffled up to her. He gently set the little girl in his arms down on the ground, but kept a protective arm around her. With his free hand, he reached out and touched Grace's shoulder.

'Maybe I can show them,' he suggested. 'You know – like I did earlier, with The Longest Night. Projecting the memories.'

'You think that could work on someone like me?' Grace fretted. 'I don't want to hurt you or… or explode your brain, or anything. I mean, no offence or anything, but I'm a Celestial, I might be too much for you to channel – it's not like I'm a mortal or a ghost, or even a Demon—'

'Yeah, but also, you're family.'

'Aww, thank you,' said Grace, 'but still—'

'So I think I'll be OK,' replied Darryl.

'I don't think it works like that though,' attempted Grace.

'Can I at least try?' asked Darryl. 'End of the world and all that. We don't have much to lose.'

Grace sighed. 'I suppose. But if I see your brain even start to explode, I'm putting a stop to it.'

Darryl closed his eyes.

Life! Life! Life! The joy of simply being Grace was projected by Darryl into everybody's minds. The pleasant, mundane sensations of brushing her teeth, scratching an itch, drinking hot sweet tea, eating crisps. Running her fingers over the hand-woven throws in her old rectory house, the feel of the uneven ribbons, the bright colours, the seams where skilled human hands had created something beautiful from scraps. Creating art for herself – making posters and banners with crepe paper and macaroni. Colours and textures.

Life! Life! Life! Thinking about what her church on the abandoned island of Coldbay should have been. Her beautiful dream of creating a thriving community on an island that was already empty and dead. A small, simple, sweet dream. A lie, yes. But the loveliest, gentlest of lies. To be human is to dream, to lie to oneself. A car pulling up. Seven strangers – five humans, a Demon and a ghost. And with them, kindness, immediately. Kindness and care and so much love. So much love in that ordinary little car. A family. Grace's heart, all of Grace that yearned to be Grace Barry, now yearned for some of that love and to be part of a family. Part of *that* family. To know that love between spouses. Between siblings. Between parents and their children, whether biological or adopted. Between best friends, living and dead.

And then... and then, this family adopted her, too. Scooped her up from a dead island like a wailing baby taken from the arms of a corpse. Took her home. Gave her a place at the table and a place in the car. Gave her her own mug, with a grumpy-looking kitten and a statement about coffee that was a lie. So many lies – so many loving lies. Grace took the loving lie that she was a small human priest named Grace Barry, and she ran with it. She turned it into something different. She did loving things with it. She made a minibus when the second car was destroyed. She volunteered in Rutherford. Helped humans, telling herself they were her 'fellow man'. She got a black eye when she was punched protecting others – a black eye that she still proudly wore, even without her suit. Her Celestial form was still taking the appearance of Grace Barry. This *was* her true form, now. This little human shape was the shape her soul wanted – no *needed* to be. It was no longer a lie. Grace Barry was the truth, now. She was what she was, because she was.

Life! Life! Life is change. Life is flux. Life is a set of contradictions stacked messily on top of one another. Leaves and milk and sugar and water could be changed to make a hot sweet drink, but the component parts would still exist. The same with ribbons, rags and thread, altered to make a rug. An island could be cold and empty and also a trap, full of the dead. A service station could be a spot for weary drivers to stop and also the desecrated mass grave of a medieval village. A baby girl could be an orphaned Xu and an adopted Rook. A man could be a frightened, lonely client called Janusz Wosniak and a capable, beloved accountant called Janusz Rook. A boy could be human and Demon and could be a clairvoyant and a conduit through which the dead could speak. A person could be Richard and Murzzzz. A dead woman could be furious and sad and loving and forgiving. A woman could be an absolute bloody nightmare – hostile, dismissive, a liar, a problem drinker... and also be brave, and loving and caring enough to go into another realm and save her Celestial friend from a debrief meeting worse than death.

And so, with all of this in mind, in life, in the mortal realm, Grace Barry could be a Celestial Executive, and also be Grace Barry. She could be a little priest who liked brightly coloured knits, cheerful acoustic guitar renditions of vaguely religious pop songs, and binge-watching competitive metalwork shows. She could feel the rain and taste cheese toasties and smell the vegetable soup cooking at the volunteer centre and stroke the little tabby cat on number 36's green bin on the way home... and live! And live! And live!

The love of it – of *living* – of getting to be Grace Barry with all her tiny human kindnesses and her fond little human thoughts, surrounded the group on the freezing mountain as Darryl projected it. It felt like a warm bath. It soothed. It comforted. To Brenda, experiencing Grace's feelings about being Grace was the emotional equivalent of taking off high-heeled shoes and a wired bra.

The projection ended. Darryl gave Grace a little pat on the shoulder. Brenda's son hadn't exploded at all – he was utterly unscathed by the experiment. Brenda reminded herself that if they did make it out of this apocalypse alive, she wasn't to let Grace live down the whole 'thinking she was so powerful she'd destroy Darryl's brain' thing.

'Oh,' said the Former Aurora after a while. They sounded strangely… hollow. Dejected, even. 'I was Aurora Tavistock for years. Why didn't I feel any of that?'

'Because you didn't let yourself, perhaps?' hazarded Grace. 'Because we all experience existence differently and mortality wasn't for you?'

'Or because you were a liar and a stuck-up dick who got other people to fetch and carry for you all the time?' called Yemisi, who was still understandably upset.

'Is that what it really feels like?' added the Manager, in the smallest voice Brenda had ever heard the Manager use. 'Stroking a cat and drinking some tea and making soup for homeless humans actually feels that… that important?'

'It does to me,' replied Grace. 'That's why I want to stay. And if it's only for five more minutes, well, so be it.'

The Manager took a moment, hummed thoughtfully to itself, then turned all of its eyes down to Brenda.

'What do I do?' it asked.

CHAPTER SIXTEEN

Are You There,
Brenda? It's Me, Not-God

Brenda stared up at the Manager.

'Me?' she asked.

'Yes, you, Brenda Rook. You're the ringleader, aren't you? You're at the centre of all of this. You think you know *all* the answers, so let's hear them. What do I do? I've tried ending things quickly and cleanly, and you got in the way. I've shown you the slow, miserable rot that happens if I don't manage the end, and still you keep inserting yourself to grind all my plans to a halt, like a… a grain of sand in a complex machine. I tried to quit, leaving matters to my clients, and look what happened. Carnage. Immediately. And now, I've had the experience of a mortal-Demon hybrid beam into my mind the importance of making soup and stroking cats and so, if I *do* manage the end and harvest its energy as I was contracted to do, I destroy all that *and* trap one of my celestial clients in a void for all eternity. So, why don't *you* tell *me* this time, hmm? Where's the off-ramp? What do I do?'

Brenda thought, for a second. She glanced around her group. 'Have you ever seen *Monsters, Inc.*?'

'What?'

Brenda realised time had stopped. It had even stopped for the Angels. For all the Angels' talk that they outranked the Manager who was just a Celestial sub-contractor, she was certain that, in Head Office and the mortal realm at least, the Manager was still the most powerful being.

'*Monsters, Inc.*,' she said. 'It's a brightly coloured film for little children, so my adult daughter loves it. I'll see if it's on my phone…'

'No, it's all right, if it was made by mortals, I can find the memory of it… Big furry biped, little green biped and a small human?'

'That's the one. There's this bit at the end—'

'Yes,' replied the Manager. 'I just watched it. They initially use terrified screams for power, and then they find out they can use happy laughter instead. You see that as a lesson I could take – you think I could fix things by simply harvesting a positive human emotion for my clients' energy needs, rather than concentrated misery.'

'Can't you?'

'Meh,' grunted the Manager, half-heartedly. 'Technically, I suppose, but it's not as good. The Celestials tried running a mortal universe once where they only harvested bliss, and it was a bit of a shambles. With no proper drive for the mortals, things fell apart really quickly, and the Demons were constantly complaining. Even Celestials found they preferred to harvest misery. It's easier, there's plenty of it to power the doors, and it's a good excuse for them to then use the doors to visit your world – to drum up more misery.'

'But *technically*, you could?'

The Manager sighed. 'I think maybe this film was put here on purpose – like how the Celestials made sure your daughter was inundated with stories about orphans who turn out to be the Chosen One in order to prime her to be Death… not that *that* worked. I think someone wanted you lot to have the idea that I can just harvest happiness instead of misery as some sort of last-ditch negotiation attempt. And it might have worked, if it weren't for two glaring issues. One, your world is dying anyway. It's the end, whether I manage it or not.'

'And the other?' asked Brenda.

'The other,' replied the Manager, 'is even more obvious, and yet it's one that I only realised when you and your silly family showed up and started smashing up my lovely office and making me experience ridiculous emotions about soup.'

'And that is…?'

'I shouldn't be harvesting you people, at all.'

Brenda blinked, and frowned.

'You mortals are intelligent. And annoying. You stole fifty suits and made an absurdly over-the-top cartoon superhero out of them. You cared about a Demon enough to protect him, even though he comprehensively fucked over your whole family – pardon my language. You loved a Celestial so much you raced into my dimension to rescue her from a meeting. Your dead friend still loves you so much, even though she's angry, and sad, and feels hurt and betrayed… You people love and care so much that it lasts beyond death and goes beyond species. Beyond reality. You're *so annoying* and… and admirable. Brave, brave, loving little meaty primates. You try *so hard*. Grace Barry tries so hard. And there's such reward to be felt just in the act of trying – Darryl Rook made me feel it. I felt the… the glow. I'd never felt the glow, before. It comes from you people. I shouldn't be harvesting you. I shouldn't be trying to control you. I tried to do so ethically, mercifully, but… but I see now there is no way to do so in an ethical manner. So, what do I do? Do I just leave you all in a dying world and let you boil yourselves to death? The harvest from that would produce an excellent yield of misery, but… but I don't want to do it. I shouldn't. You see my dilemma?'

'You respect us?' asked Brenda, surprised.

'I wouldn't go that far,' grumbled the Manager.

'You do! You respect us!' Brenda gave the Manager a small smile.

The Manager rolled its impossible number of eyes.

'Can I ask you a question?' asked Brenda.

'May as well,' replied the Manager.

'Are you God?'

The Manager paused. 'I don't think so. I mean, if I *were* "God" in the way you mean it – the ultimate sentience behind everything – then I think I'd know I was, wouldn't I? And I'm not sure. Maybe there's yet another reality, outside the ones I know about, that looks down on Head Office and the Celestials and the Demon dimension the same way that we look down on you. Who can say? Does it matter?'

'I don't suppose it does. I just liked the idea of giving God a pep talk.'

'You haven't given me much of a pep talk so far, to be fair.'

'Well, not yet,' conceded Brenda, 'but here it comes: You were right, earlier. What you said in Head Office. You should just quit.'

'That's the opposite of a pep talk,' grumbled the Manager.

'Number twelve on our street stopped mowing their garden last spring,' Brenda said. 'It was all the talk of the neighbourhood WhatsApp, I'm telling you. People didn't like it. But when we spoke to them, they told us they were doing something called "rewilding". Just leaving the garden be and seeing what happened. Better for pollinators and so on, they said. Better for nature. And it was messy – really messy. There were weeds the height of a child – but this summer I swear I saw more butterflies than usual round our way. Obviously, Darryl loved the idea, and not just because it was usually his job to do the weeding and he's a lazy sod. Him and Janusz are all about saving the bees and whatnot. So, I decided, back in the autumn, before you started your nonsense, that we'd let our garden go wild next year. If there's a next year. What if you did that? Stopped mowing. Let things go wild. What did they call it in the olden days… you could leave the world to go fallow?'

'But your world is dying.'

'It's not dead yet. So, we're not too late. You said yourself, there's a glow in the act of trying. My children are still furious with me, because I kept the truth from them. But I haven't given up on them. The family's fractured and strained, but it's not dead. We can fix it, with time and with space, their feelings need to have the chance to grow naturally – go fallow.' She paused. 'They need me to stop meddling. They definitely need Murzzzz to pack it in. They need to be the ones to process the truth and the truth of their feelings, by themselves.'

'What's that got to do with me?'

'Oh, it's all you, you, you, isn't it? Pardon me for thinking aloud about my own situation.'

'Just… your family situation even continuing to exist is sort of reliant on what I do about *my* situation…'

'Yes! I know! And, I'm saying, you should let this world rewild. Not as an act of surrender or indifference, but as an act of love and care. Wall it off and start a new mortal universe without us if you really have to, but stop meddling. And stop letting the Demons and the Angels or whatever they call themselves meddle. Let us deal with our own dead. Hell's Bells – let us deal with our own living – we're better equipped to do so, because we're mortal and you're not.'

'That's your answer to the apocalypse? I should just give up and let you deal with it?'

'Pretty much, yes. I already saved the world in the short term a couple of times over. You should definitely let me take a pop at saving it properly.'

'You saw what the end entails. Slow rot. Entropy. And all of you trapped in it. I showed you, when I let Helsbury decay and turned it to ruin.'

'You did show me. When you "ruined" that manky old service station I saw plants shoot from tarmac. I saw moss and bracken take back the wilderness that had been temporarily paved over. I saw an ancient spirit of nature finally at peace again, after decades of raging against cars and concrete in its place of rest and growth. And when you had that strop and folded Coldbay Island out of existence, I saw sea and coastline take its place. Rotted, rusted seaside attractions fell away and the place was left to the fishies and whatnot. After you stopped meddling in both of those places – after you metaphysically flipped those Scrabble boards over – the dead were at peace, and life could thrive again. There might be decay in this place and there might be an inevitable end of humanity, but "the world" is not dying. Life can survive without us humans, just as us humans can survive without you. Obviously, leaving Earth to the ants is not my Plan A, but even as a Plan B, it's better than just destroying everything now because you've given up.'

'So, "Plan A" is…?'

'You sod off – after all, you emotionally checked out ages ago so you may as well – and you seal off all the interdimensional doors for good. In turn, I… I start helping the living, as well as the dead. Start looking at ways we can stop the rot, or at least slow it down.'

'*You* want to help even more people than before?'

'"Want" is the wrong term,' replied Brenda.

'I'll say,' agreed the Manager. 'You're not exactly a people person at the best of times, if you don't mind my saying so, Brenda Rook.'

'Nor are you. And you're God.'

'I'm not God,' grumbled the Manager.

'Also, I'd like to think that, people skills notwithstanding, I rose to the challenge of being forced to help the dead a damn sight better than you rose to yours.'

'I'm sorry – are you saying you're better than God?'

'You just said you *weren't* God.'

The Manager let out a strange sound that was almost like a sigh.

'I've spent my life helping, as best as I could,' continued Brenda, 'but maybe along the way, I forgot to care. Forgot to empathise. Told myself it was self-preservation – armour – but, looking at it now, it made me too much like those Celestials, or the Demons… or you. I shouldn't be like you lot because you lot don't help – you just meddle and make it worse. I should be more like Janusz, or Charity, or Krish, or even Darryl. That's Plan A, I suppose. I need to become more of a Darryl. Nag people to grow out their lawns and eat plantburgers and whatnot. Even take a leaf out of Grace's goody-two-shoes handbook, if I can stomach it. Volunteer and so on.'

'And you think *that* can save the world?'

'Oh, almost certainly not,' replied Brenda, 'but it's worth a try. There's also the power of complaining and being annoying. That's been *very* effective these past few apocalypses. Perhaps I should find a few choice mortals to irritate in order to *really* save the world, instead of wasting my time on some half-arsed deity…'

'I am *not God*. I keep telling you!'

'I know, but calling you it annoys you and I still really enjoy winding you up.'

'And that's your idea of a pep talk, is it?'

'Yep. How did you enjoy it?'

'You *really* need to work on your people skills if you're going to persuade others to stop with the whole carbon in the air thing.'

'Yeah, I know.'

'Because you mortals really do love putting carbon in the air.'

'Yeah, yeah.'

'My clients won't like this,' added the Manager. 'Not one bit.'

'Ex-clients,' Brenda reminded it. 'Maybe while you're locking them out of our dimension you can lock them out of your office as well.'

'Oh, they would be *furious*,' replied the Manager, and Brenda wondered if that was a touch of amusement she could sense in its tone.

'You're very good at being a troublemaker,' Brenda added. 'You've caused us no end of problems. You are deeply annoying. And I mean that as a compliment – troublemaker to troublemaker.'

'Thanks...'

'You're welcome. And do you know what I have found is much more satisfying than causing trouble to low-paid service staff? Causing trouble to the management. The suits. The people with some actual power in matters. I think it's been made pretty clear over the past few months that us mortals are the grunts in this hierarchy – the cashiers and the baristas of the multiverse. You should give some grief to the higher-ups, instead. It's lots more fun.'

'Hmm,' hummed the Manager.

'Welp,' said Brenda, briskly. 'You asked for my advice, and there it is. Satisfied?'

'You *did* give me a pep talk after all, you sly primate,' replied the Manager.

'I did say so,' Brenda told it. 'So. What do you reckon? You going to do what I say?'

'I can't just wall your reality off and keep it going while starting up a new one,' the Manager told her. We only have the resources to run one at a time, at present.'

'Like humans and the Large Hadron Collider?' asked Brenda

'Yes, I saw you mortals had built one of those, it's very amusing,' said the Manager, and it *did* sound amused. Fondly so. '"God Particle" indeed. We can't start up a new mortal dimension without switching yours off, but… but maybe we shouldn't. If we did, we'd just be unethically harvesting a new reboot of the human race – or the octopuses, if the Celestials decide it's time to give the octopuses another go at being the main ones. Not that the octopuses are any better at looking after the world when they're in charge. It always ends exactly the same as it does with you primates, only wetter.'

'I thought the plural noun was "octopi",' interjected Brenda, to be annoying.

'Rewilding instead of harvesting. Locking the others out. Making them wait. Being annoying. I… *like* being annoying,' admitted the Manager. It vibrated, pleasantly. After a moment, Brenda realised it was doing something akin to laughing. 'I like being annoying. Thank you, Brenda Rook.'

'You're welcome, God.'

'I'm not God.'

And just like that, time was running again. And they weren't on Mount Snowdon. The Sunnyside leisure estate was back as it was before the Angel fight had ripped it up and turned it all into a set of crumpled balls. Even the Lamada Inn was back, its lobby lights on and its laminated signs advertising 'A night of psychic revelation with Aurora Tavistock (as seen on *This Morning*)'. Even off the top of Wales's tallest mountain, it was still bitterly cold in the car park, but Brenda was relieved to see it back.

'I'm going to stop mowing,' announced the Manager. 'I'm rewilding, and you can't stop me.'

'What does that even mean?' asked the Former Aurora, functioning within time once again. 'I thought you'd quit.'

'Not any more,' the Manager told them. 'I'm locking this dimension up, and making sure nobody interferes. Not even me. Think of it as... turning this world into a nature reserve.'

'Ooh, I love a nature reserve,' said Grace.

'If they do tear themselves apart, at least it'll be on their own terms,' added the Manager.

'But what are *we* supposed to do?' demanded the Former Aurora.

'You're supposed to be the most powerful, advanced beings in the known dimensions,' the Manager told them. 'You can work out what to do yourselves.' The Manager exuded a particularly happy glow as it said this. Oh, it was enjoying this. 'There must be plenty of other ways you can amuse yourselves and even to create enough energy for interdimensional visits to the Demon dimension if you like.'

'Ew, I'm not going *there*. It's full of Demons and it smells.' The Former Aurora turned slightly towards a nearby low-ranking Demon, who was lurking and looking put out. 'I'm sorry, my love, but it does,' they continued.

'Suit yourself,' said the Manager, cheerfully, 'but this realm and the Waste department are now shut to visitors. Mortals are to try living and dying in peace. Orders of the Management.'

'You jumped up little—' began the Former Aurora.

'Sorry,' interrupted the Manager, happily. 'Complaints department of Head Office is closed, as is the rest of Head Office. You lot never liked Head Office, anyway. Always moaning it was too purple, and insulting the ether's ideal designs...'

Charity raised a hand. 'Hate to agree with the Angels here, but your place really is horribly designed.'

'Yes, well, you lot aren't coming back again either.'

'Just, if that's the ether's idea of aesthetic perfection, and it's the same specs that were used to create the mortal universe, well... maybe that goes a way towards explaining why nothing here ever quite works properly.'

'I...' began the Manager, before dimming a little as it pondered this. 'Huh.'

Charity smiled primly at Krish, who was gazing at her with a particularly soppy expression.

'Aesthetics versus functionality comes up a lot with superheroes,' she explained with a shrug. 'Specially woman ones. The number of times I've gone, "Well, *that* outfit wouldn't actually work at all in the real world and the dude who drew it clearly just has a thing for sideboobs".'

'Well,' said the Manager, 'all the more reason for me to rewild your world. By the way, I thoroughly resent you making me just find out what a sideboob is.'

'You're welcome,' smiled Charity.

The Manager turned its many eyes back to the Former Aurora and the various unhappy-looking Demons. 'I'm locking the door in about five mortal minutes, so I'd get a wriggle on, if I were you.'

Brenda glanced upwards and saw that above her, the Hell Hole was indeed down to half the size it had been before, and was dwindling fast.

The lower-ranking Demons were the first to act, slithering wetly up streetlamps and hovering on stubby wings to get back to their own dimension. A couple of slightly higher-ranking Demons dithered a little, glancing at Richard, before following the others. The Former Aurora radiated with the very specific rage of someone who is not used to being talked back to.

'You will be hearing from us,' they warned the Manager.

'No I won't,' replied the Manager, happily.

'This is the *worst* mortal reality *ever*,' wailed the Former Aurora. 'You have ruined *everything*.'

'Well, you've ruined my New Year's,' called Yemisi. 'And… kind of my career. I mean, do I still get paid? Do I get a reference?'

'Stop whining, Whatsyername,' snapped the Former Aurora. 'You get to live, my love. That'll be enough.'

'Yemisi Kumuyi, you will find a year's wages in your bank account, and a five hundred pound bonus for your trouble tonight,' announced the Manager. 'And in your emails you will find a glowing reference from Aurora Tavistock's management.'

'You are *not* my boss,' raged the Former Aurora as they floated up towards the Hell Hole, 'I'm *your* boss, my love! You can't give her a reference! I forbid it!'

'Oh, piss off, you big fraud,' replied the Manager.

And, in one final burst of bright rage, the being formerly known as Aurora Tavistock did just that.

'I am *not* going to miss them,' noted the Manager. 'As for your New Year, it's still the 31st of December in this time zone for another ten minutes. Of course, if you were to miraculously find yourself in New York or Rio de Janero, you would have the whole evening to—'

'No, I'm a London girl, thank you,' interrupted Yemisi. 'If you could get me to my brothers…? They're probably at a bar by now.'

'They're in a rather sweaty basement in Clapham,' said the Manager.

'Nice.'

'Would you all not rather be at a high-class rooftop bar overlooking the imminent fireworks?' asked the Manager.

'Well, yeah, but we'd never get somewhere like… oh wait, is that an offer? For all of us? Can you make sure there are hotties there? I like men. I like tall men. I like hot, tall men. Who play bass. Oh! And my kid brother's single again and he likes hot, short men who write poetry. And my older brother's engaged, but he really loves cats, so if you could—'

'I'll see what I can do,' said the Manager, and Yemisi disappeared. One of the bedraggled humans from the audience and had stood next to Yemisi put up her hand.

'Um, I've had a rubbish night too. Can I go and watch the fireworks in a nice bar?'

'Yes, fine, anyone else want to go to a rooftop bar in central London where I am apparently providing attractive men of various heights and some friendly stray cats?'

Around fifty people put up their hands, and promptly vanished.

'And who would like to just go home?'

Most of the others raised their hands, and similarly disappeared.

'Um,' said one, tear-streaked woman, 'I can't go home because I can't find my little gir— oh there she is!'

The child in Darryl's care recognised and called for her mother, who scooped her up with relief.

'Can we watch *Monsters, Inc.*?' asked the kid.

'Sweetie, it's midnight,' replied the mother as she disappeared. 'Also, why's that man wearing women's yoga bottoms?'

CHAPTER SEVENTEEN

Resolutions

The few mortal stragglers hurried away, still watching the shrinking Hell Hole with suspicion. And then there were just the Rook party, the Manager and the remaining handful of lingering ghosts. The dead were no longer silently screaming in anguish, instead they looked exhausted and lost, driven from their usual haunting spots to this strange place, only to be used as terrible Celestial batteries, and now abandoned.

'The Waste dimension will remain accessible from this world,' the Manager told them, 'and closed off to the others. You mortals need a place to rest in peace, after life. You'll be able to shepherd the dead, just as you were before.' It turned its eyeballs to the ghosts. 'I imagine many of these will want to leave, now. I'm afraid you're the best ones for that job – sorry to ask you to work even more tonight.'

Krish nodded stoically, manifested his scythe and got to work, muttering, 'Evening, I'm Krish, would you like to move on?' to every ghost, before vanishing them with a swipe of his metaphysical weapon.

'If it helps,' continued the Manager, 'the changing of the year is entirely arbitrary, so you're not really missing out on anything in having to work this evening. Also, if it helps, at least for what remains of your future, no more of the dead will be specifically waiting for me. They shan't be told that I have the answers any more. After all, I never really did. It was all just a cruel trick. Apologies for that.' Its eyes swivelled up to the Hell Hole again. The portal was barely visible, now. Just an uncanny smudge in the sky, to Brenda's psychically gifted eyes. 'Almost done now. Grace Barry, if you do stay here, it'll be forever. When this world ends, you'll be walled up in it.'

'I know,' replied Grace. 'And you already know what my choice is. I've already changed my form to be the Grace Barry I want to be. Perhaps in the time I have left, I can find a way to be fully mortal, as Grace Barry should be. Live a short, meaningful life, and then go to the place of rest with my humans.'

'With your *fellow* humans,' added Brenda.

Grace glanced at Brenda, gratefully. 'You think I could be?'

'You made a minibus out of nothing but the idea of how a minibus should be,' Brenda reminded her. 'I don't see why you can't make yourself a human using the same willpower.'

'Which leaves just one more decision,' said the Manager, turning its eyes to Richard, who was no longer Richard, but Murzzzz.

Well, that was hardly going to be a tough decision, thought Brenda. Obviously those two were going to want to stay together forever.

'**Um, yeah,**' Murzzzz sighed. '**Wow, I wish I had more time for this. I know I owe a lot of people a lot of apologies, but… yeah, I think I'm actually going to shoot off.**'

'*What*??' asked Darryl.

'*WHAT???*' asked Richard… who was no longer in the same space as Murzzzz. Murzzzz had simply… stepped to one side, easy as that, and was outside of Richard. All this time – forty years – and Murzzzz had only been a simple sidestep away from not being part of Brenda's husband.

'What are you doing?' Richard continued in a panic. 'We just went through being split up, it was horrible...'

'Because that was by force. This is by choice. It's going to be OK.'

'No it isn't,' gabbled Richard. 'The emptiness... And you can't go back there, they tortured you...'

'They'll likely be too busy getting angry at this one to bother much with me again,' said Murzzzz, nodding at the Manager, who rolled its colossal eyes. **'But in any case, I need to face up to what I did. Not regarding my dimension's rules – sod the rules – but... Richard, I hurt your family. And I hurt you. I made you too used to me, too dependent on me to see that this relationship we had was parasitic.'**

'Like a good parasite,' continued Richard, 'like the kind you get in expensive yoghurt...'

'Not always,' replied Murzzzz. **'And, even at the times when it *was* beneficial like a yoghurt, it was still parasitic. We're not yoghurt, Richard.'**

'But what about the family?' Richard continued, 'Don't you want to stay with your family?'

'They are not my family. Brenda is your wife, not mine. Charity is a person I wronged, not my daughter. Even Darryl is not really my son, because he doesn't see me as his father. You're his father. You're the one he calls "Dad". Krish was right. They're all better off without me. It isn't that I don't love them. I do. I love them enough to free them from the meddling of the Demon realm – including myself. I was an intruder. A tourist who stayed too long and got too attached, but a tourist nonetheless, and it's time for me to go home.'

'But,' added Richard, in a much smaller voice now, 'what about me? Won't you stay for me?'

'**Richard Rook, I have existed for countless lifespans of your universe, and I have never known love like the love I have felt for you these forty years. I have loved you more than anything in the history of histories. You're such a lovely person to be. And you deserve to be yourself, wholly Richard, a husband, a father and a friend entirely on your own terms. Perhaps the emptiness you describe is merely a fear of embracing the wholeness of Richard and it was a fear I allowed to develop and fester in my decades of being too selfish to let you go. Richard Rook, I love you so much that I release you.**'

And Murzzzz leaped onto a lamppost, only a few feet from the fast closing remnants of the Hell Hole.

'No,' cried Richard, wiping away tears, 'not like this.'

'**Brenda, Darryl, Charity, Grace, I did love you. Thanks for being so nice to me. I know you didn't always want to be. Um. Look after one another. And look after Richard.**' Murzzzz gazed down at the agog group. '**Constance Xu,**' he added, '**I am truly sorry. I don't mind if you can't forgive me now, but do you think, maybe in the future…**'

Constance shook her head and gave Murzzzz the middle finger.

'**Yeah,**' replied Murzzzz, '**that's fair.**'

Brenda watched as he leaped again, and, after forty long years of possessing her husband, Murzzzz was gone.

Richard collapsed into a quietly sobbing ball.

The sudden quietness was exacerbated since it was at this moment that Krish stopped quietly asking the dead if they'd like to be reaped, with the polite tone of an air steward and sent the final lingering ghost on their way. The Nice Reaper allowed his scythe to dissipate into the night again, and stood next to Charity, watching the sorry sight of her father.

'Wow,' he said after a moment. 'That's... um...'

'"I love you so much that I release you"?' repeated Charity, incredulously, putting on a poor impression of Murzzzz's demonic voice. 'Did he just pull the same line that Darryl's crap first boyfriend used to dump him?'

'Hey,' complained Darryl, 'Simeon wasn't crap, he was just—'

'A dick,' interjected Janusz.

'It's a dickish line,' agreed the Manager, 'but I'm afraid Murzzzz is kind of a dick.'

'Don't call him that,' wailed Richard.

'If it helps, I think you're all kind of dicks,' said the Manager. 'And you'll get over him, Richard. Just give yourself time – which you have now.' In the distance, a single, sad garden firework went off. It was midnight. The new year. 'You have until the ends of the Earth,' added the Manager. 'Whenever that might be.'

The single firework petered out in a disappointing shower of green.

'Well then,' announced the Manager, 'Red Sticker Issues all sorted so that's me done and dusted. I am officially away from my desk. If you have any urgent enquiries about the nature of your universe, please invent a deity to send all your queries to. Just don't try to come running to me because I won't answer. Goodbye forever, you annoying monkeys.'

And then the Manager, along with the Hell Hole, was no longer in the world.

The group stood around in the car park, staring up at the sky. A strange sense of emptiness gripped Brenda. Was that... was that it, then? They'd saved the world properly this time? She'd expected it to feel a bit more satisfying than that. For a moment, the only sound was of Richard, still crying. And then, she became aware of singing. Whether the revellers in the pub across the car park had had their memories of the Angel fight wiped when things had been put back, or whether time outside of their bubble had frozen as the Celestials had flung land at each other, she did not know, but the people who had chosen to spend their new year at a Harvester pub on a leisure estate now seemed perfectly happy with their night, and were cheerfully 'Auld Lang Syne'ing.

A couple of lyrics in, she realised she was humming along. Darryl, too. It was Grace who joined in with the words.

'Should old acquaintance be forgot...'

Charity and Darryl joined in.

'And days of auld lang syne?'

Darryl took his sister's hand, crossed his arms and grabbed Janusz's in the other. Janusz reciprocated, taking Brenda's hand. It really was the world's most ridiculous, static, basic and boring dance – just stand in a circle, cross arms, join hands and then pump your elbows up and down, in a futile attempt to keep some sort of rhythm. And yet, Brenda joined in, not really sure why.

'For auld lang syne, my dear, for auld lang syne!'

She found that she couldn't grab the hand next to her, her fingers went straight through it. Constance smiled, next to her, and crossed her arms, taking up a gap in the circle that Krish thoughtfully left for her, and waved her elbows about ridiculously with the rest of them.

'We'll tak' a cup of kindness yet, for auld lang syne!'

Why was Brenda crying? She had no idea. Possibly because she hadn't had nearly enough to drink for a New Year and didn't even have a glass of fizz to hand, so this was very far from ideal. Terrible, actually.

Krish tried launching into a second verse, and the others sportingly joined in, even though nobody knew the words.

'We ner nee ner the ner nee ner,

And something ner ner nine!

And ner nee ner nee dum dee dum,

FOR AULD LANG SYNE!'

The elbow pumping reached a fervour for the return of words the people actually knew. This was awful. Stood in a rubbish car park at the rubbish end of their rubbish town, singing a boring old song that nobody even knew the words to and doing a weird cross-armed chicken dance to it. Brenda stood with her dead best friend and her family, and sobbed, and sobbed.

'For auld lang syne, my dear, for auld lang syne!

We'll tak' a cup of kindness yet, for auld lang syne!'

'Happy New Year!'

Brenda noticed that Darryl too was crying, which set Janusz off as usual.

'*Szczęśliwego nowego roku*,' managed Janusz. 'And whatever it is you say in Canada.'

'Usually we just go with "Happy New Year",' replied Krish. 'Um. So. Is that… like… Did we do it? Feels like we did it.' He pointed at Richard, who had joined in with the circle, but not actually managed to get any singing done due to falling apart all over again at the mention of 'old acquaintance'. 'Is he going to be OK?'

'It's been an emotional one for us all,' said Brenda, wiping her eyes. 'Lot to take in. We should get out of this car park.' She looked around the circle, hopefully. 'All back home, then? Need to do first footing. Krish, you're tallest, you can take over from Janusz this year and be the first one through the door for the new year.'

Janusz opened his mouth, annoyed for a moment, then closed it again, and nodded in agreement.

Darryl wiped his face on his sleeve. 'OK, but we're not "going home", are we? We don't live with you any more, Mum. "Home" is the flat.'

Urgh. Yes. That old problem was still rumbling on then, thought Brenda.

'Also,' added Charity, 'I don't think we did do it, not properly.'

'But the Manager...' began Krish.

'Yeah,' replied Charity, 'but I would like to wish every one of you a very merry "scroll through any news website right now and tell me the world isn't still ending". The Manager just made it an Us Problem instead of a Manager Problem.'

Krish looked dejected. 'I guess.'

And yes, *that* was another old problem that was going to continue to rumble on, Brenda supposed, and she'd just volunteered to try to sort it out. Bugger.

'We can drop by on the old house though, right?' Janusz asked his husband and sister-in-law. 'I'm freezing and hungry, and I want to watch *Dinner for One* and the TV there connects to my phone better...'

'Yeah, I'm on team "back to Mum and Dad's",' added Charity. 'This hoodie's all bloody, and I could murder some cheese on toast right now – the grill at ours is filthy.'

Brenda tried to look haughty, even though on the inside she felt a strange little fluttering. Hope. She didn't try to stamp it down, this time. She allowed it to open its fragile wings.

'Good thing for you we took a white loaf out of the freezer this morning then,' she said, 'and there's bicarb for blood stains as usual and yes, Janusz, you can watch your strange little comedy show.'

'*Skål!*' replied Janusz, happily, and turned, hand in hand with his husband, to start heading home.

'I don't get *Dinner for One*,' complained Darryl. 'It's just an old man falling over.'

But Janusz was already snickering to himself. 'The bit with the chicken!'

It really was just half an hour of an old man falling over, but for some reason it made Janusz happy as much as it baffled the rest of them. As for Charity, well, she was delighted just to get a mountain of cheese on toast and not have to clean the grill. She ate it next to Krish, but gave him a quizzical glance when she saw he was creating a gap between them on the sofa. It was only after she tried to shuffle closer to him and he shuffled aside a little more, maintaining the gap, that she realised what the issue was.

'Constance, sorry, no offence, but could you move? I want to sit next to the boy.'

'I'm not a boy, I'm thirty-three, but thanks,' Krish replied, finally shuffling right next to Charity. 'I don't like sitting inside ghosts, least of all the ghost of the birth mother of someone I kinda… someone I'm… Are we dating, now?'

'You haven't actually taken me on a date yet,' smiled Charity through the cheese. 'Buy me dinner and I'll see.'

Honestly, even though it had been a Hell of a day, and there were quite literally a world of problems still to be addressed, and they had just seen the closest thing their universe had to a creator-maintainer-destroyer deity officially abandon them for good, Charity spent that New Year's night rather elated. True, there was an edge of falseness to it – it was a 'pushing all the actual problems to one side to deal with another time and doing fun stuff to try to distract from the fact the problems were still there' sort of an elation – but that was pretty common for New Year's anyway. They'd survived the latest apocalypse. That would do, for now. That was enough reason to raid her mother's impressive wine rack and play increasingly rowdy card games until the small hours. Richard sat looking withdrawn and sad, but at least he stopped crying after a while. He just looked numb. Numb and hurt. Everyone knew why, but, well, they'd deal with it later. Murzzzz was gone. And he'd not been forced or ripped from this world against his will, he'd just pissed off – and, yeah, it was probably for the best, but it was complicated. Charity was pretty sure that she did feel a sense of grief for the loss of Murzzzz, deep inside of her, but it was the grief like the grief for the ending of a relationship that had already gone bad. She felt like Murzzzz had maybe actually done the right thing for once, there was a lightness to her sadness about his departure. A relief. But she obviously wasn't going to tell her dad that, right now.

Brenda played a few card games before giving up and going to the kitchen. Charity assumed it was to get some heavy solo drinking under her belt. Another tomorrow problem. It was only when she went into the kitchen herself for a cheeky 3 a.m. top up that she saw what Brenda was really doing. She was perched on the worksurface, talking to what looked to Charity to be thin air. She and Constance had gone for a kitchen chat – perennially the cool girls of any houseparty. She had also, Charity noticed, drunk only half a bottle of wine in two hours. That was extremely conservative consumption for a Brenda with a house full of booze and a whole night to kill.

The thirty-somethings hung around playing cards with an equally elated Grace until 4.50 a.m., on the grounds that that was the absolute latest one could still count it as still being the night before, rather than the morning after. Only in the ten minutes between the night and the dreaded five o'clock line did they begin even glancing at tomorrow problems such as 'Where is Krish supposed to stay?'

'There's plenty of beds still,' Grace said, 'You could all stay over. Krish can have the sofa. I can sleep on the floor.'

Charity looked at her brother. They both knew that staying the night in their old beds was the start of a slippery slope that would end with them moving back into their childhood bedrooms.

'Thanks, but it's nice to greet the new year with a bracing walk,' announced Janusz. 'Home's not far away.'

Charity noticed the emphasis which her brother-in-law put on the word 'home', and she silently thanked him for that. And then, a few seconds later, her adrenaline and wine muddled brain reminded her that, when a married couple talked about somewhere as 'home', they didn't generally include an adult sibling still living with them as a part of that equation. She was reminded of just how small her room was, and how much the men complained about her stuff lying all over the flat. And about how she kept mentally referring to it as 'the flat', not 'home' the way they did. Oh well. Another tomorrow problem.

She turned to Krish. 'You know, we have a sofa, too. You'd probably fit on it.'

The four of them walked back to the flat together in the strange stillness that descends when the night proper has ended but the morning hasn't quite yet begun. The husbands walked ahead together, their arms wound tightly around each other in a way they still rarely dared to do in public. The empty streets and the wine in their systems emboldened them, as well as the knowledge that they'd just saved the actual world, dammit. Sometimes Darryl would kiss his husband on the cheek, or rub his hands over Janusz's waist. Urgh, they were so blatantly about to do it. Charity would have to listen to a white noise app or something.

Charity and Krish walked behind, themselves in a strange and exciting space where they were not quite yet one thing nor the other – a space where it was a heart pumping, rollercoaster thrill to brush the backs of hands together and pretend you'd just done it by accident. The pre-dawn of a… of a something. As soon as they got in, Darryl and Janusz disappeared to their room, leaving Charity to find a pillow and a throw for Krish.

She handed Krish her Pikachu throw without embarrassment or apology.

'Pokemon,' said Krish, with genuine enthusiasm. 'Neat!'

They stood together, awkwardly, neither wanting to be the one to break the spell.

'Well,' said Charity, 'it's so late it's early, so...'

'It's not New Year's in Winnipeg for another half-hour,' blurted Krish.

Charity smiled. 'Do you want to see in Canadian New Year together, then?'

'That'd be nice.'

They got underneath the throw together on the sofa, collectively deciding to ignore the soft noises coming from the husbands' bedroom, and watched cartoons on Charity's phone beneath Pikachu's warped face. They toasted the Winnipeg New Year in with some of Darryl's peppermint tea, and then, since it was traditional, they kissed. He tasted of unsweetened peppermint tea – a sort of bitter old chewing gum flavour. It was delicious. Only afterwards did Charity think to check with Krish that Constance wasn't watching them, and so it was only then that Krish realised Constance wasn't with them at all. And she hadn't been since they'd walked back to the flat. Last he'd seen her, she'd been with Brenda in the kitchen. Charity supposed that was probably progress, and kissed Krish one more time before going back to her own bed to sleep.

CHAPTER EIGHTEEN

Happy New Year

And with that, the world carried on. Ghosts still lingered; a job in Andover confirmed that Stonehenge was still a horrendously haunted nightmare of a place; the planet's atmosphere and seas still got clogged up with various pollutants; and war, pestilence and famine still did their dreadful things. The Demons had gone, but it became quickly clear that this didn't actually make all that much difference. Misery still begat misery, cruelty still begat cruelty – even without beings from dimensions beyond to revel in it all and harvest what they could of it for their own ends. The Celestials and the Manager could no longer waft about uncaringly, but there were still plenty of humans who reacted to fixable problems and reversible misery by simply shrugging and turning away.

Plenty of other humans, however, did not. Very many people, Brenda realised, turned towards the problems and asked how they could help. They organised. They did good things, and in return they received only the knowledge that they were helping. People like Grace. And it wasn't that Grace's presence on Earth in human form was leading the way – it was the other way around. Grace was following. This was Grace's idea of what it meant to be human, and she'd learned it from humanity. What Grace's presence had changed was that Brenda could see it now. As Grace went straight back to her Grace-ish nonsense – helping at homeless centres and that silly charity cafe, shaking buckets and doing food bank drop-offs in her daft minibus – Brenda started noticing more and more others who were doing that nonsense with Grace. And they were ordinary humans, not simpering Angels disguised as priests. Brenda started learning their names. There was Zainab, at the cafe, with her biscuit addiction. And Tony at the homelessness centre, who was surprisingly spry for a man with a prosthetic leg. There was Grace's food bank driving partner Kenji, with all those bloody photos of his bloody cats. It wasn't that Brenda *liked* those bloody do-gooders, goodness no. She'd just get talking to them while waiting for Grace to finish up and come with her to do the big shop, or Grace would invite her new friends over, which was a horrible imposition, of course. And then, over an otherwise perfectly nice curry, Kenji had told Brenda about some of the environmental campaigning he was doing as well, and that was that – she got roped in, she supposed. Although, well, wasn't that sort of her remit now? Wasn't that the responsibility that the Manager had passed on to her, as part of their deal? She still had to save the world, only now she wasn't supposed to do it by fighting a horde of Demons armed with nothing but an ethereal minibus full of psychics and an accountant. Now she was supposed to save it by taking on some of the wealthiest corporations on the planet, armed with nothing but a homemade placard and a retired British-Japanese man in orange corduroys. True, she'd fought harder battles for the future of the planet, but still, it was a pain.

Richard was quiet. Richard was quiet for almost the whole of January. He took to skulking silently in corners all sad

– haunting the place while still very much alive. Brenda tried pulling sad faces for her husband's benefit for a while – she even wished quietly several times that she could feel the same loss as him, to share the pain and in doing so, soothe it – but she found that she couldn't. She wasn't sad about Murzzzz. It was strange because, in many ways, Murzzzz had just broken up with her. Murzzzz had, after all, been in there on her wedding day, saying 'I do' along with Richard. He'd been with her all those decades, shared all those moments with her, of grief and of joy, and then he'd just... gone. Barely a word of farewell for Brenda. No 'Thanks for the last forty years, doll face, see you around'. She should, she thought, feel bereft. Hurt, even. But, no. She felt... freed. Like a weight had lifted off her. She found herself silently approving of Murzzzz's decision... and then, seeing the sadness etched on the face of her husband, and feeling bad about it.

'I don't blame you,' he said, quietly, one night.

'Why on earth would you blame me?' she replied.

'Because. You know. You didn't... you didn't love him.'

'No. I didn't.' And she realised she'd never said this out loud before.

'You resented him. Even after all he did for us.'

'Yes. You're right. I resented him.'

Richard snorted. 'Why even tolerate him, then? Why tolerate *us* all these years?'

'Because I love you. With him or without him. I love you, Richard. And you loved him. So, I lived with Murzzzz rather than not live with you.'

Richard cried, again, and she cried, too, that night. Things weren't immediately OK afterwards, but the week after that, Richard started kissing his wife again. And, on Valentine's Day, the traditional annual card and box of Thorntons were signed 'Love from your Richard (and only your Richard) xxx'.

Krish didn't go back to Canada for some time. He'd only been given a one-way ticket and, he rationalised, he had been sent to the UK to deal with the end of the world – which was still ongoing, just at a slower pace than he had first assumed. Janusz helped him apply for a visa for the short term at least, and to start looking into longer-term options. He did go back for a quick trip to Winnipeg – after all, there was a big build-up of ghosts in that city he needed to deal with. And he wanted the grandmother who had raised him to meet his new girlfriend. Even without the interference of the Celestials or the Manager, Krish could still manifest his scythe, and still do all the work of the Nice Reaper. Perhaps, the family pondered amongst themselves, the role of a psychopomp was a basic human need. Perhaps humanity had created the concept and the Celestial Executives had run with it, rather than the other way around. Or, perhaps it was just that no high-ranking beings had thought to revoke his scythe and powers before the dimensions had been closed off and now he just had them by default. Whatever the reason, he was now an extremely useful member of the family business, especially with Brenda having to go off and do sit-down protests on ring roads quite so often, and Darryl... well. Darryl was a different matter altogether.

In late February, Darryl Rook quit his job – the only proper job he had ever had. His husband, he insisted, would continue to work as the family's accountant and administrator, but Darryl, at thirty-six big years old and, after failing most of his GCSEs two decades ago as a result of constantly being pulled out of school for work, was going to go to Rutherford FE College and finally get a BTEC. His mother was, obviously, appalled. His father was quietly pleased for him. His sister, who had managed to actually pass her GCSEs while working for the family, teased him mercilessly about it. Darryl maintained a dignified stance throughout. He was good at stuff, he maintained. Not just psychic stuff, but stuff-stuff. The work he'd done with the family had showed he had a strong track record for helping people who were in need and who were at their lowest ebb, so he was going to get a BTEC in social care and devote himself to helping both the dead and the living. So *there*. Brenda scoffed. Richard nodded, proudly. Grace got to her feet and applauded him, and then went out and bought him a cake. The family could continue to hire him occasionally, he insisted later, over slices of the chocolate cake, for the seances and big, difficult jobs and so on, but it would be part-time only and they would pay him a decent rate. He was going to need the money, frankly.

A few days later, it became clear to Charity just how much her brother was going to need the money. He and Janusz had a quiet chat with her, over breakfast. The husbands had decided that they were going to adopt. Adopt *properly*, Darryl added to his mother pointedly, as they broke the news to her, later – not just scoop a baby out of a dead friend's arms. Krish said that Constance had laughed at that. As much as Charity relished the idea of becoming the coolest aunt in the world, the husbands' decision meant that they would be needing the flat's small second bedroom. Her room. It wasn't that they were kicking her out, it was just that they'd really appreciate it if she didn't live with them any more.

Charity had, if she was being honest with herself, seen this coming down the track, ever since New Year. Her old bedroom in her parents' house was immediately offered to her, and polite-ly rejected. She was a grown woman and she wasn't moving back to her mum's house. She needed her own space, for her own comic books, kawaii plushies and collectable figurines. Besides, it would help with Krish's visa applications if he were living with a British citizen as her partner as soon as possible. There was a perfectly nice little one-bed basement flat not far from the Sunnyside estate, which was in their price range... provided her mother gave them both a pay rise. Brenda vocally refused to do so, and complained that they were selfish and greedy and then quietly upped their wages that night anyway. All three clairvoyants in her family told her cheerfully that the basement wasn't even a little bit haunted – unless one counted Constance, who had come along to check that her birth daughter had a nice place with a nice boy. Krish told Charity, after everyone had finished helping them move into the basement, that Constance had, again, gone home with Brenda, rather than lingering around the new couple. Charity found that she didn't feel that sad that the ghost of her birth mother was spending less and less time around her. That was good, right? That was healthy. Especially now that she had a new, psychic boyfriend.

Charity had always been adamant that she was the Chosen One. And then she'd refused to be the Chosen One, because she didn't like the terms. The one thing that her steady diet of comic books and superhero movies had made her absolutely certain of was that, while it was a glorious thing to be the Chosen One, one of the worst things one could be was the Chosen One's girlfriend. Chosen One's girlfriends sat at home looking prettily worried, got kidnapped loads and often ended up being killed to give the Chosen One motivation in the third act. This was very definitely not something that Charity wanted, and yet, here she was, girlfriend to the second choice Chosen One. But she was not sitting at home, prettily worried and she was not getting kidnapped and certainly not getting murdered any time soon if she had anything to do with it. Perhaps, she reasoned to herself, this was simply *her* second act, now she had rejected the status given to her by meddling outside forces and had to build up her own heroic status on her own terms and by her own rules. Maybe she could become her own, self-chosen Chosen One. Maybe in accepting her boyfriend's powers and status as the psychopomp, she was showing a new sense of humility that would shape her on *her* hero's journey. Or, maybe – just maybe – superhero stories were oversimplified, comforting nonsense that helped mortals find patterns and moral codes in the cruel chaos of a dying world filled with frightened, miserable mortals and even more frightened, miserable ghosts, and that they were not to be taken as any kind of gospel. Yes, that was a very real possibility, she thought to herself as she binge-watched yet another Marvel series. It was a real possibility, but a boring one, so she was just going to ignore it.

None of them saw it as a fracturing of the family. More of a dispersion, a growth. They weren't really one unit any more, but three. The ties that had bound Darryl and Charity to their parents and the business hadn't been cut, as such. They had simply found that the ties were more elastic than they'd previously thought and there was some give to their bonds. They could stretch away a little, find more space – physically, emotionally, economically. Charity started taking on a few psychic jobs by herself, or just with Krish, which Darryl immediately decried as 'copying his idea to do his own seances'. The family would still work together regularly. Once every few weeks, the children and their partners would go to the house for dinner, with Brenda, Richard and Grace, who had since moved into Charity's old room but still wasn't paying any rent, much to Brenda's noisome chagrin. They would talk and laugh. They did not exactly avoid the sensitive topics, it was more that they treated them with a lightness. They'd been through the end of the world, three times. That gave them permission to laugh and joke about subjects they used to avoid. Most dinners would involve an anecdote from Janusz about how, in spite of his insistence that the itty-bitty Demon form was to be for emergencies only, Darryl kept using it as a cheat mode for overcoming increasingly trivial problems. Clambering up a stadium wall so he and Janusz could sneak in to watch the

Lionesses play the Eaglesses. Using it to carry Janusz at a bound over the rooftops after missing the last bus home. The family always laughed, and Darryl laughed along with them, after giving his husband the most cursory of gentle whacks to the arm for bringing it up. Janusz had already decided that Demon Darryl was going to become the baby's favourite teddy, and had nicknamed the Demon form 'Bukowski'. Charity, for her part, had started calling the Demon form 'Gizmo', and was hoping that would stick.

By spring, the only aspect of the family's past that they avoided bringing up was Murzzzz. It wasn't Murzzzz himself that was the elephant in the room, more the general sense of relief since he had gone. Nobody wanted to mention that in front of Richard, because it felt cruel. They spoke to him about the garden, and the best route to get to Wolverhampton, and who his favourite was to win the latest series of the *Great British Metalworking Challenge*, and other subjects that relaxed and engaged him, and they allowed him to get over Murzzzz quietly, in his own time. And by the time the grass and dandelions in the newly rewilded back garden were high and humming with fat furry bees, the family had a new elephant in the room not to discuss – Richard had a new lightness to him, that they'd never seen in him before. A new sense of direction. He'd started joining Grace at her volunteering, and Brenda at her protests and was, Brenda told them in hushed tones when he went to the toilet, really enjoying it. He was discovering, after forty years, a new sense of what he truly wanted Richard Rook to be. Richard Rook, in the singular, his own person, truly independent… as long as Brenda didn't mind.

Brenda very much didn't mind. Brenda would smile about a 'second honeymoon', much to the embarrassment of her children, their partners, and her Angelic housemate whose bedroom shared a wall with hers. Brenda didn't mention it often, but Richard's change of attitude wasn't the only contributing factor to the rekindling of their physical relations. The therapy – which she had only admitted to twice, but which Grace confirmed Brenda was attending on a weekly basis – was definitely helping. And on both occasions when she'd stopped drinking all together, her children had been able to tell, from her demeanour as well as from the way Richard proudly hugged and kissed her. She had, to her children's knowledge, lapsed in her sobriety after both attempts, around a month in, each time. Charity had noticed a link between how tragic Krish's description was of whatever ghost they'd helped into the Waste this time, and whether Brenda was going to start drinking again. Maybe in time there'd be a reliable enough early warning system for the family to prevent slips from the wagon before they began. For now, they were all proud that after every tumble from sobriety, Brenda would dust herself off and try it again.

And me?
I stayed in the kitchen with Brenda, on New Year's night. We talked until eight in the morning. Well. She talked. I mimed, which was time consuming and annoying, but it got the job done. She said she was sorry, for everything. I already knew she was sorry. I always knew she was sorry – at least about my death. With my Charity – our Charity – I always knew it was more complicated than that. She said that she was truly sorry for going against my wishes, and promised she'd help Charity get in touch with my sister so she could find out more about her birth family if she so wished. I believe her. She also told me that she could never feel absolute remorse over taking Charity that night, because being her mother had brought her so much joy. And it continued to bring her joy. I believe her. She was honest with me, and with herself. I feel as if it helped us both.

What happened happened. She has grieved, and I have grieved. As flowers began to open in the wild garden, painting it haphazardly with the early spring colours of white, yellow, blue and purple, I found myself feeling a strange new sensation. I felt it, long, long ago, in the nineties. Joy. I was feeling joy. The grief and the anger were still there, but they had receded enough to make way for joy to sprout, and open up its bright yellow petals to the sun.

Still, I stayed with Brenda, not with Charity. Charity was making her own life, with Krish, in a basement full of her toys. Harry told me to watch Charity, all those years ago, and I watched her. But she doesn't need watching any more. She doesn't need any parent helicoptering around her. She's her own deeply silly and childish adult woman, and she and Krish remind me so much of another young couple. Sometimes when I visit, I get flashes of them, in another little flat, thirty years ago, watching cartoons on a little telly with a crap aerial and a VHS instead of on a little laptop with crap WiFi. One day I was surprised, on visiting them with Brenda, that their duvet cover had anthropomorphic fried eggs on it, and not Transformers *as I remembered. Maybe the* Transformers *bed set had been mine and Harry's. Brenda, Krish and Darryl all asked why I was crying. I had no answer for them, even if I could speak. I wasn't entirely crying out of sadness, but it wasn't entirely happiness either.*

Sad happy.

Sappy. Had.

I watched the flowers more and more. I stayed in the house whenever the living went out to try to save the world using their twin powers of showing kindness to the powerless, and excruciating levels of annoyingness towards the powerful. The bright cold colours of March and April gave way to explosions of pink and peach hollyhocks and snapdragons. Lilacs found cracks between paving slabs and quickly grew to the size of armchairs, their purple cones noisily teeming with insect life. I wished I could smell it all. Grass. Flowers. Pollen drifting around, making eyes itch and noses run.

Today is midsummer. The others are out, saving the world, inch by difficult inch, but the house is far from empty. Here is a fly. There is a spider. Dust motes dance in the sun. Grace's mug, washed and drying upside down on the draining board. An upside-down kitten warns me in upside down English not to speak to them until they've had their coffee. Kittens don't drink coffee, but then I suppose technically neither do Angels, and yet Grace diligently has one every morning, because she feels that's what Grace is meant to do.

I drift through to the living room and see photographs, everywhere, fading ever so slowly in the bright mid-morning sunlight. They put up a good photo of Harry and me. He was so handsome. I really punched above my weight, with that one. A new photo of Brenda and Richard, from this year. You can see in Richard's eyes that Murzzzz is gone, and Brenda's eyes look brighter, clearer. A photo of Grace, finishing a sponsored half-marathon for the food bank. They all teased her over that, asked how hard could it be for an Angel to run thirteen miles. She'd insisted it had actually been really tough, although she tended to only puff and pant and complain of sore feet when reminded. The family all sponsored her twenty pounds each anyway. A photo of Charity and Krish, on a visit to see his grandmother in Winnipeg. Charity has said that next, they're saving up for Wellington, maybe with a stopover in Jingzhou, where Harry's parents were from, and his cousins still live. She's trying to learn Mandarin through Duolingo. She's absolutely terrible at it, but I was expecting that. In twenty years of being addicted to anime, she has barely learned a word of Japanese. Brenda and Richard's wedding photo, next to Darryl and Janusz's wedding photo, and then the newest picture, taken just the other week. Darryl and Janusz, with Halina. A suspiciously fast turnaround from applying for adoption to actually adopting a baby girl. Nobody yet has had a quiet word with Grace over whether there may have been some Celestial administrative intervention at play.

I suspect it's run through everybody's mind so far, but nobody wants to be the one to bring it up.

I drift again, to look out of the big back window. The former lawn is a knee-high sea of grass and wildflowers. Cabbage white butterflies flit past, and bees so big and fuzzy they look like hamsters with wings.

At the side of joy, a new feeling has blossomed within me, with the pastel summer flowers.

Calm.

Peace.

It's so beautiful. This world is so beautiful, for all its faults. For all its lack of care, there are the people who care. There are people who love. There are people who take up what others have abused or neglected or abandoned, and they nurture it, let it grow, let it heal. My grief over my daughter has been allowed to heal. My friendship with Brenda has been allowed to heal. My pain over my loss of self has… OK, that's not completely healed. I don't think it can be, in this state.

I think…

I think I want to go.

This story isn't over. The Rooks still need to save the world. They still need to move the dead from this realm to the next. They are still the team working with the world's current psychopomp to help him fulfil the destiny of every Grim Reaper. The family business is still 'ghost hunting', although that's definitely a misnomer. They don't hunt the dead, they find and gently guide them. They're not hunters. They are carers. Yes, this story is far from over.

It's just… I don't think I want to tell this story any more. It was never my story. None of this was ever really about me. It was about my baby. My baby and my friend. And now my baby is an adult with her own life, and my friend is my friend is my friend and I love her. I never stopped loving Brenda, even when it hurt.

It doesn't hurt to love her any more.

It doesn't hurt to love any of them any more.

It doesn't hurt. This doesn't hurt. The thought of leaving doesn't hurt.

They'll hurt, I think, later, when they come back and I'm not here. They'll grieve, and that's OK. They'll grieve, and then they'll feel lighter, like with Murzzzz. I'm not going to apologise for their grief. I have nothing to feel sorry about.

Love you. Bye.

I don't need help leaving. I don't need Death's gentle hand, even though he really is such a nice boy. I've been around them long enough, seen it happen enough times, to know how to go through. It's just a push backwards, just a little pressure against the thin fabric between the living world and the desert of the Waste. And off I pop.

And off…

I…

I thought the Waste was supposed to be a desert with no up or down, no sky or land. Maybe that's just what it looks like from outside of it, because on the inside, it has forms – like a nice dream has forms. It has shapes, it has solidness… or at least, a memory of solidness. It has a bed with a Transformers *duvet, and a tiny telly with a crap aerial and a VHS, and the smell of breakfast, and a face, such a handsome face… and a voice! A voice! The touch of a hand and his voice!*

'Hey, baby. Where the Hell were you?'

The End

Also available

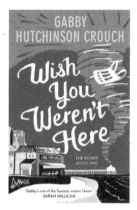

Wish You Weren't Here
(The Rooks series, Book 1)

The Rook family run a little business: ghost hunting. And things have picked up recently. Something's wrong. It's been getting noticeably worse since, ooh, 2016?

Bad spirits are abroad, and right now they're particularly around Coldbay Island, which isn't even abroad, it's only 20 miles from Skegness. The Rooks' 'quick call-out' to the island picks loose a thread that begins to unravel the whole place, and the world beyond.

Is this the apocalypse? This might be the apocalypse. Who knew it would kick off in an off-season seaside resort off the Lincolnshire coast? I'll tell you who knew – Linda. She's been feeling increasingly uneasy about the whole of the East Midlands since the 90s.

OUT NOW

Also available

Out of Service
(The Rooks series, Book 2)

En route to a new investigation, family ghost hunters the Rooks find themselves in a motorway service station where something appears terribly wrong – more than usual. It's empty, completely empty… apart from all the ghosts…

Can the Rooks close the Hell Hole that is forming above their heads? Surely keeping the underworld from pouring into the living world shouldn't be outsourced to a chaotic family business? Or is the world on its way out anyway?

OUT NOW

Also available

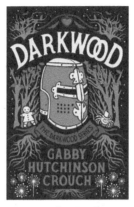

Darkwood
(Darkwood series, Book 1)

Magic is forbidden in Myrsina, along with various other abominations, such as girls doing maths.

This is bad news for Gretel Mudd, who doesn't perform magic, but does know a lot of maths. When the sinister masked Huntsmen accuse Gretel of witchcraft, she is forced to flee into the neighbouring Darkwood, where witches and monsters dwell.

There, she happens upon Buttercup, a witch who can't help turning things into gingerbread, Jack Trott, who can make plants grow at will, the White Knight with her band of dwarves and a talking spider called Trevor. These aren't the terrifying villains she's been warned about all her life. They're actually quite nice. Well… most of them.

With the Huntsmen on the warpath, Gretel must act fast to save both the Darkwood and her home village, while unravelling the rhetoric and lies that have demonised magical beings for far too long.

Take a journey into the Darkwood in this modern fairy tale that will bewitch adults and younger readers alike.

OUT NOW

About the Author

Gabby Hutchinson Crouch (*Horrible Histories*, *Newzoids*, *The News Quiz*, *The Now Show*) has a background in satire, and with the global political climate as it is, believes that now is an important time to explore themes of authoritarianism and intolerance in comedy and fiction.

Born in Pontypool in Wales, and raised in Ilkeston, Derbyshire, Gabby moved to Canterbury at 18 to study at the University of Kent and ended up staying and having a family there.

She is the author also of the acclaimed Darkwood trilogy, a modern fairy tale series for grown-up and younger readers alike.

About The Rooks

The Rooks is a series of supernatural horror comedy adventures, about the Rook family, who run a little family business. Ghost hunting. And gracious, business has certainly picked up recently. Something's wrong. It's been getting noticeably worse since, ooh, 2016? Bad spirits are circulating…

The full series –

Wish You Weren't Here
Out of Service
Home Sweet Hell

Also by Gabby Hutchinson Crouch – the Darkwood series

Darkwood
Such Big Teeth
Glass Coffin

Acknowledgements

Thanks to Dom Lord and everyone at Farrago and Duckworth. Thanks to everyone who read, reviewed and recommended Wish You Weren't Here, Out of Service, and The Darkwood Trilogy.

Huge thanks to Nathan, Violet & Alex for being a brilliant family. There's no point thanking Spooky the cat, because she can't read.

These books are for the families – no matter how traditional or otherwise, no matter whether you're bound by blood and love or by love alone, it all counts. Here's to the ghosts of my family, and yours, wherever they may be.

Note from the Publisher

To receive updates on new releases in The Rooks series – plus special offers and news of other humorous fiction series to make you smile – sign up now to the Farrago mailing list at farragobooks.com/sign-up.